ESCAPE FROM ENLIGHTENMENT

ESCAPE FROM ENLIGHTENMENT

MARLEY'S JOURNEY

◆ ◆ ◆

Tessa Rose

ISBN: 0996534407
ISBN 13: 9780996534406

Falling Pine Publishing
www.fallingpinepublishing.com

DEDICATION

◆ ◆ ◆

This book is dedicated to all young L's, B's, G's, T's, and Q's. My attempts to empathize with you by imagining society the other way around directly inspired this story. I wish you all a good journey.

Acknowledgments

◆ ◆ ◆

THIS BOOK MIGHT NOT EXIST at all, and certainly would not be as good if not for the assistance, support, and encouragement of the following people:

Don Traub, who encouraged me with $1000 to finish the first draft.

My husband Larken and daughter Elyssa, who suffered in various ways while I worked at writing instead of getting a job, cooking, or cleaning the house.

Aven Rose, whose editing vastly improved the book.

Amanda Rogers-Petro, who gave me useful feedback on an early draft.

Natalie David, who gave me useful feedback, medical expertise, and great encouragement.

Peter O'Connor at Bespoke Book Covers, who created an amazing cover.

My Gold Level Contributors:

Thomas J. Buford

Anonymous

John Michael

Many others who contributed money, encouragement, and enthusiasm that kept me going on the long and arduous journey from inspiration to publication.

Escape From Enlightenment

MARLEY'S JOURNEY

by Tessa Rose

Of course we should try to make things better, insofar as it lies within our power. But we should probably not try to make things perfect, especially not ourselves, for that path leads to mass graves.
— Margaret Atwood

Prologue

◆ ◆ ◆

God help us. New York, Philadelphia, and Washington, D.C. have
been devastated by nuclear bombs. Now men are being removed
from positions of power and authority by any means, including
outright assassination. Illegal oligarchies of women have grabbed the
reins of the North American Confederacy and the United States.

–Marlena Madison, unpublished journals, 2062

September 2062, Indiana:

THE MAGNETIC ROAD OUT OF Indianapolis was completely disabled. Indian
Air Force bombers had pelted it throughout the night as they blazed their way
through the heartland of the United States of America. Now cars and trucks
were crowding, bumper to bumper, on Old Route 75 in the rush to flee the
city and suburbs of Indianapolis.

In a fourth-floor apartment, Marlena Madison hurriedly filled her backpack with bottles of water, bags of trail mix, and the stun gun she'd found yesterday on the street with a full clip. Gun shops were empty. Food shops were
empty. Her mother, dying in the hospital, had begged her only daughter to get
away from the city while she still could. Lastly, the young woman grabbed her
electronic journal from the kitchen counter and threw that into her pack too.

Shrugging on the backpack, she heard the roar of airplanes. Seconds later, a squadron of Chinese bombers screamed over the city. She heard explo-
sions and the rumble of collapsing buildings. Terrified, she sprinted for the

stairwell, ran down the stairs two at a time, and threw her body against the door into the front lobby, opening it and sliding on the tiles in her panic. She heard a deafening roar and felt the whole building shake. Parts of the lobby ceiling fell and broke in pieces on the floor, and the middle of the room collapsed as she pushed through the front door and bolted across the street.

Shaking and breathing hard, Marlena turned and looked back. A tall black man, just behind her, had come through the door only to be knocked to the ground by an avalanche of falling debris from an overhanging section of the crumbling structure. With wide eyes, she watched him struggle to remain conscious as the rubble rained down on him. He would be buried in a minute. She knew him only as a friendly neighbor who had always smiled at her in passing. She struggled with indecision for a moment, and then ran back to help, frantically lifting and heaving away chunks of mortared bricks and broken cinder block while some detached part of her brain marveled at her own strength and daring.

Choking on concrete dust, she heard creaking, crashing, and glass shattering as the high-rise folded in on itself, and more chunks of masonry plummeted down to replace what she had moved. Suddenly fully conscious, the man fought to free himself as the young woman strained to lift a section of brick wall pinning down his leg. Another lethal chunk tumbled from far above, sending up a blinding dust cloud as it hit the rubble inches behind her. Pulling his bleeding body free, the big man crawled desperately toward the street, then, grabbing Marlena's arms, hauled himself up onto his battered feet, his skin ghostly gray with dust. Marlena staggered under his weight as they crossed the street, now littered with chunks of masonry. The deadly avalanche ceased—the ruined building creaked and groaned, enveloped in its dust cloud. Gasping and coughing, they paused for a few moments while the man tested his limbs. They were bruised and bleeding, but bore his weight.

"Mensch," he said to Marlena. "You're safe with me, for now. But I have to get to the men's camp before that changes. Where are you going?"

"I don't know," Marlena said. "Somewhere with women—and guns."

"I know such a place. Let me take you there. We need to find a car."

CHAPTER 1

◆ ◆ ◆

Evolution gave the male human a violent and competitive nature.
For much of our time on this planet, those qualities helped our
survival. But competition in war has come precipitously close
to annihilating our species. The time has come for women to
take control, and men must never be allowed to wield power
again. We must extinguish our desire for them. We must
learn to live without them, or none of us will live at all.

Women will create a new, enlightened society
from the ashes of patriarchy.

–Iolanda Voorhees, 2063

May 1, 2217, Fair City, Pennsylvania:

Marley had lost track of time, as fourteen-year-olds do, in the midst of
making up her face. Her elbows rested on her lace-trimmed dressing table,
and now her chin came to rest on her fists as she pondered her own reflection.
Her decorative tasks forgotten, she lost herself in the contemplation of her
own luminous dark eyes. An uncomfortable sense of longing persisted, but she
did not know what she longed for, and those eyes were not telling her.

Her golden-brown face blended the genetic heritage of the planet: full lips
and glossy waves of deep brown hair that could easily be lightened to gold

when she so desired. Marley was just one more young, beautiful, healthy specimen of North American womanhood, a species that had gradually improved since scientific reproduction began in the late 21st century.

Early morning sun peeked through lace curtains, and specks of dust drifted on the yellow light, falling onto a hanging fish net and its plush occupants. Cats, dogs, and bunnies were packed in with cute, toy versions of extinct species—polar bear, otter, lion, and tiger—gathered from numerous visits to the animal museum. Vivid scarves spilled from a shelf where a grouping of dolls cuddled together, childish things still holding a place in the changing heart of a young woman.

Oversized tropical fish added splashes of bright orange, black, and white to walls of pale aqua and blue—lovingly painted fifteen years ago by two happy women anticipating motherhood. On the dressing table, the happy moms-to-be laughed and smiled at Marley from a worn photo frame. Mama Jo's head was thrown back in laughter—mouth open, showing perfect teeth— her thick, dark hair falling freely over her shoulders. Mama Sue's adoring eyes peeked out from under wispy blonde bangs.

This picture was how Marley thought of Mama Jo, who had died when Marley was very young. In the slang of the day, she was Marley's egg-mama, the one whose egg had been fertilized to make her. Her mother's partner was her heart-mama. And the sperm donor? Well, they never told you which breeder male the sperm came from. He was undoubtedly a strong, healthy specimen, or he wouldn't have had his manhood preserved to pass on his genes. His progeny would now be scattered around the 102 states of North America.

Marley had seen vids of those huge, muscular young men brawling in their high security camps, shouting with deep, angry voices. She had no wish to meet one of them, ever.

◆ ◆ ◆

"Breakfast, Marley. Hurry up or you'll miss all the girls on the walk," Mama Sue's voice carried up the stairs, and Marley bestirred herself to finish her face and come down.

Marley's room was the tidiest room in the house, despite the cohabitation of childhood things and growing-up things. There was no place in the house to store away the treasures she no longer played with, because Mama Sue had filled up every available space with things she bought, salvaged, or just failed to throw away. The dwelling Marley shared with her heart-mama consisted of five rooms stacked on top of each other, one of twenty such homes forming a circular city block. Marley expertly found her footing down two stairways littered with boxes and stacks of things. Clothes hung on every railing.

"G'morning, Mama Sue," said Marley, flashing a brief smile. She did not run over to hug her heart-mama, as many girls would. As her friend Maddy would hug her moms, for instance. She just slid herself into the space in the dining booth where Mama Sue had pushed over some bags of recent purchases to clear a place just big enough for Marley to sit, and whisked away some dirty dishes to make room for her plate, stacking them precariously on top of the dishes already on the counter.

Mama Sue was not the huggy, kissy type. She set a plate of eggs and fried potatoes in front of Marley, with a cool, distant smile. Her eyes glanced over the girl with what felt to Marley like vague disapproval, but she said nothing. Marley was used to that look. She'd been getting it forever, but much more since she'd gone through puberty and gotten curvy. There was nothing wrong with Marley's looks—she knew that. She had streaks of metallic turquoise in her deep brown hair, and soft glitter brought out her dark eyes. Her clothes were the current teen fashions—mostly soft, form-fitting outfits in highly saturated colors that allowed a girl to move freely and showed every curve of her young body. Mama Sue let her buy and wear whatever she wanted without a word of judgment or praise or any other expression of interest.

I wish she would smile at me like she did at Mama Jo in that picture, Marley thought. The blonde wisps of the photo upstairs were gone now. Mama Sue wore her graying hair short and unkempt, her hands and ears unadorned, her squarish figure concealed in sensible, comfortable clothes. She used to wear flowy, colorful things when Mama Jo was alive. At the edges of Marley's memory were hazy scenes of friends and parties, singing, laughter, and dancing. Now, just an oppressive absence, and stuff on every surface.

Mama Sue would not talk about the fatal accident. When Marley asked about it, she answered tersely and changed the subject. Why was Mama Jo driving a car by hand on the old roads? Was it just a thrilling adventure? Many people knew how to drive a car by hand, as it was sometimes necessary to get from one mag road to another, especially in rural areas. But city folk like Marley and her mamas had no reason to be in those areas, except to cut across them on a mag road. Moving walkways got you around the city, and for longer trips, you just hired a car when you got to the mag road, or kept your own car in the garage there.

The condition of the old roads was unpredictable and deteriorating. The government invested in new mag roads rather than the maintenance of those relics of centuries past, when driving deaths were an epidemic. There were a lot more people, too, long ago, before World War III. Hundreds of cars, independently controlled by people who had to pay attention every second. What a bad idea that was. Those old cars had to be equipped with seat belts, air bags, and steel cages to protect their occupants. Now you just programmed in your destination and settled back to read a book or play games or eat lunch. And the car just took you there—smooth as your silk thong, fast as your mother's eye, and safe as your own bed.

What business did Mama Jo have driving on those rough old roads in a fragile mag road car? And why wasn't Mama Sue with her?

Maybe it was a mystery to Mama Sue as well. She had never remarried. She never seemed remotely interested in sharing her life with another woman. And so it had been Mama Sue and Marley, alone together all these years, in five rooms filled with random purchases and disorganized collections.

CHAPTER 2

◆ ◆ ◆

Voorhees is encouraging both women and men to embrace same-sex relationships. Hetero sex is all about lust, but same-sex love can be a meeting of minds and souls and everything. So she says. This idea that you can choose to be gay or straight was thrown in the dustbin of history a long time ago, and now she wants us to believe it again. But there are rumors that the Reproduction Centers are going to make all the babies gay. It's hard to know what to believe.

–MARLENA MADISON, UNPUBLISHED JOURNALS, 2065

MAY 1, 2217, FAIR CITY, PENNSYLVANIA:

MARLEY ATE THE EGGS AND potatoes, gave Mama Sue a quick kiss on the cheek, and bounced out the door to catch the walkway to her school. It was Sunday, a day when, in centuries past, people would have gone to various churches to worship the old deities. But to Marley, it was just another day—a day to take an exam, meet her friend Maddy for lunch, and play hockey in the afternoon.

Outside the back door, shrub gardens and lawns sloped away from the circle, shaded by a walkway two stories above. A pebbled path took her a few yards to a hollow pillar. She stepped inside, and an elevator raised her up to the slowest, rightmost track of the walkway. She looked around for friends in the moving throng of girls, women, and yunies.

"Marley, over here," a familiar voice called, and a hand waved from farther up the track. "I'll slow down for ya." The girl ahead stepped over to a slower track, while Marley stepped to a faster one until they met up. The taller girl, blonde with Nordic features, embraced her friend.

"Hey, *man-lover*, where you been?" she asked cheerfully.

"Fuck yourself with a carrot, Stace," Marley returned, taking the slur in the intended spirit of friendship. "I've been around. Online. Offline. Nowhere special. I messaged you yesterday. Guess we've just missed each other lately."

The girls held hands and stepped easily from one track to the next until they were on the fastest, leftmost track. The rain cover was retracted, leaving the walkway open to a cool, fresh, spring breeze and morning sunshine. The girls did not notice the dull hum of the machinery under the track. They walked at a leisurely pace past commuters who chose to sit on benches and move along with no effort. On one bench, a woman lay on her back, basking in the spring sunshine with eyes closed, her warm outerwear draped over the back of the bench. A Natural woman sat with her legs tucked up on the bench underneath her long skirt, reading something on her electronic device. She looked up and gave the passing girls a smile.

"Hard to get you away from Maddy these days," the blonde girl said in a teasing voice. "Is she converting you?"

"No, silly." Marley squeezed the hand of her sister-like friend and laughed. "Maddy doesn't try to convert people."

Marley and Stacey had spoken their first words together and taken their first steps together in the circle café while their moms drank chai. Stacey lived across the circle, and the girls had played together in the open space inside the circle of homes. Circle girls shared a playground, pool, and trampoline. Women shared the community kitchen and dining room, café, gym, general store, beauty salon, baths, and laundry.

Stacey and Marley had grown up in the homes of circle friends as much as their own. From their earliest days, numerous women welcomed them in, fed them, and tended their scraped knees. Many circle-dwelling mamas worked at businesses downtown, but many others worked from their computers at home, and women with new baby girls usually stopped working altogether for a year or two.

The girls grew up knowing that a decent standard of living was everyone's birthright, and no one had to work for basic housing, medical care, food, or clothing. But one did need Ameros to purchase luxuries. So Stacey and Marley had learned how to earn Ameros—first inside, and then outside of their own circle—so they could purchase the stylish clothing, makeup, and electronic toys they craved.

"It would be so weird if you joined the Naturals," said Stacey, with a trace of anxiety.

"Don't worry, silly. I'm not joining anything," said Marley. "Maddy is *glossy*, and so is her family. But I could never live their way. And maybe Maddy won't either, when she grows up. But anyway, I'll love you always. You know that, right?"

"Of course," said Stacey. "But I just don't understand their ways. Seems so *backward* to reject all the rep tech we have now." The girls swayed a little with the subtle movement as the walkway curved into the city center. "Something I love about you, Marl," she continued. "You don't care at all who's *hot* and who isn't, or what anyone thinks. You just like who you like, and hang out with who you like. I know we're supposed to be tolerant, but most people just won't hang with Natural girls."

"I know. They're different," said Marley agreeably. "Their ways are different. But they're women and girls underneath, just like us, right? They're not hurting anyone else, and they should be allowed to live their way, don't you think? Even if other people don't understand them. It's a free country."

"Course it is." The blonde girl twisted her long, straight tresses into a rope and then let them go again. The tall buildings of Fair City passed quickly on either side. People stepped onto the walkway, drifted over, spread out to give each other space, hurried up or slowed down to meet up with friends, or relaxed on the benches and just rode along, gazing at passing skyscrapers above and trees below, gorgeous with pink and white spring blossoms.

"It was really nice of you to make friends with her, anyway," Stacey continued. "I've never dared to say more than 'hi' to those girls. My questions would probably offend them, and I wouldn't know what to talk about. Like, why are they so modest and so, well, *bestial* at the same time? Why would *anyone* want to give birth in that horrible way, and suckle babies from their breasts? Ugh. It's so *disgusting*." She shuddered convulsively. "I mean, that's like having sex with your baby. It's perverted. But then they won't get naked with other women? Just what the fuck? I don't get it. Are you *lovers?*"

"What?" said Marley, startled.

"You and Maddy. Are you lovers?"

"No. No, I just like her. She's interesting and nice."

"So you're still not doing it with *anyone?*"

"No," said Marley. "You *know* you'd be the first one I'd tell if I were."

"Well, why the fuck not, girl? You're almost fifteen already."

"I don't know. I just … just haven't felt that way about anyone yet, I guess."

The blonde girl smiled. "Well," she said, in a knowing way, "maybe your hormones just haven't got going yet. Takes longer for some girls, I've heard. Even fifteen's not *really* old or anything. It's just such a delicious thing."

But Marley could feel some anxiety behind her friend's words. She knew there must be gossip that her loyal friend was not passing on to her.

The conversation paused as a group of hurrying girls caught up to them. Marley was left to her own thoughts as the other girls greeted Stacey and pulled her into the group. A couple of them smiled at Marley, but the group pulled Stacey away. Until the last year or two, Marley had felt right in step with the girls around her. But their growing sexual interest in each other was making her uncomfortable. She *was* having some sexual feelings, but she didn't feel like sharing them with anyone else, and she found the advances of the other girls vaguely repulsive. She knew she had hurt some feelings with her rejections. And her social status was not improved by hanging out with a weirdo Natural.

"How do you tell a girl Natural from a boy Natural?"

"The boy one has a beard?"

"No, silly. The girl one has a belly out to here!"

Marley took a deep breath and slowed her pace, letting Stacey move ahead with the other girls. She knew the lame joke was aimed at her, but she would not engage with their ignorant bigotry, which didn't even make sense. There was no such thing as a *boy* Natural. And those women were not pregnant *all* the time.

◆ ◆ ◆

Left to herself again, Marley thought about the exam she was taking today to pass Level Thirteen in history and social studies. History was her best subject, and she was several levels ahead of her age-mates. She'd read all of the writings of Iolanda Voorhees and the Second Enlightenment writers who built on her work. She mentally rehearsed the essay she would have to write today from memory.

In the old days before World War III, aggressive males ran rampant through society. Women could not have children unless they physically mated with men, which was a painful and disgusting procedure. Men were not capable of love, and had little interest even in pleasure. Their humanity was overpowered by their biological drive to impregnate women and pass on their genes. Women had actually tried to live with them through all those centuries—but mostly because men had all the power and money, and a woman had no way to live on her own. This abuse of women and children was bad enough.

Even worse was that men controlled governments and armies and constantly made war on each other, torturing and killing countless people. Men fought over the world's resources, destroying much of what they were fighting over. They fought over things that were patently ridiculous, like *skin color*, for *godssakes*, or petty disagreements about creation myths and gods. But the real reason they fought over those ridiculous things was that their hormones made them uncontrollably aggressive. And this happened for many, many centuries before the last devastating crisis of World War III, when women finally took all political and social power away from them.

◆ ◆ ◆

Marley's mind continued to wander through all the facts and ideas she had so readily absorbed throughout her young life. Before World War III, women were the property of men, to do with as they pleased. Men used to burn women at the stake, or drown them, or throw stones at them until they died. In some countries, they did not allow women to abort embryos they didn't want. In others, they forced women to keep their bodies covered up, even more than the Naturals did. Women were not allowed to leave the men who owned them, and not allowed to marry other women with whom they could have real love.

Not all men were abusive or stupid. Like the modern yunies, some men had lower testosterone levels that allowed their humanity to shine through. Some of these men had intelligence on par with that of women. Such men had used their power and privilege to help women advance in science and technology. But it was touch and go for a century or two when these advances allowed the creation of massively destructive weapons and governments were still controlled by men: the recipe for disaster that led to three world wars.

But women were not all innocent in those bad old days, either. The lust of hetero females for powerful men was as much to blame for the near-destruction of the human race and the planet as the men were themselves.

Marley's historical reverie ended with the girls' arrival at one of their school buildings. The massive moving highway was now six stories above the ground, and the girls stepped off it onto a smaller walkway leading to the sixth floor entrance of their school building. Marley hurried inside, ready and eager to ace her exam.

CHAPTER 3

◆ ◆ ◆

I have showed you the way. Together we have constructed
a new society free from the dangers of patriarchy. Now it is
up to you, and your succeeding generations, to preserve and
improve on what we have done. You must never forget the
horrors of the past. You must never become complacent.

—LAST SPEECH OF IOLANDA VOORHEES, 2102

2188-2206, NEW YORK CITY, NEW YORK:

VANESSA SILVA IOLANDA HAD WANTED to work in law enforcement as long as
she could remember. Both Mama Coopa and Mama Silva were on the force,
fighting pornography and subversion from their home in a circle community
in the sprawling metropolitan area of New York. As a toddler, Vanessa sat near
her mamas, sucking on her bottle as they worked on their computers, and
listening as they talked about their work. Defending the Enlightened Society
from its internal enemies was, to her, the best work a person could do, and
Vanessa never had any other ambition.

She learned to read sitting on Mama Coopa's lap, watching words on the
reader as her mama read them out loud. Vanessa was about four when the
words began to make sense, and she started reading on her own.

At about eight years old, she began to lose interest in her friends, and the
older Vanessa got, the more she found the girls her age boring and silly. She
preferred to spend time with her mamas and their adult friends.

Other law enforcement professionals lived in the circle, too. Work colleagues became friends, and friends nominated friends to live in their circles when there was an opening. On a typical evening, some of these friends gathered in their small sitting room, with wine and snacks, and Vanessa, now eleven, drew pictures and listened to their conversation.

"If our society were any more perfect, we wouldn't have jobs, would we?" Mama Coopa was saying, as she refilled her friends' wine glasses. The other women nodded in agreement.

"But after all this time, there are still so many bad apples," another woman sighed. "It's like there are people who just can't be happy anywhere."

"Those bad apples have no perspective," said Mama Coopa. "Humanity has gone through so much bloodshed and horror to get to where we are. And we've come closer than ever before to creating a society that makes *everyone* happy. Our criminals are spitting in the face of all that effort, and in the face of all the suffering that went before. They would take us back to the Dark Ages."

"Why do people want to go back to the Dark Ages?" asked Vanessa, looking up from her pencil drawing. She was redesigning the living room on paper.

"Different people have different reasons," Mama Coopa said, including her youngster in the conversation without hesitation. "There are men, for instance, who want the power and control that men used to have. There are women who are shortsighted and selfish. There are people who are unhappy or mentally disturbed, lashing out and blaming society. And of course the heteros who want to act out their lust and don't care about the ramifications of what they do."

"What are ramifications?"

"Consequences, results."

"Are heteros bad people?" Vanessa asked.

"Not necessarily. I mean, some of them are quite nice and hard-working," Mama Coopa said. "But they're infected, or rotten, like bad nuts or bad apples. If they're not separated out, they can infect other people with their sickness. Maybe they can't help having those feelings, but some choose to act on them, and then they want to justify that. If that starts, our whole society could become infected and fall apart. Someday we'll find a way to identify hetero-sexuality at birth, or even sooner, and then they won't be a problem any more."

"So even if they're really nice people, you have to find them and put them in the camps?" Vanessa asked.

"Yes, exactly," her heart-mama replied. "But we don't need to find every single one. They don't do a lot of damage if they keep quietly to themselves. Mostly we need to suppress advocacy and solidarity—"

"What's advo-cassy?"

"Finding each other, getting together, telling people it's okay to be hetero."

◆ ◆ ◆

Through her teen years, Vanessa used the resources and facilitators at her local school to research all the major areas of modern crime, looking for something she could spend her life fighting.

She studied economic crime. Barter, alternate currencies, and black mar-ket trading were crimes because they hurt the Amero system that provided a decent standard of living for everyone. Some law enforcement professionals worked online looking for these activities, and others went undercover to look for illegal trading. Vanessa was intrigued by the idea of befriending people, learning their secrets, and then bringing them crashing down.

She loved arguing online with people all over Canusaco.

Barterisbest: Why should the government care what we trade with? People in communities trade things all the time— goods for services, and services for goods. Why should anyone care if we use silver, gold, shells, or goats to facili-tate this?

Van79: If people don't trade with Ameros, the system doesn't work.

Barterisbest: Trading has no victim. Only winners on both sides. How can that be a crime? Ameros suck. They lose value constantly. They're worth a tenth of what they were when I was 20.

Van79: Of course. That's how the system works, stupid. You also get everything you really need for nothing: food, housing, medical care. If you destroy that system, you bring back poverty, and all the crime and suffering that went with it. You don't think that's a crime? That's the biggest crime I can think of.

◆ ◆ ◆

When Vanessa was fifteen, Mama Silva showed her how to participate and cast her votes in the official ongoing conversation about what constituted a decent standard of living. What should the government provide, and what should people have to work for and pay for?

"It's a subjective thing," Mama Silva explained. "And it changes with technology and overall prosperity. It's important for everyone to have a voice in it."

For months, Vanessa was almost constantly on her computer, expressing her opinions. It was exciting for her to participate in this highly democratic system.

Van79: Of course free homes should have climate control. People can die without that.

Barlane642: Lots of people out in the countryside don't have climate control. It's too much. If you give people too much, they won't want to work. And then everything else costs a fortune because you have to pay people so much to induce them to do a job.

Van79: Everyone I know has a job. People aren't just going to stop working. What would they do if they didn't work? Nobody wants to sit at home watching screens all day. They'd get bored to death.

Barlane642: I know people who watch screens all day. Because free housing has screens and Web access. There's nothing they want enough to work for it.

Van79: Well, good for them. They're content, right? If they ever want new furniture or cool clothes or something, they'll get a job. Why does it bother you?

Barlane642: Because they're getting all that and everything I buy costs more because of it. I just think screens and climate control are too much.

Van79: Well, vote against them, then.

Violent crime was almost nonexistent, and this was, of course, one of the crowning achievements of the Enlightened Society. For centuries, everyone had known that young males were committing the vast majority of murders, rapes, robberies, and assaults. But before the Second Enlightenment, an irrational concept of civil rights got in the way of effective prevention. Now that young males were humanely contained and controlled, every murder that happened in Canusaco was national news.

Child abuse and neglect had of course been widespread and common before the Second Enlightenment. Fertile men naturally abused the women and children who belonged to them, and victims who escaped fell into poverty. Vanessa knew a few moms who yelled at their girls, or even slapped them or pulled their hair. But now, communal living and public nudity made more serious physical abuse almost impossible to hide. Some moms were just fucking mean or uninterested in their girls. But a girl could always go and live with someone else. Girls had rights and respect in the Enlightened Society.

Before Voorhees, people had valued all the wrong things, Vanessa decided when she was sixteen. They valued the independent nuclear family, the private home, the rights of parents, and modesty—values that allowed abuse to go on for years and years without anyone noticing. But most of those weird values came from their crazy old religions. No wonder.

But even now, with fertile men controlled and contained, crimes happened. Vanessa read about women who had poisoned their little girls to get them out of the way. In some cases, the mother had a new lover who did not want the child. In others, the mother just didn't like motherhood, and wanted to garner sympathy instead of disapproval.

There's absolutely no excuse for that, Vanessa thought with angry disgust. *When so many other women would have taken her child. Mothers in the old days had to deal with pregnancy, horrible childbirth, postpartum depression, ruined bodies, poverty, social isolation, and violent men. Children could be sick, deformed, or retarded. They had to raise boys, too, and try to keep the girls safe from the boys. It's a wonder any children survived at all.*

Everything is so easy now. In our society, criminals have no excuses.

CHAPTER 4

◆ ◆ ◆

The modern woman is many generations removed from the necessity of carrying, birthing, and suckling babies. She thinks with horror of the pain of childbirth, and the ruination of the pristine beauty of her body. She thinks that surely we are too technologically advanced to endure such things. What the modern woman misses is the astounding wonder of another human life growing inside of her, and the intense bonding that occurs as a baby girl suckles from her breast. Artificial womb technology has taken this away from us. But we can choose to take it back.

–MADELAINE SAIRA AMAR, *THE NATURAL WAY*, 2146

JANUARY 2216, FAIR CITY, PENNSYLVANIA:

MARLEY HAD NEVER MET A Natural girl until Maddy appeared at school in January of 2216 after the winter break. She was accompanied by two older girls dressed in the same odd fashion. Maddy looked shy and out of place, and stayed close to the older girls. Their dresses were pretty, just not at all fashionable, and they covered up the girls' bodies as if they were something to be ashamed of. The dresses were made of lovely fabrics, but over-decorated with ribbons, buttons, or lace, which was not at all the current thing. The girls looked like they belonged in a period piece for some period Marley couldn't quite place. Not 23rd century Canusaco, certainly.

Fascinated, Marley had flipped open her computer to learn something about these girls and their strange subculture. Naturals believed that the biological processes of pregnancy and suckling were essential to mother-daughter bonding, creating a stronger family and healthier, happier girls. Naturals did not have their eggs removed like normal people. The sperm selected by the Breeding Program was injected into their bodies, fertilizing their eggs right inside them. When the babies came out, the mothers suckled them at their breasts, which swelled up and made milk like the udders of cows.

Naturals also believed that sexuality belonged only inside of marriage, and that girls and women should dress modestly to inhibit sexual interest until they were committed to one person. They did not participate in sports or public bathing for this reason. The mothers kept their young daughters very close, rarely allowing them outside of their circle communities until they were ten or twelve.

So this is why I've never met any before, Marley thought. *I wonder if all the Natural moms don't want people to see their ruined bodies, and they dress all the girls like that so they never get used to looking good.*

Naturals tended to live and work inside their own circles, and never went out in public in that offensive state of advanced pregnancy. And Marley supposed that they kept the girls close so they could indoctrinate them with their odd ideas. Because who would chose to live like that if they knew better?

Marley knew that in the bad old days before the Second Enlightenment, people believed they had the right to indoctrinate their children with their own way of life. Religions, nationalities, political parties, feminists, and patriarchs all had their own worldviews, myths and gods, rituals, and sacred stories. They all thought it was dreadfully important for their children to grow up believing the same things, living the same way, and often hating those who believed differently.

Maybe it's a nice lifestyle if you're really into it, Marley thought. *But don't they get how wrong it is to brainwash little girls to make them think like you? Girls have a right to their own beliefs and choices.*

The worst thing about natural pregnancy was that women could not be sure that they'd conceived a girl until they were a few months along. If the embryo tested male, they had to abort and try again. And some Natural women even rejected abortion, believing that it was wrong to deliberately terminate any human life. Marley could not understand how women could embrace an idea that had been so central to patriarchy. But some of these women insisted on birthing the males they conceived, after which the authorities would take them and deliver them to a boys' camp. Then the poor woman had to start all over again trying to have a girl.

More disturbing than the Natural Way itself were the subversive links that popped up as she researched it. Subversive sites were illegal, of course, and girls could get in serious trouble if they were caught looking at them. The authorities continually shut them down, but new ones appeared just as fast. She had heard girls talk of the site called *Man Power* that the authorities apparently couldn't kill, and now she was curious. She touched her screen and went to the site.

"WHY MEN MUST WAKE UP AND TAKE BACK POWER" was the title of the top vid.

Well, that's a bit frightening, Marley thought, imagining the breeder males she'd seen in vids rampaging on the walkways. Then she tried to imagine the gentle yunies who lived in her circle waking up and taking back power. Why the hell *would* they? Why would they want *power*? She almost laughed out loud at the thought. Her "uncles" knew as well as anyone that breeders, yunies, and women had their proper places and roles in life.

She'd seen badly crafted vids like this in history class—relics of the 20th century. An older male with facial hair and crooked teeth began speaking in a deep, belligerent voice that Marley found so grating that she muted the sound. The words were transcribed, and she read them quickly instead.

City Woman think there enlightened, but everything they think is bullshit propaganda that the government stuffs into their heads through their corrupt school system. There so spoiled and lazy that they don't want to think about what hippocrits they are. They live in lazy luckshury while breeder men and work campers do all the work and have nothing. They put innocint children in work camps so they can live in luckshury without working at all. And they give girls to their breeder man-slaves to keep them working.

THE NATURAL ORDER IS FOR MEN TO HAVE POWER AND WOMEN TO HAVE BABIES AND BE SUBJECT TO MAN. That is why GOD made us stronger then them. Woman are being misled by the DEVILS of Science and Enlightenment.

Reproduction Centers must be destroyed! City schools must be destroyed! Woman must be forced to give up these DEVILISH ideas and fulfill her natural function. Subscribe to *Man Power* now, and join the fight.

LIBERATE MAN!! SUBJUGATE WOMAN!!

Fucking hell, Marley thought. *Why are the authorities even worried about this crap? Who would believe this? Nobody wants men in power, and this is all so obviously wrong. Of course women work. And we pay for our luxuries. And our society is all about taking care of girls, and breeders don't even want girls. And God and the Devil? That's just wacko stuff from the 20th century. And forsakes, he can't even spell the words right.*

As Marley wiped the history of her search off her computer, she wondered if there was some connection between subversives and the Natural culture, aside from the frequent use of the word "natural." But Naturals did not appear to be interested in forcing their lifestyle on anyone except their own girls. And Naturals never spoke of destruction or giving power back to men.

She continued to see Maddy and the other girls at school through the spring, summer, fall, and into the winter.

January 2217, Fair City, Pennsylvania:

A year had passed since Maddy first appeared at school, and Marley returned from the winter break eager to embrace new things in the new year. The older Natural girls had moved on, and Maddy now went quietly about her business by herself—doing her studies, eating her lunch, smiling and being polite, but never approaching the other girls with invitations for friendship. The other girls had smiled back politely and avoided her, as always.

One day Marley couldn't stand it anymore. She approached Maddy in the lunchroom.

"Can I eat with you?"

"Of course," Maddy said.

"I don't like to see you alone all the time," Marley said. "The girls just don't know what to make of you. But you seem so nice. Why couldn't we be friends?"

"No reason at all," said Maddy. She was tall and slender. Her eyes were hazel, and her light golden brown hair fell straight past her shoulders. Marley loved how her wide smile lit up her face. Her face was not the most classically pretty, but was somehow tremendously appealing. Marley liked her instantly.

Maddy accepted the ostracism of the other girls as a matter of course, and was amused that Marley got so angry about it. She seemed entertained by the looks that passed between Marley and the other girls: disdain from the girls, and daggers from Marley.

◆ ◆ ◆

Through the rest of the winter, the two had met up at school and gone to the School Mall for lunch or shopping. This ground level walkway extending away from the school buildings was lined on both sides with shops, salons, and eateries, staffed mostly by girls learning trades and earning Ameros. When the trees sparkled with ice, or carried loads of snow, the Mall was covered over and kept warm. Marley wished she could invite Maddy to her home, but she was too ashamed of the cluttered mess there. She hadn't invited a friend over for years.

"It's not you," she told Maddy. "It's my house. It's just not ... well, good enough for you."

"Well, you'll have to come to mine, then," said Maddy.

"Really? Your moms wouldn't mind?"

"Why would they mind?"

"I thought Naturals didn't like other people," said Marley, embarrassed.

"My moms like everyone," said Maddy.

And Marley was surprised and pleased at the warm welcome she got from Maddy's moms and sisters. Still, she sensed an undercurrent of wariness in looks that passed between the moms or between Maddy and a mom when they thought Marley wasn't looking.

They're afraid, she thought. *They think I will take their daughter away from their way of life. And, to be honest, I want to.*

"I want to see your room," said Marley.

Maddy showed her the small, simple room where she slept and studied. "It's so plain," Marley said, and then wondered if that was rude. But Maddy was not offended.

"I don't like fancy things," Maddy said. Marley thought her room was at odds with her clothing style, but kept that to herself.

"Shall we watch a show?" Marley asked.

"Sure," said Maddy. "Downstairs, though. I don't hang out with friends in my room."

MARCH 2217, FAIR CITY, PENNSYLVANIA:

Marley felt herself drawn into a nest of affection that warmed her heart. These moms didn't need a good reason to hug and kiss their three girls. Marley and Maddy rarely watched a show in the den without a sister or two snuggled up on the couch with them. Mama Denissa sometimes sat with them, too. Once, Marley was astonished to see the smallest girl, about three years old, run up to Mama Denissa and put her head under her mama's shirt to suck on her breast after getting hurt on the circle playground. Mama Den scooped her up with an embarrassed laugh. "We'll be back in a bit," she said to the teens, carrying the child out of the room.

"Sorry about that," said Maddy. "I know you're not used to it."

"It's okay," said Marley, trying to sort out her feelings. It was tender and sweet, yet revolting. And now they had a few minutes alone.

"I love your family so much," Marley said. "Me and Mama Sue ... we're nothing like this. You're like a bunch of friggin' puppies. It makes me cry, almost. I want a family like this."

"But," she went on, "do you ... or do I ... really have to go through natural birth to have a close, loving family like this? Isn't there another way? I mean, Maddy, do *you* want to ruin your body by having babies like your moms have?"

"No, I don't," Maddy said without hesitation. "And I really think that babies from the Rep Center could be raised with just as much love."

"I do, too," Marley said confidently, happy that Maddy seemed to agree. "It wouldn't have to be like me and Mama Sue. I don't think she really loves me. But I think my Mama Jo did. All that stuff your Mama Lara says about the physical basis of love ... I think I could ... *we* could ... me and my partner, I mean ... we could do a lot of it without being so unreasonable. We could hold our baby every minute, and sleep with her, and all that good stuff they talk about. Just leave out the pregnancy and the suckling thing."

"You want to have life all figured out, don't you?" said Maddy, with gentle amusement. "Having babies is so far off."

"Oh, I know," said Marley. "I think it's *you*, actually. I want to convince you. I'm afraid you'll go your moms' way, and I just can't stand to think about you going through all that. And I'd love to see you in regular clothes, and playing sports and stuff, too. Your moms are so sweet, and I don't understand why they can't just let you be yourself and do what you want."

"This is just their way of life," Maddy said. "I'm just going along with it for now. They totally love me. Someday I'll get to be myself more."

"Your moms wouldn't be mad if you grew up to be like us?"

"No. Not at all," said Maddy. "They don't try to push Naturalism on me or anyone else. Can we watch this fucking show now?"

CHAPTER 5

◆ ◆ ◆

Shame was the invention of a patriarchal male god, and
served the abuses of patriarchy. Countless bruises inflicted
on women and children were hidden under clothes.

—IOLANDA VOORHEES, 2102

MAY 1, 2217, FAIR CITY, PENNSYLVANIA:

MARLEY READ THROUGH HER HISTORY essay one more time, did some final
edits and additions, and hit the Send button. Six other girls, all two or three
years older, were scattered around the room in comfortable chairs, typing on
special devices that did not allow them to access outside information. The
exam was designed to test the knowledge in their heads, not their research
skills. She'd been at it for two hours, and she knew she'd done very well. She
closed the device, got up, and went to trade it for her own device at the facili-
tator's desk. The woman gave her a smile.

Outside the room, Marley messaged Maddy, who was wandering the
Mall waiting for her to finish. They met up in their favorite Thai lunchroom.
Marley caught her friend's eye and her wide, warm smile from across the
room, and hurried over with her tray.

"How are you, sweetie?" she asked before she dove hungrily into her
Weeping Tiger salad.

"I'm good," Maddy returned. Marley was pleased to see Maddy wearing a dress they'd picked out together. It was long and simple, in pleasing shades of brown and intense green, with wings on the shoulders. Wings were the latest thing. Maddy had always worn clothes made by the women in her circle, and it had never occurred to her to look elsewhere. But Marley had quickly discerned that this homemade clothing was not really Maddy's style. They'd done some searching together online, and found modest enough clothing in vivid colors with wings, stylish and flattering to Maddy's tall, slender figure.

"So how's the math going?" Marley asked.

"Almost finished Level Thirteen," Maddy said.

"You're way ahead of me," said Marley. "I got to Level Ten before I got more interested in history and horticulture."

"I quit history at Eight," said Maddy. "History annoys me. Math makes a lot more sense. Horticulture sounds fun."

Marley was happy to have a friend who liked academics at all. Many of her friends studied very little, and spent most of their time socializing in the lounges and eating rooms, or playing games or watching movies. The school offered all kinds of arts, crafts, and practical skills as well. Girls were encouraged to try many things and follow their own interests.

"I like the bigger boobs," Marley teased. On their last shopping spree, she'd helped Maddy pick out a new padded bra.

"I like fake better than real," said Maddy. "I can take them off when I want to."

Marley laughed. "You're right. I wish I could take mine off for hockey."

"I saw you coming in with the mean girls this morning," Maddy smirked playfully, changing the subject. "I avoided you all like the plague."

"Oh, *them,*" said Marley, rolling her eyes. "I was walking with Stacey, and they chased her down. Stacey's the only one I really hang with. They're okay people, though. They just talk about the same stuff all the time—sex, clothes, and how popular they are. Like there's nothing else in life."

"Seems like they want you in their crowd, though."

"I don't know," Marley mused. "I guess they do. I used to hang out with them a lot, but it just doesn't feel as comfortable now. I feel more comfortable with you." *Which is weird,* Marley thought. *Weird that I feel so close to a girl who was brought up so differently from me.*

Marley met Maddy's eyes, and she felt mesmerized, like she could look into her friend's eyes forever.

Gods, am I attracted to her? Is this actually happening to me?

"You gonna watch my game this afternoon?" Marley asked.

"Sure, if you want me to."

"I want you to."

◆ ◆ ◆

Marley looked up from the hockey field to find Maddy in the stands. Her friend looked wistful, and Marley suddenly felt guilty. Maddy wasn't allowed to play sports at school.

But she wishes she could, Marley thought indignantly. *Why don't her moms let her do what she wants?*

After the game, hilarity and abandon pervaded the locker room. Girls shrieked, and water was everywhere. Marley stripped off her protective gear, and then her purple and turquoise uniform, which she threw into the laundry chute with the others. At her own locker, she took off her underwear and shoes and walked naked to the shower room. The textured floor was soft as carpet under her feet, pulling the water into itself and away.

Nine girls stood under the shower heads near the walls, watching two more who were playfully attacking each other with sodden towels. Hot water sprayed from the twelve showerheads, streaming down nubile bodies and still-childish bodies that glistened in every shade from palest peach to deep cocoa. Water turned all hair dark and straight, except on a few heads where droplets clung to unsinkable curls. Onlookers shouted encouragement as the shrieking combatants scored hits on each other's slippery bodies. Water pooled on the floor briefly before disappearing into the textured flooring that drained it away. A little scream pierced the air as one girl slid suddenly, grabbing at the slippery body of the other. Both went down with a splash, gasped, and then wrestled on the floor, the towels cast aside and the spectators egging them on. Marley watched with amusement as she waited for a chance at a shower.

"What is going on here?" A stout, older woman, fully dressed and with frumpy hair, had seemed to materialize at the shower room entrance while the girls' eyes were on the show. The shrieking and laughing stopped like a plug had been pulled. The running water was loud in the sudden stillness. The frumpy woman clapped her hands authoritatively. "Get your showers, get dressed, and run home," she said. "You've all got more energy than anyone deserves." She stood there glaring to make sure hilarity did not break out again.

The girls finished showering in a more subdued manner, until there was room for Marley. She showered quickly, and picked up a towel in the drying room. Warm air caressed her from all directions, drying her body while she toweled her hair. She was too impatient to dry her hair all the way. She pulled her clothes on quickly, wondering if Maddy was waiting for her.

She was.

CHAPTER 6

◆ ◆ ◆

Immature girls can be confused by the presence of the younger
yunies, and curiosity can turn to full-blown heterosexuality. Girls
should never be exposed to any male person younger than thirty.

–BRANDA WALTENE, *PRESIDENTIAL ADDRESS*, 2122

MAY 2217, FAIR CITY, PENNSYLVANIA:

LALLAINA LIVED ON THE OTHER side of Marley's circle. Marley liked to hang
out there because Lallaina's mom made glossy cannabis cookies, there wasn't
a speck of clutter in the whole house, and there were so many cats.

Lallaina's long, straight hair was a dark, iridescent green. She wore loads
of black makeup around her almond-shaped eyes, and had little stars tattooed
all the way down her arms and legs. She and Marley had reached menarche
at about the same time, and they went to the MediSalon together to get all
their body hair permanently removed and receive implants to immunize them
against sexually transmitted diseases and inhibit their monthly cycles. A first
tattoo at this time was traditional—a visual reminder that one had reached
this threshold of womanhood. Marley had conservatively stopped at one: a
Celtic knot on the back of her right shoulder.

On this particular springy, warm afternoon, Marley entered carefully, pushing away cats with her foot while squeezing her body through the space to pre-
vent the felines escaping. They never ceased to be curious about the outdoors.

She loved this sparsely furnished, uncluttered home. The walls, painted bright shades of green and blue, were adorned with catwalks, cat-stairs, and cat-shelves. Cats lounged, slept, and jumped from one to another. No other decoration was needed, nor would any other decoration survive long here.

Marley found Lallaina upstairs in a screened-in balcony overlooking the expanse of the center garden. Cherry, apple, and dogwood trees bloomed white and pink. Petals had just begun to fall, like spring snow. An old woman bent over in the vegetable garden, weeding the first crops of lettuce and spinach. Two small, giggly girls chased each other through the playground, climbing the slide and spiraling down, over and over again, under the eye of an older girl with short blue curls.

"Who *is* that?" said Lallaina, concentrating. "Oh, it's Dallas! Love the hair. When did she do that?"

"Must have been yesterday," said Marley. "I think I saw her the day before, and it wasn't blue then."

"Wanna see something fucked up?" Lallaina asked.

"Sure."

Lallaina took out her device, and touched a few places on it. "I just got past the controls," she said. "Funny. I always thought it would be *hard*. It's pretty simple, really. I found all this hetero shit. And boys."

Marley was interested. "Gross," she said.

"You wanna look or not?"

"Hell, yeah."

Lallaina pulled a slender telescoping pole out of her device, and a screen unfurled, big enough for them to watch together.

"Oh," Marley gasped at the illicit images of teenage boys.

Vids smuggled from boys' camps showed boys running and playing on a summer day, boys from about five to fourteen years of age. They wore simple khaki shorts and muscle shirts, with caps covering their shorn heads.

Other vids showed teenage boys kissing and fondling each other. And teenage boys with teenage girls.

Where did that happen? Marley wondered. *That's not supposed to happen anywhere.*

Then there were vids of grown men and women. Big breeding males were sticking their cocks into women. Mating. Rape. But the women were acting as if they *liked* it.

Fascination, revulsion, and arousal knocked against each other inside Marley's mind and body. *I'm not aroused by this,* she insisted inside herself. *It's horrible, weird, and wrong. How can women let men do that? Aren't they scared? Is someone threatening them? Is someone protecting them?*

"There's tons of it," Lallaina said. "I think a lot of people secretly like it."

"Really? But it's so *disgusting*," said Marley vehemently, opening the next vid. "They're like animals. It's not like you could have a *relationship* with a male. I wonder if they do it with animals, too?"

She felt a flush in her cheeks, and hoped it didn't show.

"You can read articles here too," said Lallaina. "History-you-won't-learn-in-school kind of stuff. Our facilitators would call it wacko bullshit. But these people say that we've all been brainwashed and *they're* the ones telling the truth. They say that in the old times, they used to persecute women for being together, and men for being together. They thought this hetero stuff was normal, and women were happy with it."

"I saw something like that on *Man Power*," said Marley, happy that she had something illicit to share as well. "It was obviously total bullshit, though."

Lallaina's brow was furrowed. "I know women had to do this to make babies back then, but how sick is it to enjoy it? It's like killing real animals for fun when you can just buy meat from the factory."

"Why do you think so many people want to watch this stuff?" Marley asked, keeping the conversation academic, as if they were studying the reproductive behavior of animals. She pushed away a young black cat that was insistently getting between her and the screen. The kitten playfully attacked her hand with his little teeth and claws as Marley rubbed his soft belly.

"I think there's a primitive part of the brain that still likes it," Lallaina theorized. "Because, you know, our species wouldn't have survived before without people doing it. There had to be *some* pleasure in it, right? For someone? Maybe we're not as evolved as we think—not all of us, anyway. And there's no real harm in watching vids, right? It's not like you're bringing a big scary breeder male in to live in your circle, or letting them control society. You're just watching a vid."

"Can you show me how you got through the controls?" Marley asked. "I want to see what other fucked-up shit is out there."

◆ ◆ ◆

Later on, in the privacy of her own room, Marley disabled the barriers on her own device, and guiltily explored this forbidden territory for herself. She knew that the morals of her society were grounded in science, not based on ancient superstitions or the dictates of ferocious male gods. Rationality had at last won out over fairy tales. Humans had endured centuries of bloodbaths and bombs before enlightened scientific morals came to the rescue. And here she was, violating them.

But I just want to look at them, Marley told herself again. *It can't hurt to just look. It's not like I'm actually doing it. It's not like there are any boys to do it with. And I think I'm attracted to Maddy, so I'm okay.*

"Photos of boys! Vids of boys! *Boys! Boys! Boys!*" the websites screamed at her. "Photos of boys from Pine Barrens Boys Camp in New Jersey." She clicked on that one, and the pictures slid past her eyes. Laughing, smiling faces. They didn't look like the yunies she knew, or the hulking breeders, either. Their faces were young and smooth like girls' faces. Their bodies were slender.

She clicked on a slideshow that said, "Watch a boy grow up." A little naked baby boy was kicking and waving his little arms, studying his own fists with great concentration. He looked just like a baby girl except for that funny little noodle between his legs. The video showed the baby crawling around, and then walking. She watched as he grew older, and he still looked a lot like a girl, except for the simple clothes and the shorn head. Then she saw him reach puberty. She saw him shaving his face. The muscles developed, and he was definitely not like a girl anymore. But not like a yunie, either. She had never seen a yunie unclothed, but she was pretty sure that her uncles were not so beautiful and slender under their clothes. The flat belly, the beautiful curves of buttocks and thighs ... she wanted to reach out and caress those curves

... and his chest and shoulders ... *oh.* A closeup showed laughing eyes with long, dark lashes. She watched the young man playing with the others: batting baseballs, running races, wrestling. Then she saw two young men in the grass, kissing each other. She felt a tightness in her belly. Arousal, revulsion, and envy. She didn't like them kissing each other. She clicked past it quickly.

But why not? They belong with their own kind. We belong with ours. They're not like us. This is just immature lust. This is why we're not supposed to watch this stuff. She felt a rush of intense shame.

Brightly colored links popped unbidden onto her screen.

BOYS! BOYS! BOYS!
HOT BOY-ON-GIRL ACTION!
HOTTEST HETERO SEX PICS!!!!
Meet Other Heterosexuals.
Chat With Heterosexuals. Private. Discreet. Fully encrypted chat rooms.
Help for Heterosexuality. You are not alone, and you have the power to change. Free, confidential counseling and hormone treatment.
Porn Addiction. Is hetero porn destroying your life? Get help now.

Marley suddenly felt wrong and dirty, and she cleared her screen and pulled up her history project: *Iolanda Voorhees, The Early Years.*

CHAPTER 7

◆ ◆ ◆

We believe that marriage love is stronger when sex has been saved
for it. When a bow is pulled back strong and hard, the arrow flies far
and true. Holding back one's sexuality requires strength, but ensures
that all of one's sexual passion is poured into one relationship, giving
it the best chance to succeed. We fear that girls are wasting and using
up their passion on too many relationships at such a young age.

—Aurelie Madeleine Saira, *Beyond the Natural Way*, 2167

May 2217, Neshoba Boys' Camp, Mississippi:

At Neshoba Boys' Camp in Mississippi, dim firelight glowed softly on the
faces of three boys. James, a wiry boy of thirteen with dark hair, light brown
eyes, and a few freckles scattered across his nose and cheeks, stirred a pot of
stew over the smoldering embers of a small campfire. Da Zack, the yunie father in charge of their dormitory, had prepared the stew and sent it with them.

"Is that ready yet?" asked Peter, a strong, dark, stocky boy of fourteen.
"I'm starving."

"Almost hot," said James.

"I don't care," said Peter. "Give me some now."

James served some out into a metal bowl.

Robert—blond, blue-eyed, and thirteen—was engrossed in a book illu-
minated by a small battery lamp on a clip. Two boys a couple of years older

33

were snuggled up in a double sleeping bag, watching the stars and talking quietly.

"You crushies want some stew?" said James presently. Bryan was the eldest in James' dorm, and Keiran one of the eldest in Peter's. A month ago, they were just buddies like the rest of them, and now they were crushies. James idly wondered what that felt like. He loved his dorm brothers, and many of his camp brothers, but he'd never experienced that crushy feeling.

◆ ◆ ◆

Neshoba Boys' Camp in Mississippi sprawled over almost 1,000 acres of rolling hills near the origin of the Pearl River, in what used to be the heart of the Choctaw Nation before the Choctaw were sent on their Trail of Tears. The nearby city of Philadelphia was a hotbed of conflict in the Civil Rights Movement of the 20th century. In the late 21st century, Chinese bombers razed half of the city to the ground. To the boys growing up there, these ancient conflicts were merely quaint historical facts. The blood of all the continents mixed in their veins, their features combining gracefully in mostly light-brown faces, though the Reproduction Centers also took care to preserve some physical types based on recessive genes.

This beautiful and sturdy race of mongrels played outside in the warm sun, climbed the maples and magnolias, and fished for black bass, perch, and mullet in the streams. They took binoculars and went hunting for glimpses of opossums, armadillos, coyotes, minks, skunks, and white-tailed deer. The ubiquitous raccoons invaded their campsites and made off with their food if they weren't careful. Neshoba was a refuge for native species of plants and animals, and many of the yunie fathers worked in conservation as well as caring for the boys.

James had some vague memories of older women who had cared for him in another place until he was about five years old. Then he was told that he must go to school, and he was brought to Neshoba to live in a dormitory with fourteen other boys. He missed his mamas and dadas, and cried under his covers for a few nights, but he soon bonded with the other boys and his new fathers at the dorm.

It didn't seem odd to him that the boys never left the camp. There was plenty of room to play and explore, and his days brimmed over with sports, school, raucous meals, and chores.

All the boys were tested and observed for physical and mental aptitudes, and educated accordingly. Medicals, coaches, and teachers scrutinized them for their breeding or career potential. But the boys would not be told who had been selected for breeding and who for amendment until it was time to leave the boys' camp for a breeder camp or a career training camp for yunies. Both kinds of future were described to them in the sunniest terms.

◆ ◆ ◆

The boys polished off the stew along with the sweets and drinks Da Zack had packed for them. A breakfast of nut bars was safely packed in a small, metal, raccoon-proof box. Peter banked up soil around the smoldering camp-fire while the other boys zipped themselves into sleeping bags. Thankfully, the night was comfortably cool—cloudless under the wide panorama of Mississippi stars. Robert knew all the constellations.

They would be up before dawn to fish in their favorite fishing hole.

June 2217, Fair City, Pennsylvania:

Marley watched boy porn for many days, every chance she got. But afterward, she felt wrong and guilty. And there was just no use in it. She was finally feeling her first flicker of interest in a girl. What if watching the boy porn killed that feeling? She mustered all of her will to stop watching it. But she couldn't stop thinking about it.

She'd been kissing girls in a friendly way since she was very small. It was all normal and nice until some friends had started getting that crushy look in their eyes and wanting to prolong the kisses. And when a girl had slipped her tongue into Marley's mouth, she'd had a strong feeling of revulsion. After that, she became wary of the crushy vibe, and learned to avoid and gently deflect advances. And she waited, hoping to meet a girl who would make her feel something.

And now ... now she wondered what it would feel like to kiss Maddy. Would her normal feelings wake up then? Would the boy fantasies stop plaguing her? Or would it go all wrong and ruin their friendship?

CHAPTER 8

◆ ◆ ◆

Heterosexual lust—like jealousy, rage, and the hunting
instinct—is a biological relic. We do not need it anymore,
and it does not serve a peaceful society. The hetero woman
is a woman who has failed to evolve and mature fully.
She confuses an archaic mating instinct with love.

–IOLANDA VOORHEES, *SCIENTIFIC PRINCIPLES OF HUMAN SOCIETY*, 2068

2206-2208, NEW YORK CITY, NEW YORK:

AT EIGHTEEN, VANESSA WAS HELPING Mama Silva track down subversive writers on the Web. She enjoyed the challenge of this cat-and-mouse game. The writers and vidsters developed new strategies to hide their identities and spread their messages, and law enforcement had to work hard to keep up with them.

"But why do they want to wreck everything?" Vanessa asked Mama Silva. "Are they just stupid? What do they get out of it?"

"Some of them are making money," said Mama Silva. "Subversives who hate our society fund these fraudulent research foundations, often with illegal currency. They're up and running for a while before we find out what kind of 'research' they're doing. Their followers, though, I think they're just stupid, ignorant people who don't understand why things are the way they are. A lot of them are heteros who can't think past their own desires. They'd rather blame society than do the work of changing themselves.

"We're always going to have some people like that," Mama Silva said philosophically. "But our society makes more people happy than ever before in history, and we have to protect it from those who don't see the big picture. Look at this one," she said, indicating the website that she'd just pulled up on her screen. "They've got all these stories about people who are unhappy, or don't fit in. This stuff isn't helpful. These people should be getting treatment—drugs and therapy to make them feel happier. Not blaming the system and trying to change it."

"But don't we want to listen to everyone, and make as many people happy as we can?" Vanessa asked.

"Oh, of course we do," said Mama Silva. "But these people are the oddballs, and they want to change things that work for everyone else just to suit them. Look, here's a man complaining that he wants a woman and a family all to himself. But that's patriarchy. We can't go back to patriarchy just for him, *forsakes*. These people just don't understand what we've *done* here."

"This one wants to get rid of Rep Centers, and make all the babies at home," said Vanessa. "That's so dumb, though. Like they think a man and a woman can make a good baby just because they're attracted to each other. They could end up with a freak. And imagine *being* that child. It's just cruel and stupid to leave it all up to chance like that."

Modern Reproduction Centers employed the best scientists in human reproduction, who worked together to ensure that every child was beautiful and healthy—easy to love and raise. A potential egg-mama would have many eggs extracted, and could be blissfully unaware of all the imperfect embryos, fetuses, and even full-term infants that did not survive the baby-making process. Cutting-edge scientists continued to work on prevention and detection of undesirable traits such as heterosexuality, obesity, and mental illnesses.

"A society has to share core beliefs and values, or it falls apart," said Mama Silva. "The First Enlightenment gave us freedom of religion and speech. Those were really good ideas at the time, because so many *horrible* ideas were entrenched and powerful in those days. Those freedoms shook things up, and a lot of those bad things went away: slavery based on skin color, patriarchy, persecution of same-sex love, child abuse, and even religion itself. And that shaking-up paved the way for the Second Enlightenment."

"Oh, I see," said Vanessa thoughtfully. "Now that we've got *good* ideas in place, we don't need freedom of speech."

"Well," said Mama Silva, "I wouldn't say that, exactly. We want people to express all their feelings and ideas about the system so that we can make it better and better. But we don't want people attacking the foundations. That's not a useful conversation. And some of these people go beyond talk. The worst are the subversive predators who lure people with talk of a hetero utopia, and offer to take them there. Teenage girls are especially vulnerable. They often go through a phase of having hetero impulses before their sexuality matures. These people lure them away from their homes and abuse them and kill them."

"That's monstrous," Vanessa exclaimed.

◆ ◆ ◆

Mama Silva's job was to identify the criminals behind the websites and writings. She reported them to the Justice Department, and professionals there decided what measures to take. She often followed up on the cases to see what had been done.

"See," she told Vanessa, pointing to a line in a section of her big screen, "this offender is a yunie. He's been apprehended and taken to a lifer camp. His Amero account is closed out, and all the money goes back to the government. Men are not citizens, and living in the cities is a privilege, so they don't get second chances. This one's a woman. Her account was reduced to zero, but she can start over. This one here, account reduced to zero, and work licenses cancelled. This one is a license violator. She was caught publishing subversive material, lost her work license, and then continued to work, so she's going to a work camp now.

"Cancelling their money is easy, and slows down our inflation, so that's done for almost any offence. They like to keep people working, though.

Licenses are revoked for more serious things, like hiding boys. And work camps for serious or second offenses. Women can be sent to work camps for a few months or a year. The lifer camps are separate from those."

◆ ◆ ◆

At twenty, in the year 2208, Vanessa was well on her way to obtaining her professional licenses. She decided to round out her education by investigating boy porn and hetero porn. She'd never felt any physical or romantic attraction to either girls or boys, and she had no empathy for people who got themselves into trouble over sexual matters. Although she had no desire to actually look at the porn, she loved the online discussions.

> *Balagirl:* Hetero porn is a harmless outlet for closet heteros. It prevents them from acting out in real life. Who cares what people are looking at? That doesn't change society or harm anyone else.
>
> *Van79:* Porn inflames hetero feelings. That can lead to actual crime. At some point, looking won't be enough. Heteros should be getting treatment and learning to suppress and redirect their urges. They shouldn't be stirring them up by viewing images.

Tracking down websites was a never-ending task. New ones were created every day. Stamping out the problem seemed hopeless.

"Remember that the fines reduce inflation," said Mama Coopa. "And we can send some of the producers to work camps where they're forced to do something socially useful. So maybe we'll never stamp this stuff out, but we're doing good work."

CHAPTER 9

◆ ◆ ◆

Girls should be encouraged to be active in normal sexuality
from its first awakening. Any flickering of heterosexual lust will
be extinguished by the pleasure of being with other girls.

−IOLANDA VOORHEES, 2082

JULY 2217, NORTH CAROLINA:

THE SUN WAS SETTING OVER the ocean in pink and orange clouds in a fading blue sky. A cool ocean breeze promised a comfortably cool evening.

Marley lay on a large blanket, catching the last rays on her brown skin, her top discarded, wearing only the briefest green thong. She'd just arrived, and she missed Maddy already. Gama San and Gama Ny relaxed nearby in their folding beach chairs, under huge blue umbrellas stuck into the sand. The remains of their picnic dinner had been put away in the rolling cooler. The sandcastle Marley had built in the afternoon had been flooded, crumbled, and finally flattened down to nothing by the incoming waves of the rising tide.

A girl with long red hair strolled along the wet sand at the edge of the water.

"Hi Osanna, hi Nyimbo," she called, coming across the dry sand to their little camp. "Oh, Marley's here! Hi, Marley."

Marley lifted her head from the blanket. "Oh, hi, Swanni." She knew this girl from previous summers. Swanni lived in her gamas' circle.

"When did you get here?"

"Yesterday," Marley said.

"*Dulce*," said Swanni. "Are you ready to party?"

"Absolutely."

"Are you girls going to steal her from us already?" said Osanna with a mock pout. Gama San was Marley's great-grandmother. Her eyes were sparkly blue in her sun-weathered face. Her white hair fell in a long braid over her shoulder. She was 82. Her daughter, Nyimbo, was 62. Her hair was short and dark, and everyone used to say that Mama Joselanna was the spitting image of her.

"Of course, Gama San," said Swanni, laughing. "But we'll give her back, I promise."

"Well, it's time for us to pack up and go back, anyway," said Nyimbo.

Marley put her top back on, they packed up their little camp, and Swanni helped carry some of their things. At the top of the beach was a long row of pretty sheds, painted pastel colors, many of them sporting gingerbread trim. Gama San called theirs "the beach house." They stowed the umbrellas, the chairs, and the big blanket, and Marley pulled the rolling cooler up onto the beach walkway to go back to the circle.

◆ ◆ ◆

Summers at the beach with her grandmother and great-grandmother had been part of Marley's life as far back as she remembered. Mama Sue used to bring her until the summer she turned ten, when they'd decided that Marley was old enough to go by herself. She remembered Mama Sue walking with her to the garage and programming the car. Mama Sue had tracked the car all the way, and checked in with Marley on the car speaker, and the drive had given Marley a thrilling sense of freedom.

She'd done that every summer since. She had lifelong friends in the gamas' circle and the neighboring ones. The beach girls took days or weeks off from work and school to hang out with all the friends who came to stay. There were always summer romances and usually a bit of drama.

In recent summers, kissing and making out at parties or on the beach had become a favorite pastime, and Marley had grown increasingly anxious. She'd allowed a few girls to kiss her, and it just wasn't fun, and she didn't want to go further. She knew that some of the girls she'd rejected were gossiping about her.

In the required sex education course at school, teachers had warned the girls that some of them might go through a phase of struggling with heterosexual lust. Any girl who had these aberrant feelings should not be too ashamed to tell her medical and get treatment. But this assurance was always followed by derisive laughter and an outbreak of rude comments from Marley's peers.

The teachers stressed that a girl must never, ever succumb to the temptation of boy porn. And now Marley knew why. Ever since she'd watched that stuff with Lallaina, she could not get those boys out of her head. She just wanted to watch more and more.

Oh, gods, please, I want to be normal.

AUGUST 2217, NESHOBA BOYS' CAMP, MISSISSIPPI:

"D'you think Da Wan made us a cake?" James' dorm brother Sam asked as they strolled back to the dorm from the dining hall.

"Of course he did," said James. "He never forgets our birthday."

"Yeah, and the older guys are leaving tomorrow, so I guess it's for them, too," said Sam. "Time to start wondering what they're going to do with us."

"Why wonder?" said James. "It's not like you can do anything about it."

"Still, don't you care?"

"Sure, a bit. I'd really like to live in the city some day. Just seems like it would be more interesting than living in camps all my life."

"Yeah, me too. Women, ya know. They're interesting. Not in a gross way, of course. But hey, wanna see something I got?"

"Sure. What?"

"I was unloading trucks yesterday, and a delivery guy dropped it. I think he did it on purpose. It's a picture book of girls."

◆ ◆ ◆

James and his four age-brothers had been taken from their artificial wombs at the Rep Center on the same day, and delivered to the same Baby Camp. They'd come to Neshoba together at the age of five. Today they were all fourteen. And tomorrow, the three eldest dorm brothers would be leaving Neshoba.

"Have they told you where you're going?" James asked Bryan, stuffing cake into his mouth in Da Wan's room.

"Yeah. Breeder camp. Same one as Kieran."

"Wow, you guys got lucky! But damn. I'm gonna miss both of you."

"Me, too, little bro," said Bryan. "Maybe you'll come there, too, in a couple of years."

"Yeah, maybe," said James. Being selected for breeding was super cool. But Bryan and Kieran would never live in a city or meet a woman who wasn't a guard.

◆ ◆ ◆

In the darkness under Sam's bedcover, James and Sam looked at the picture book with a flashlight.

"Damn," said James. "They're the prettiest people I've ever seen." He barely remembered the older women at the Baby Camp. Here at Neshoba, there were women in the administration building and guard house. Stern-faced, unapproachable women in black uniforms.

These girls were entirely different creatures. Their grace and beauty stunned him. Their enticing smiles and friendly eyes reached right inside him. Oh, the pretty hair. Black, chestnut, gold. And even green and pink. There were long mops of curls, and long, straight, shiny locks, and short hair styled in all sorts of cute ways. His fingers wanted to touch and feel it. The girls wore vividly colored clothing that fit them like a second skin. Some wore wings behind their shoulders, or flowing half-skirts hanging down behind them. In some pictures, they wore nothing at all.

James stroked a picture reverently, and Sam laughed.

"You're not a woman-lover, are you?" he teased.

"Of course not," said James indignantly. He was ashamed and confused and didn't know what he felt. These lovely beings were so far above him. He imagined those pretty expressions turning to horror and disgust at the sight of him. And only a despicable het would want to touch them and defile them. In the old days, men used to rape them, making babies grow in them until the babies forced their way out, causing horrible pain. Thank the gods the Enlightened Society had changed all that, and those men who still harbored that despicable lust for mating were kept far away from them.

No, no, no, James thought. *I'm not one of those. I just like to look at them.*

AUGUST 2217, NORTH CAROLINA:

Marley's last night at the beach was warm and breezy. Girls had been drinking on the beach, listening to music and watching the waves roll in. They were celebrating Marley's fifteenth birthday and the sixteenth of another girl in the gamas' circle. Now everyone had gone home to bed except for Swanni and Marley.

Swanni put her arm around Marley, and kissed her on the cheek. "I don't want you to go home," Swanni said. "I wish you lived down here."

"Sometimes I do, too," said Marley. She felt Swanni's desire for her. She loved Swanni. She didn't want to reject her and hurt her, and she acquiesced to the kissing. Her state of mild intoxication was helpful.

"I really thought we'd have a thing this summer," said Swanni, kissing her cheek and progressing down her neck.

Just make out with her, Marley. She'll be happy. You can tell people you did it. But what if she's in love with me? What if making out makes it worse? I'll be leaving and going home tomorrow. She'll get over it.

Marley relaxed back onto the blanket, and Swanni lay down next to her, pressing against her body. Swanni's mouth suddenly captured Marley's in a long, penetrating kiss. Marley's feeling of revulsion was softened by alcohol and affection. Yet she stuffed down a sense of violation.

I don't want this. Why am I doing it? I don't want it. I don't want it. But I want to make Swanni happy. And my reputation … if I reject one more person, everyone will be calling me a dirty het man-lover. I wish she didn't want me like this. I wish I could feel something.

Marley closed her eyes and thought about boys. Beautiful, laughing, playing boys. She imagined that Swanni was a boy, kissing her … that it was a boy's hand cupping her breast, a boy's mouth sucking on her nipple … a boy's mouth moving down her belly … a boy's hands removing her thong.

When Swanni's tongue found her clit, at first she felt nothing. And then slowly, the feelings began to stir, and the boys she imagined when she was alone were gazing into her eyes. She imagined a boy on top of her, with smooth skin over lean muscles that she so longed to touch, and a beautiful mouth that she longed to feel on hers.

Wow … this feels much better than my fingers. I could let her do this for a long, long time.

Marley knew that Swanni wanted her to climax, but there was a point when she knew that it wouldn't happen—not with the underlying awkwardness that asserted itself through her fantasies and physical feelings.

I must make her climax. I must satisfy her, and give her something to tell the girls.

She wiggled away from Swanni's ministrations and took the dominant role. "That was super nice," she said. "But it doesn't always work for me. I want to make *you* feel good now."

Swanni smiled and lay back on the blanket, and Marley returned the favor—not enjoying it but knowing what to do. She stuffed down the revulsion she felt, thinking of her friend's pleasure and her social standing, and, strangely, she found that pleasuring her friend felt less violating than those penetrating kisses. Thankfully, Swanni climaxed in minutes, whimpering and arching, and both girls dissolved into giggles at her loss of control.

But at home in her bed, Marley shed tears and hated herself, and hated Swanni for wanting her.

CHAPTER 10

◆ ◆ ◆

The attraction to males is not a personal choice, but a political one.
The hetero woman worships strength and power. She loves nothing
better than to see men fighting over her, bloodying each other to
gain the right to mate with her, like wild animals. She therefore
encourages the worst in men. A moral woman shuns this primitive
instinctual lust and embraces a spiritual love for her own kind.

—IOLANDA VOORHEES, 2070

SUMMER 2208, NEW YORK CITY, NEW YORK:

BY THE SUMMER OF 2208, Vanessa had been working at shutting down porn
sites for about two years. She was bored with the futility of it, and tired of
spending so much time on her computer, and she was intrigued by the hetero
hook-up sites that popped up with the porn.

She carefully crafted an identity and a look, and posted a profile of herself
as a hetero woman looking for action. When the first one was perfect, she
posted several more profiles with different looks and personalities, and began
to work all of them.

She found it amazingly easy to get a man interested, and the number of
hetero yunies who had slipped through the cracks in the system was shocking.
The Young Men's Camps were tasked with expunging the sex drive of heteros
before they were let out, but apparently they were not doing this well enough.

She marveled that even after amendment, these yunies just could not leave women alone. There were also some who had grown up in Natural communities and passed as women right into adulthood. Only their families and their lovers knew they were men.

The Natural lifestyle should be outlawed, Vanessa thought. *Those circles are not just hotbeds of subversion, but literally breeding grounds for it.*

Her mothers knew nothing of these activities until Vanessa told them that she was going to a restaurant to meet a hetero yunie and get him arrested.

"Wow," said Mama Coopa with consternation. "So you just went right ahead and did that without even telling us?"

"Well, I'm telling you now. And I'm twenty years old, for godssakes. And it's not dangerous. I'll have cops right there. All I'm doing is meeting a man for lunch in a public place."

"You've got to admire the initiative, Coop," said Mama Silva, smiling.

◆ ◆ ◆

The small street-side lunch shop was sunny, with bright green and yellow décor. Vanessa was going as Cassandra, who had straight blonde hair with long bangs, dark eye makeup, and long red fingernails. It was exhilarating to Vanessa to put on a different personality and use herself as bait to reel in a criminal. She saw the man come through the door—a tall yunie, not much over thirty, with straight brown hair to his shoulders—and she waved him over. They talked for a while and ordered lunch. She'd been conversing with him online for a week. He'd told her that he had always dreamed of leaving the camp and working with women in the city. In the young men's camp, he'd been amended and educated, and he had paired up with another hetero to fake out the authorities there. But now he was looking for a hetero woman to love.

Vanessa had scoffed inwardly at the word "love." Of course he was just looking for sex. What would a hetero man know about love?

These men think the city will be their playground, Vanessa thought. *After everything society has done for him, he thinks nothing of breaking one of our most essential rules. And he's about to lose everything because of that arrogance. And because he refuses to control his aberrant sex drive. He's probably taking illegal doses of testosterone, too. He looks suspiciously masculine. Yuck.*

Two cops in normal clothing were having lunch at another table. All Vanessa had to do was to play her part. The plain-clothes cops would signal for the uniformed ones to come in. Vanessa felt a rush of excitement when the uniformed cops walked through the door and right up to her table. All the color suddenly left the yunie's face. One moment he was happily anticipating a sexual interlude and a new relationship, and the next moment he was horrified, realizing that he was outed and had lost everything he had hoped for. Male sex offenders were always placed in segregated lifer camps.

◆ ◆ ◆

Vanessa did not feel sorry for the hetero yunies she snared. They knew that what they were doing was against the law. They were deceitful and sneaky and driven by a disgusting sexual appetite that they were probably deliberately enhancing. Vanessa felt nothing but revulsion and disdain, but she enjoyed the game of making them like her.

It's so easy to attract them because they aren't looking for a real relationship, she thought. *It's all about that perverse, animalistic appetite. What else would hetero sex be about? Mental and emotional connection can only happen between people of the same sex.*

Vanessa thrived on undercover work, and she continued to bait and reel in men under the supervision of her mothers and their colleagues as she completed her professional training. Her first independent job was tracking down subversives online. She did well at this, but she longed to work in the real world again, face-to-face with criminals. After a few years, she was able to get an assignment to work undercover with Naturals.

Naturals had been permitted to have babies their own way for over fifty years. But they had become increasingly private, and espoused vaguely patriarchal values. Citizens were calling on authorities to keep a closer eye on them. So in 2211, at the age of 23, Vanessa went into deep cover as a Natural to look for crime and abuse from the inside. She crafted an identity named "Ariel." She extended her hair, making it long and light golden brown. Her licenses in home decorating and organizing gave her a profession to cover her real work. She adopted the dress and habits of the Naturals. She sought them out online, made friends, and moved out of the city to Colchester, New York, where the concentration of Naturals was higher. She made it known that she wanted to live in a circle. But this was not just a matter of buying a home. She would have to be nominated to live in a circle, and accepted by all current residents, and Naturals did not accept people quickly.

CHAPTER 11

◆ ◆ ◆

Modest dress and avoidance of public bathing are simply our ways of
encouraging our girls to save their sexuality for an adult, committed
relationship. We chaperone adolescent girls for the same reason,
and we keep girls at home longer to instill these values. We are
being criticized for indoctrinating them with patriarchal ideas, but
our values only promote bonding between women and girls. The
mainstream has its own form of indoctrination. Every society does.

—AURELIE MADELEINE SAIRA, *DEFENDING THE NATURAL WAY*, 2177

SEPTEMBER 2217, FAIR CITY, PENNSYLVANIA:

SWANNI DID NOT KEEP THE interlude with Marley to herself. Back at home,
Marley saw her experience with Swanni run through their circles of mutual
friends online. Marley's wavering reputation was vastly improved. Which was
nice, except that a few girls at school were looking at her with renewed interest.

She signed up for history, horticulture, sports, dancing, and fashion de-
sign. She tried to fill her schedule so full that she was too busy to hang out
with other girls.

Maddy's home had become a haven for Marley. She felt more comfortable now in this bizarre subculture where teens were not allowed, let alone
expected, to have sex. She was rarely even alone with Maddy, and though

Maddy was snuggly, she did not make further advances. And Maddy wasn't friends with the whole world online.

OCTOBER *2217,* FAIR CITY, PENNSYLVANIA:

The last leaves had fallen, the bite of winter was in the air, and Marley was visiting her medical for the third time in a month. She waited on the examining table, hugging her own knees. This time, she was determined to tell the truth to this medical, who had cared for her all her life.

"I don't usually see you so often," the woman said. "Are you still feeling ill?"

"I have problems with sexuality," she said. "I keep thinking about …."

"Boys?"

Marley nodded, happy that she didn't have to say it herself. She watched as the medical glanced over her notes on her device.

"But you've been active with girls," she said.

"A bit," said Marley. *Only once really, and it was kind of awful.*

"Did you want it and enjoy it?"

"Not really, and not very much."

"So you really don't feel attracted to girls?"

Marley shook her head.

"This is just a phase, Marley," said the medical sympathetically. "It does not mean that you're het—that you're not normal. You must never seek out boy porn or it will get much worse, do you understand? I'll give you some medicines, and set up some counseling for you."

DECEMBER *2217,* FAIR CITY, PENNSYLVANIA:

The first big snow came in December, turning Fair City into a white wonderland. Walkways were covered while the snow fell, but opened up the next day, which was mild and sunny. Fluffy snow clung to every twig of every tree, and sunshine bounced off the snow. Marley's spirits lifted as she walked out into this bright world with Maddy, heading back to her house after school.

"You look happy today," said Maddy.

"Of course," said Marley. "I love sunshine and snow, don't you?"

"Yes," said Maddy. "But you haven't been as happy. You're taking too many classes. I think you're too tired."

"I'm okay," said Marley. She couldn't tell Maddy what was really going on. She'd been taking the medicines. She felt flattened out. Her sexual feelings were all gone. No desire. No boy porn. No orgasms. No nothing. She was doing the right thing—seeing the counselor, taking the medicine. She had the power to make the right choices, and she was making the right choices.

She slipped her hand into Maddy's as they walked along the track.

FEBRUARY 2218, FAIR CITY, PENNSYLVANIA:

The short days of the cold, snowy winter passed quickly as Marley struggled to keep up with all the courses she'd signed up for. She met with the counselor a few times, and then stopped. The counselor was just telling her what she'd already learned at school.

Lying in her bed alone one night, Marley felt a surprising flicker of sexual desire. It was weird. She hadn't felt that for so long.

Oh no, I haven't taken my meds—for how long?

She'd been writing papers, and taking exams and completing projects, and somehow taking the meds had slipped her mind. The sweet feelings were like a long-lost friend, wanting her back. Her fingers found her clit, and the feelings suffused her body as boys slipped, laughing and smiling, into her mind.

After an exquisite orgasm, Marley thought, *Those medicines didn't change anything. They didn't make me stop wanting boys and want girls more. They just suppressed everything. Totally. What the hell am I going to do? I'm so tired of feeling nothing at all. I like Maddy, but I can't do anything about it, and I can't tell if she likes me that way or not. And she wouldn't like me at all if she knew that I watch boys online.*

Marley got up, threw her medicines in the trash, and clicked through to a boy porn site on her device. The boys were a welcome sight.

Maybe it's possible to be turned on by boys and love a girl, too.

CHAPTER 12

◆ ◆ ◆

The hetero utopia in the Pacific Ocean was never anything
more than a subversive fairy tale, a siren song to lure out
people with aberrant feelings and lead them to a bad end.

—MALOREY MAHIMA, *PRESIDENTIAL ADDRESS*, 2187

MARCH 2218, NESHOBA BOYS' CAMP, MISSISSIPPI:

JAMES HAD BEEN WONDERING ALL afternoon why Da Zack wanted to talk to him. He knew he hadn't done anything seriously wrong, and Da did not seem angry or excited. So why had he asked him to come to his room at eight o'clock that night? His manner had been serious, and maybe a little sad. James showed up in the doorway right on time. The father waved him in and closed the door.

"James," he said, "I want to tell you some things. But you must promise not to tell anyone else, or to tell anyone that I told you, because if anyone found out, we would both end up in a worse prison than the one we are in now."

"Prison?" said James, puzzled. "We're not in a prison."

"In fact, we are," said the father. "It's a mighty comfortable and beautiful and big one, I'll admit. But you're not allowed to leave it, and that makes it a prison. But I *cannot* tell you more unless you really want to know more, and will swear that you won't tell a soul."

"I won't, Da," said James. He'd never seen this dear man so deadly serious. He was intrigued and frightened. "I want to know whatever you want to tell me, and I swear on my life I won't tell." He crossed his hands over his heart.

"One thing I want to tell you that you're not allowed to know is where you'll be going when you leave here. Do you want to know?"

"Yes!" said James. "I thought it was still too soon."

"We know long before you do," said Da Zack. "You've been selected for amendment. Your artistic talent is impressive, and the authorities want you to use that talent in the city."

I will never see Bryan and Kieran again, James thought. *But I will see women and girls, and the world they live in.*

"I guess I'm glad," he said. "The women's world seems more interesting."

"Yes," said the father. "Now, James, I want you to think about something very personal. You don't have to tell me anything, though I'm a pretty good guesser. Just think about it inside yourself. You've been taught a lot of things here that are not true. *I've* taught you things that aren't true. I'm required to do so, and I couldn't be here if I refused to teach what I'm required to teach. But listen carefully now, because *now* I'm telling you the truth."

James was completely entranced. He wouldn't have left the office then if his arm were on fire.

"You've been taught that being hetero is unhealthy, and destroys society," said the father. "That's a lie. You just told me you like the idea of living in the cities with women. Do women hold some fascination and attraction for you? Have you ever felt a crush on a boy? Don't tell me if you don't want to. Just think about it. If you've never felt attracted to another boy, there is a good chance you're a hetero. Lots of boys are, many more than you realize. And it's nothing to be ashamed of."

A sense of relief washed through James. The images he'd seen had stirred an intense yearning to see, and talk to, and *touch* those mysterious, beautiful girls. But he still felt ashamed. Whatever Da was saying now didn't erase a lifetime of learning that sexual feelings for girls must be shunned as a sin against society and women.

"Go on, please," he whispered to his father.

"What we don't teach you here," the man went on, "is how beautiful and good the love between men and women can be, how intensely wonderful sex with a woman can be, for both you and her, and how amazing it is to father your own children with someone you love. What they're planning on doing to you, James—the castration—will permanently destroy your ability to do that. You can still have some sexual desire, but you can never father your own children."

"But," said James, confused, "but nobody has their *own* children."

"Women do," said the father. "They give their eggs to the Rep Center, and they get back their own child. But the men who become our Honored Breeders never know and never see the children they've helped to create. Never get to raise them, never get to love them. You've been taught that this is the enlightened way. But James, what it really is is a heinous crime committed against every single boy and man, those who breed as well as those who don't. They're going to take away your manhood, James, and you have no choice in the matter, do you? Nobody asked you. They just put you on a list. You have no choice in the matter because you are a prisoner with no human rights, by virtue of being born male."

James was dumbfounded. This same man had been teaching him all these years that the Enlightened Society had all this figured out—scientifically, rationally, fairly. Maximum happiness for all, both male and female. And now this. But James could not doubt him. He was as serious as a diamondback in your sleeping bag.

"My next question, James," he went on, "is whether you would like to escape that fate and go to a place where you can remain whole and love a woman if you so desire."

"Wow," said James, stupidly. *Next he'll be telling me there's really a heaven with winged angels and trumpets.* But he trusted this man absolutely, and his Da certainly looked both sincere and sane. "I think ... *yeah*. I think I would like to do that. Is it possible?"

"Yes, it's possible. I can only do this for a very few boys. You can't imagine how heartbreaking that is. But if I got too many out, I would be discovered and removed, and then I couldn't help any at all."

For some moments, they were silent. Then the father said, "I'm sorry this has to be an immediate decision. But I don't want you walking around here with a secret in your heart that could destroy us both. You cannot say goodbye to anyone. You must act completely normal. And you must leave tonight."

James had to think fast and hard. He had to decide whether or not to leave everything and everyone he had ever known, all the brothers and fathers and friends he loved, without even saying goodbye—to keep his manhood intact and to have the chance to love a woman and have children. Those possibilities were strange and vague, and yet their pull seemed stronger than anything else in this now-or-never moment—tantalizing possibilities he had never imagined before. He felt queasy, like something was jumping around in his stomach.

"I want that," he said, softly, but with conviction. "I want to escape."

"All right, then," said the father gently. "Go to bed with the other boys tonight, but don't fall asleep. At midnight, come down to my room. Bring nothing with you."

◆ ◆ ◆

At midnight, James slipped quietly out of his bed and crept down to his Da's room. The man met him at the door with a finger on his lips. "Be quiet," he said. "I have a surprise for you, but don't make a sound." James entered the room and suppressed a yelp of joy at the sight of Robert and Peter. "You three are leaving together," said the father with a smile at James. "That's much better than alone, isn't it?"

He sat them all down in his small private sitting room, where the worn, comfy armchairs were stuffed with silent memories of innumerable conversations. In this room, these boys had been encouraged, comforted, scolded, or forced to shake hands and make up.

"One of the many things you've never been told is that you have microchips implanted in your bodies," said the father. "The camp authorities use those check your locations every day. So you must get out of this camp and have them removed before someone wonders where you are. The chips are embedded too deep for me to get them out, but there will be a surgeon waiting for you when you get through the fence. Also, we have to consider dogs. They'll probably be set on your trail tomorrow, and if they find where you got through the fence, that route can never be used again. You must follow these instructions exactly so that doesn't happen." He unfolded a map of the camp on the coffee table, and the boys crowded around with rapt attention.

◆ ◆ ◆

After many quiet instructions, hugs, and tears, James, Robert, and Peter donned black, hooded cloaks and went quietly out the door of their Da's room for the last time. They carried nothing but small bags of nuts, dried fruits, and meat jerky to sustain them on the way; small, powerful flashlights; and a light nylon rope. Silent as smoke, they crept beyond the light of windows where fathers sat up late reading books, and past the dark dorms where lights went out at 10:00. Then they ran in the moonlight along the dirt road to one of their recreational spots, about a mile and a half on a diagonal through the camp from corner to corner, not hard for boys who ran several miles on most days. They pushed themselves as fast as they could in the uncertain light, and reached the familiar spot in about fifteen minutes.

The boys loaded up a canoe with fishing gear and pulled it to the water. James was the best of them with canoes, so the others let him man the back and steer the craft. Robert sat in the middle, and Peter took the front. The canoe slid silently in the darkness down the lazy creek where they had fished and dunked each other for the greater part of their lives.

Gliding a half-mile down the creek between dark banks of overhanging bushes, the boys came upon a familiar spot where the stream wound and splashed through boulders. Grotesque heaps of driftwood made spooky shadows under the moon, piled up by flooding waters. The boys drove their paddles against the rocky bottom to stop the canoe mid-stream. They disembarked in the shallow water, pulling and carrying the canoe by turns through the rapids, wrestling it down to where the water flattened out into a pond. They placed the paddles in the canoe, put on their black cloaks again, and set the little craft adrift in the current, watching it glide away in the moonlight into the shadow of the trees downstream. Then they turned back, splashing and struggling over the slippery rocks to find the place their father had described to them.

After some searching, they found what they thought was the place, and removed some driftwood to see a dark, uninviting hole. James, who was smallest, wiggled in first. He turned on his flashlight and crawled in deeper. After a few feet, he found himself in a buried steel pipe just big enough for a man to crawl through on hands and knees. He backed up enough to tell his friends that this was it. Then he crawled on, and his friends followed.

Good thing none of us are claustrophobic, James thought. They crawled through the damp pipe for a long time. Finally James' flashlight beam hit on something. It looked like the pipe was blocked by underbrush. What looked like an obstruction was a bramble patch covering the end of the pipe, which opened onto a stream bank. The boys crawled out into the thicket. Thorns scratched their skin and tore their clothes as they slid down the bank. Then they tramped upstream in the water.

About twenty minutes of sloshing uphill through the shallow water brought them to a place where the stream was dammed by a pile of rocks. They helped each other climb these slippery obstacles into the pond above, not without throwing some longing looks at the dry land close by. But their Da had told them to be careful not to set foot on land after abandoning the canoe. James slid down the other side of the rocky dam, where the water came up to his armpits.

Now came the scariest part. "The entrance should be right there," James said, pointing. "Right next to the dam, down at the bottom." They would have to go under to find the tunnel entrance, and swim through until it rose above the water level. It wasn't far, their Da had said. They were all capable of doing it. They were all good swimmers, and would be under the water for less than a minute. But the darkness gave James the creeps. He'd never swum into something where he couldn't see where he would come up again. It felt like swimming into death. He glanced over at his brothers. He could see that Robert was even more creeped out than he was. In fact, he looked simply terrified.

"I'll go first," Peter announced. The biggest and most athletic of the three, he'd always had a way of taking the lead when no one else wanted to. He tied one end of the rope in a loop and put it over his shoulder. The other two boys held the other end. "I'll go in, find the air, and tie in the rope. Then I'll come back," Peter said. He walked to the edge of the pond and felt around under the water with his feet.

"It's right here," he said. "You can feel it with your feet before you go under. Easy as whacking off, boys." He grinned at his brothers, who smiled back weakly. Peter took a deep breath and went under. James and Robert clung to their end of the rope and waited, holding their breath as well. Anxious minutes passed. Then Peter's head broke the surface again with a splash. He stood up, pushing water from his face and catching his breath.

"The rope's tied on the other side," he said. "How 'bout if you go first, James? You don't even need to swim. Just pull yourself through with the rope. I left my flashlight on over there, so you'll see the light through the water when you're getting close. Take a good breath, but don't worry. It's not far. I'll come after Robert."

James pulled himself through, hand over hand, and was grateful for the light at the end. About a minute later, Robert's head broke through the dark water into the cold, eerie pool of light. They both moved back in the tunnel to make room for Peter, who followed a few seconds after. Peter untied the rope from a ring on the tunnel wall and put it back into his sopping wet bag.

James led the way now, crawling, his flashlight illuminating the darkness for about twenty feet ahead of him. Nothing but tunnel, tunnel, tunnel ahead. He felt like he'd been crawling for hours. He wondered who had built this, what risks they had taken to do it, and how many boys had disappeared this way. He remembered some other boys who had disappeared. But they had drowned when they snuck out to swim at night. Some others had fallen from the rocks that the boys weren't allowed to climb. Or had they? Were those just the stories they'd been told? The fathers had recovered the bodies and buried the cremated boys in the graveyard. James remembered the burial rites. But he hadn't actually seen the bodies. Was it possible that there were just wood ashes in those urns, and those boys were alive and free?

Crawling, crawling, crawling. At first they'd gone up, away from the water. Now they were going down. James didn't like going down, headfirst, like a worm burrowing into the earth. Would they ever see daylight again? How could they reach the surface by going down?

Then his light fell on something, and the tunnel ended at a T. They were supposed to go right. He turned right, and the other boys followed. They were still going down. Then there was a curve to the left, and then James could see what looked like an opening at last. They crawled out into a drainage ditch next to a road. They scrambled up, happy to be on their feet again, happy to be in the moonlight, and happy to be, for the first time since they were brought here, on the other side of the fence. They felt like they'd come miles underground, but the fence was just there, over the hill, rising tall and electrified, with its spiral crown of razor wire.

A prison, albeit a large and beautiful one, Da had said. The boys rarely wandered near the fence. There was plenty of room inside to run and play and hike and canoe and fish. *The authorities didn't want us to know that we were prisoners,* James thought. *But we were. Only prisoners live behind fences like that.*

They wandered along the ditch for maybe a quarter mile. Then Peter got out the soggy rope again, and threw it into the road. As they settled into the ditch to wait, a cloud drifted over the moon.

CHAPTER 13

◆ ◆ ◆

The patriarchal man had to have his own castle. He competed
with other men to have the biggest and best. He hoarded resources
for his own progeny while others starved. Without men, women
will find the perfect balance of community and privacy, and will
share resources to provide a decent standard of living to every
woman and girl. Women will cooperate in the care of children,
allowing every woman to pursue her own ambitions. The feminism
of past centuries was a bud that has now fully flowered.

–IOLANDA VOORHEES, 2063

MARCH 2218, FAIR CITY, PENNSYLVANIA:

ON A WINDY, RAINY DAY in March, Maddy and Marley stepped onto a covered
walkway in the direction of Maddy's circle.

"You should take fashion courses with me," said Marley. "I'm designing
fashions for Naturals, and you're such a great model."

"Am I?" said Maddy.

"Yes. You're beautiful, and you're statuesque. Everything looks awesome
on you."

In the past year, Maddy's straight, golden-brown hair had grown longer,
and she was taller, too. But Marley seemed destined to be petite.

"Isn't that course almost over?"

"For now, yeah," said Marley. "Maybe next year?"

They found the fast track and walked, enjoying the early breath of spring in the cool air.

"I want you to come with me to the shore this summer," said Marley. "Come stay with my gamas. You'd love them. They'd love you. Have you ever been to the shore?"

"I've been to the Jersey shore. But Naturals aren't really into going to the beach. Swimming. You know. Too much nudity."

"Oh, Mad," said Marley, with a slight edge of frustration. "You're fifteen, for heaven's sake. Don't you think it's time to start doing what *you* want?"

"*Marley.*"

"What?"

"Just *don't*. I can't go this summer. I don't want to talk about it."

"Okay. Maybe I won't go, either," she said. She was a little hurt at Maddy's firm, almost angry tone. "Last summer I just missed you the whole time."

"I missed you, too," said Maddy. "I'm sorry. I'm sorry I can't go with you. I would love it if you didn't go away this summer."

"I won't then," said Marley. "The gamas will be disappointed. They love having me there. They still miss Mama Jo. Seems like a lot of old people in the circle look at me and see Mama Jo. I don't know why. She was so much prettier."

Maddy was silent, so Marley went on. "After Mama Jo died, her moms broke up and Gama Ny went back there to live with Gama San. I like to hear them talk about Mama Jo, because Mama Sue never talks about her at all. I used to think about moving there a lot. They have glossy parties on the beach all the time."

"I'm glad you didn't move there, Marley," said Maddy, putting an arm around her and pulling her close. "We never would've been friends."

"Well, I don't wish I lived there anymore," said Marley. "It's kinda been hell living with Mama Sue, but I wouldn't change anything if it meant not meeting you."

"Me, neither, Marl," said Maddy.

March 2218, outside Neshoba Boys' Camp, Mississippi:

James, Robert, and Peter crouched together in the ditch, waiting, listening to crickets and frogs chirping. Headlights appeared far down the road, bobbing up and down as the car came along slowly over the bumps. The car stopped where the rope lay in the road. They watched a man get out, pick up the rope, rewind it, and throw it into the ditch. That was their signal. Hearts pounding, the boys came up off the ground, Peter grabbed the rope, and they scrambled out of the ditch and ran to the waiting car.

"Get in, boys," said the man, and the boys piled into the back of the car, thoughtless of their soggy and muddy condition. It felt utterly luxurious to James to have a man in charge again. "You all okay?" the man asked. They all said yes. "We need to get you to the medicals ASAP," he said then, "before you're missed."

James noticed a slight lightening of the sky in the east. He had written a note, now lying on his Da's desk, saying that they'd gone off to the fishing hole so they could fish early in the morning, and they'd be back late morning or noon.

They rode in the car for maybe ten or fifteen miles, fast on the gravel and dirt roads. The man used a small device to talk to someone who wasn't there. A *phone*. James had heard of them, but never seen one. A few minutes later, the car pulled into a driveway and parked behind a large, white clapboard house with a front porch covered in wisteria. The boys were ushered quickly inside.

Two more men greeted them quickly, and hustled them into two different bathrooms to shower off. The men were friendly, but wasting no time. "We need you guys clean for surgery," James' escort told him, pulling James' shirt off as he spoke. "Get these muddy clothes off and shower quickly and thoroughly. There's a towel." He got the shower started while James took the rest of his clothes off.

James left his soggy, muddy clothes and his little bag on the bathroom floor, and enjoyed the feeling of warm, clean water running over his body and his close-cropped head for a few minutes. Then he got out and wrapped himself in a big fluffy towel. His man was waiting to usher him into another room, to a cloth-covered table, where he lay down and one of the men scanned his body with a hand-held instrument. He heard the gadget bleep.

"It's here in the right quadriceps," said the man. "Pretty deep, damn them."

They came at James with needles. After a minute, he could not feel his leg at all, but he was still wide awake. The two men worked on him, wearing masks and gloves, their heads close together, speaking to each other and ignoring James completely. James wondered if any boys had died of this.

"A little deeper," James heard.

"Okay, there's the bugger."

"Got it."

"Okay, sew him up. I'll destroy this."

One man left the room. The other stitched. James couldn't feel a thing. He watched the man put bandages on what seemed like someone else's leg. "Okay, you're done," said the man, taking off his surgical mask and smiling at James for the first time. "You, all of you, and nothing *but* you. Just lie here. You won't be able to walk for a while."

The man went to assist with Robert's microchip removal. Peter was finished, too. How fast these men worked! Soon all three boys were bandaged up, resting, and all three microchips were destroyed. And the sun was just peeking over the horizon.

The man who'd picked them up in the car now came back into the room. "We need to get you boys away from this place now," he said. "There's a slim chance you were located before we got the chips out. But after that trip you can rest and recuperate. It'll be a pretty comfortable ride, anyway. Now don't anybody move. We'll carry you out. We don't want any of you trying to walk just yet."

The men loaded the three boys into the back of a small van. They'd removed the back seat and put in a mattress that filled up the back. The boys felt a bit like sardines, but were comfortable enough. The pillows and blankets smelled good. James breathed in the fresh, relaxing scent. Before they'd gone a mile, all three boys were fast asleep.

James woke up in a king-size bed with Robert on one side of him and Peter on the other. He could feel his leg again, and it hurt. When the other two woke up, he discovered that their microchips had been removed from their buttocks. He teased them.

CHAPTER 14

◆ ◆ ◆

Patriarchy obscured the fact that women are superior to men in every aspect of intelligence. But of course there is a bell curve for each sex.

–IOLANDA VOORHEES, *SCIENTIFIC PRINCIPLES OF HUMAN SOCIETY*, 2068

APRIL 2218, FAIR CITY, PENNSYLVANIA:

"WE'VE BEEN FRIENDS FOR MORE than a year, and you've never had me over," Maddy said. "I really want to see where you live. I think of you at home, but I don't know what to imagine."

"But I'm so embarrassed, Maddy," said Marley. "Your moms keep your house so nice. I love hanging out at your house."

"I want to see your room. Where you sleep. Come on, Marley. Do you really think I care if your house is messy?"

Marley relented. But shame suffused her as Maddy picked her way carefully through the piles of objects on the stairs on their way up to her room. Mama Sue was out.

"It's so pretty up here. I love it," Maddy exclaimed, inside Marley's berth at last.

"Aw, thanks. It's full of kid stuff. I can't pack away my kid stuff. Our top room is packed full."

"I like your kid stuff. It's so cute. Look at all those animals."

Marley laughed happily, wondering what she'd ever been afraid of. She turned on the wall screen and flopped onto her bed. Maddy flopped next to her.

"It's more snuggly here, too," Maddy said. "No rules about guests in bedrooms."

Marley snuggled up to Maddy, and loved the feeling of being up against her long, slender body, the warm solidness of her. A lovely, heady feeling washed through her. She never wanted to be anywhere but right next to this girl. Maddy was laughing at the show, and her laugh made Marley's heart skip.

'Maddy, I think I love you. I think we are soul mates.' Why can't I say that? I say everything I think. Why can't I say that to you?

◆ ◆ ◆

For the next few days, the feelings in Marley's body were heightened. She often had to get into bed and give herself release, sometimes in the middle of the day. When she sat across from Maddy at lunch, she felt herself getting wet. She wanted to kiss Maddy's mouth. She wanted to get under Maddy's clothes. She felt relief and elation.

I don't even care that we can't have sex. I'm finally, really in love with a girl. I'm really normal after all.

But the boy fantasies still plagued her.

Maybe the boy feelings will go away when I can really be with her. Maybe they'll turn into girl feelings. I must never tell her about them. She wouldn't like me if she knew that I'm turned on by dirty boys. Gods, I'm awful. I don't deserve her.

And she felt suddenly extremely vulnerable.

Does Maddy feel this way about me? I think so, but I'm not sure. What if I tell her, and she tells me she just wants to be friends?

Was it just her imagination, or was Maddy withdrawing from her as Marley's feelings became more intense? Perhaps Maddy could sense that Marley had feelings that were not mutual. Perhaps she was trying to pull gently away, as Marley had done so many times with girls who wanted her.

Maddy was not being her usual sunny self. Marley saw sadness flit across her face, and her smile was not reaching her eyes. But she was hugging Marley longer and harder than usual, and she kept saying that nothing was wrong, and wanting to spend time with her. Maddy's moms seemed sad lately, too. There was a family thing happening, Maddy said, but what could it be? It was just confusing.

April 2218, Arkansas:

James, Robert, and Peter had traveled, well hidden in the back of a van, to a safe house owned by a normal yunie couple whose names were Kenzie and Faustus. Their large, antique home was isolated on a large property, and they worked from home offices—an ideal situation for hosting escapees.

Groves of black walnut, sugar maple, and oak shaded the property around the house, and the boys could go out under the trees where satellites could not see them. They spent hours in the shady groves cracking the black walnuts harvested the previous fall, working hard for small pieces of the delicious, smoky meat. Soon their pain subsided and they could walk again with minimal discomfort.

Faustus took them to the basement and showed them a bookcase that opened into a secret library of subversive books and vids. Robert devoured the literature and shared the highlights with his friends.

What they learned was that amended boys were not simply rendered unable to make babies. Castration had many effects, both physical and mental. Before the Second Enlightenment and the segregation of the sexes, some men had chosen this for themselves for various reasons, and had usually been happy with the results. But having no choice in the matter, many modern yunies suffered from depression and a deep sense of loss that persisted throughout their lives.

"Voorhees celebrated yunies as a third sex and a new, civilized kind of man," Faustus told the boys. "But we're still firmly second-class, legally and socially. Those of us who live and work with women every day know that we're just as rational, intelligent, and capable as they are. But it's hard to demonstrate that. Their privileged position allows them to steal our ideas, take credit for our accomplishments, and keep us out of the best jobs."

"Are women awfully mean, then?" Peter asked.

"Not really," said Faustus. "They're just born into these privileges, and taught from birth to think they're better and smarter than men. But some of them have serious struggles, too. Especially those who are attracted to men."

"Are there really girls who like boys?" James asked. Da Zack had told him there were, but he still found it hard to believe.

"Yes," said Faustus. "Many of them. But they have to keep their feelings carefully hidden."

CHAPTER 15

◆ ◆ ◆

We choose strong, healthy, intelligent boys to pass on their genetic
heritage. And talented yunies contribute greatly to society as well.
Boys do not form strong emotional attachments, therefore there
is no cruelty in placing them wherever they will be most useful.

—IOLANDA VOORHEES, 2092

NOVEMBER 2217, OSCEOLA BOYS' CAMP, FLORIDA:

ON A MILD, SUNNY DAY in November of 2217, a shirtless 15-year-old boy
called Kevin unloaded boxes from a truck—heavy boxes of paper goods, food
staples, and cleaning supplies for the camp. The boy and the yunie driver went
up and down the ramp, in and out of the truck, piling the boxes into three
small, open vehicles to go to various parts of the camp. The truck was almost
empty, and the boy walked up to the front to pick up the last box. The yunie
driver handed him a printed pamphlet, folded up.

"Hey, boy," he said, with a serious look. "Hide this in your pants. Read it
later. Don't let anyone see it."

The boy took the folded pamphlet and hid it inside his underwear. Then
he picked up the last box and carried it down the ramp.

◆ ◆ ◆

Osceola Boys' Camp was a spacious camp nestled into the west side of Osceola National Forest in northern Florida. Swimming made the hot, humid summers bearable, and the winters were mild and pleasant. Kevin had never seen snow. Sometimes black bears came out of the forest foraging for human food, and alligators wandered in pretty often to bask in sunny places. Little boys new to the camp were taught to treat these creatures with respectful caution.

The camp was just north of Lake City, originally a Seminole settlement called Alligator Village. Buried there were the Confederate dead of the battle of Olustee, the only American Civil War battle fought in Florida. But this cemetery was dwarfed by a vast necropolis south of the city containing the region's dead from the Third World War. Florida had been hammered by Chinese air assaults on all its coasts, and then all but demolished by the Indian Air Force before the United States withdrew from the conflict. The boys were taken to this sobering place on field trips so they could see with their own eyes what happened when men controlled nations and armies.

The camp farming operation produced citrus fruits, vegetables, berries, corn, and melons year-round in the subtropical climate, and a bit of forestry was done, mostly for educational purposes. A large part of the fresh produce was shipped east or west to the metropolises of Jacksonville and Tallahassee, but some also went south to Lake City or north to Fargo City on the border of Okefenokee Swamp.

Kevin did his share of farm work, but had more of a knack for wires, circuits, and electricity.

Before finding a safe place to look at the pamphlet, he went to find Gerald, the boy he had loved since the age of twelve. Kevin was tall and pleasant looking, but Gerald was like a young god with blond hair, deep brown eyes, and a perfect physique. He excelled at every sport he tried as well as every academic subject. Many boys had crushes on him, but Kevin was the one he loved. The two were inseparable.

Kevin located his friend, and they found a secluded place to look at the pamphlet. The boys had always assumed that they could stay together if they wanted to. They'd been led to believe that what the boys wanted for themselves was of primary importance. But this pamphlet told a different story.

> At Osceola, boys are led to believe that their own wishes will factor into their placement. They are not told where they are going until after removal from the camp, so boys in the camp are never aware that they have no choice. In fact, boys are assigned according to current social needs, their wishes are not considered at all, and the decisions of the authorities are final.
> ....
> Boys are not aware that a vast information network exists outside their camps, and that they are deliberately deprived of information about the world outside as well as information pertinent to their own lives.
> ....
> No one should attempt escape without help from the outside. A failed attempt will not be punished in the normal ways that boys are used to. Escapees are considered irrevocably tainted, and will be consigned to work camps for life to keep the subversive taint safely contained.
> ....

"We need to find out what they plan to do with us," said Gerald.

◆ ◆ ◆

Over the next few months, Kevin and Gerald tried without success to hack into the camp authorities' files from their school computers. They decided they would have to break into the administrator's office. Gerry had figured out some hacking tricks, and Kevin seized an opportunity to steal a key. Then they watched and waited.

On a cool night in February, when the office was empty, they slipped in, and Gerry hacked into the files. They found their names on the lists of older boys scheduled to leave the camp in the near future. Gerald was on a list of boys going to a breeder camp in June. Kevin was to be amended and study electronics at a Young Men's Camp. He was scheduled to leave in July.

"This is *not* going to happen, Kev," said Gerry angrily. "We've just got to get out of here before then."

"You mean break out and run away?"

"Yes. Now let's get out of here before we get caught. We'll figure it out. They are *not* going to take you away from me." And he gave his friend an emphatic kiss on the mouth.

◆ ◆ ◆

The boys brainstormed plans over the next couple of months, and finally settled on something they believed would work. They were not allowed inside the inner fence around the delivery area unless they were working with the yunies, loading and unloading. They scouted the inner fence and found an unkempt place where tall weeds grew on both sides. Kevin stole wire cutters and hid them under a bush. They crept out of their beds late at night and made cuts in the chain link fence where the tall weeds obscured it, making a flap that they could push open to get through. They had been learning the schedule of deliveries as best they could, but outgoing produce did not have a set schedule. They waited for a good day to make their move as June crept ominously closer.

CHAPTER 16

◆ ◆ ◆

Segregated education is not a new idea. Boys molest girls and disrupt
their learning. Women have always struggled to raise and teach boys.
We are educating boys according to their nature. We give them
plenty of space to run around and play their bloodthirsty games.

—IOLANDA VOORHEES, 2073

APRIL 28, 2218, OSCEOLA BOYS' CAMP:

IN APRIL, PRODUCE WAS GOING out daily from the farm. Kevin and Gerald
chose a day when several other deliveries were scheduled as well. They told
their dorm fathers that they wanted to go camping and fishing for a few days
in the part of the forest that belonged to the camp, and that they would set out
early in the morning. They'd done this many times before. But this time, they
packed up their gear, and set off hiking in the darkness before dawn. They
started out in the direction they would normally take until they were out of
sight of the camp buildings. Then they changed direction and approached
the delivery area along the perimeter fence, crawled to their chosen spot, and
waited, hidden under the palmettos as the sun rose.

They waited for hours, and the day grew hot. It was nearing noon when
men and boys arrived to open the gate and begin working. Kevin and Gerald,
itchy and restless, watched them unpacking and repacking trucks. Two trucks
would be leaving with loads of fresh produce. Two others would be leaving

empty after their cargo was unloaded, one of them towing trash. The boys' immediate problem was how to slip unnoticed into the back of one of those trucks before it was closed up and driven back out through the perimeter gate.

The men and boys broke for lunch, but unfortunately did not choose to go away. They sat around in the delivery area eating sandwiches. Two trucks left the camp empty. In the late afternoon, a camp vehicle drove in from the farm, loaded with crates of fresh berries and melons from the fields. The boys watched men talking, and guessed at their conversation. City folk would be eagerly awaiting these early blueberries, which were delicate and perishable. But the men and boys had been working hard for hours on a hot day. The farm truck parked next to the open delivery truck, and the men and boys left, locking the inner gates.

"They're prob'ly getting dinner and coming back," Gerald whispered. "*Hot nukkies.* This is our chance, Gatorbait."

Dragging their camping gear, they pushed hard on the cut fence and squeezed under, getting a few bloody scratches, and trying not to bend the metal so much that it wouldn't go back. They pushed the flap of chain link back into place in the weeds. They climbed aboard the outbound truck and rearranged some crates to make a small hiding place. They'd eaten nothing but trail mix all day, and now assuaged their raging appetites with oranges and tomatoes from the crates. Then they waited, in an agony of nervous boredom, for the workers to return.

The men came back after a leisurely dinner, chatting and joking as they loaded crate after crate of blueberries and melons into the back of the truck. Finally the boys heard the blessed sound of the doors closing, and their hiding place became dark. Minutes later, the driver climbed into the front, and at last the truck was pulling away.

The back of the truck grew even darker as the sun set. Kevin's lighted compass told them they were going north—to Fargo City, then, or perhaps beyond. But they were only about thirty minutes out when they heard sirens, and the truck pulled over and slowed to a stop, tilting a little on the shoulder of the road. They heard voices outside, officers talking to the driver.

The back door rumbled open, and a voice shouted, "Okay, boys, come on out. Time to go home."

"They're going to act like they're taking us home," Gerry said. "But they're not." And the boys made a hurried, whispered plan.

They climbed down from the truck with an air of embarrassed defeat. Two female police officers stood outside the truck, glaring at them as they came down, with a couple of uniformed male grunts for backup. The officer waved them toward the open door of the police van. "Just hop on in there, boys," she said curtly. "This joy ride's over."

Kevin and Gerald walked slowly toward the van, holding hands and carrying their camping gear. Then Gerry squeezed Kevin's hand, and at the same instant, they dropped everything, spun around, and bolted into the dark field next to the road. The officers and grunts collected their wits and pursued them, firing stunners. The boys zigged and zagged to avoid the shots. They were much faster than the older cops. Once out of firing range, already invisible in the gathering dark, they ran straight and hard, quickly increasing their distance from their pursuers. The cops gave up, panting and cursing. The boys ran on and on and on, finally collapsing next to a clump of trees, exhausted and breathing hard.

"Damn," Gerald said. "I should have done more hacking and more homework. I'll bet they found us with those goddamned microchips. I couldn't find out what their range is, or how often they check them. I didn't think they'd check on us, though … we go camping all the time, and we've never tried to run away. Damn it, we're so *fucked*."

The night was cloudy, and they were in the middle of nowhere without a scrap of camping gear, not even a flashlight or a knife. They had only a vague idea where they were, and they were likely still within the range of the microchip locator.

"I think," said Kevin, "that we should head north toward Fargo, keeping off the road. We should get to Okefenokee and go deep enough that they don't want to bother coming in after us. If they locate us in there, they'll probably just keep an eye on the towns and try to snag us when we come out. Not a great plan, but I can't think of a better one right now. We gotta figure out how to get rid of these blasted microchips."

"Seems like a plan to me," said Gerald. "But we need to get deep enough in there while it's still dark. I wonder how far away we are. It's about forty miles to Fargo, right? But we must be more than halfway already. We'd better get moving."

They could see lights from the road, so they trudged and jogged parallel to the road going north, as fast as they could manage in the dark. Along the way, they went through some old developments of single homes, set far apart. Skulking through backyards, they found a home with no lights on and unlocked doors. They raided the backyard shed for tools. When that raised no alarm, they stole into the kitchen and helped themselves to a full market bag of food, taking another bag for their tools. Kevin wished they could leave a note to explain and apologize, but Gerald said that would be a terrible idea.

They trudged through a few miles of timberland, where tall, slender pine trees grew in perfect straight rows out of a blanket of palmettos. The moon played hide-and-seek with the clouds. At times the boys could see fairly well, and at other times they were blundering through the blackness with nothing but the feeble beams from their stolen flashlights. Deer snorted and stamped to warn their fellows of human presence before bounding off unseen between the slender pines. Flashlight beams caught the occasional armadillo, scurrying away, or a raccoon sitting up and boldly watching them pass.

"We may as well eat all the food we have on us," said Kevin, "cause those coons will take whatever's left after we go to sleep."

Abruptly, the timberland gave way to swamp, and they decided that the road was less risky than blundering into a wetland in the dark. They were very close now to the official parkland, where for centuries these wetlands had been preserved as habitat for American alligators, migratory birds, and many other wild creatures.

◆ ◆ ◆

Along the park road was a tourist center with a store and canoe rental. Canoes were simply stacked up near the water and easy to steal. But the tourist shop and storerooms were locked. They found an unlocked tool shed in the back, and used a pry bar to force open the back door of the shop and the storage area.

Bug spray, a small tent, swamp maps, caps, and packaged food came out of the shop, and paddles from the canoe rental store room. The boys loaded up a canoe and paddled out along the trail, exhausted from their long trek, but not daring to rest so close to where people would come in the morning.

"We should get off these tourist trails," Kevin said. But they couldn't see most of the trail markings in the cloud-obscured moonlight, and they had to go where they could. Along the canoe camping trails were big wooden platforms where campers could set up a tent for the night. But the boys did not dare to use them. When they finally reached the point of utter exhaustion, there was no solid ground anywhere near them. They slept side by side in the bottom of the canoe, very uncomfortably, for a few hours.

Early daylight found Kevin and Gerry stiff and sore and still bone tired, with nowhere to stand up and stretch their aching bodies. They picked up their paddles and moved along the waterway until they found a clump of trees on some fairly solid ground. Gratefully they clambered out of the canoe, stretched, and ate some of their food. At least sleeping on top of the food bag, in a canoe on the water, was one way to keep it from the raccoons.

◆ ◆ ◆

Day after day, the boys camped in the swamp, wondering how to get out of their predicament. They stole two more canoes and some lumber to build a floating platform far away from the tourist-traveled trails in a part of the swamp that had been burned recently and wasn't so picturesque. The islands and lakes were not safe for them, but they watched the overnight canoe parties, and paddled through the trails between parties of tourists.

Sometimes they pushed their worries to the back of their minds, and enjoyed being together in the wild spring beauty of Okefenokee. Water lilies covered the deeper lakes and ponds like snow, blooms reflecting perfectly in the smooth black water. The boys heard the strange bellowing of male alligators attracting females. They paddled along narrow trails bordered by wild rhododendron, and through open prairies where clumps of pitcher plants lured insects to a sticky death. Anhingas posed on trees with wings spread out wide to dry in the sun, and sometimes disconcertingly poked their heads up out of the water. Green anoles ran up the boys' legs and regarded them with their tiny eyes.

Cypress trees towered into the skies with their bumpy knees sticking out of the water in rough circles around them. Protected since the 20th century, many of these trees were several hundreds of years old, and of great girth. The boys found smaller islands of solid land, where they could stop and explore. They saw a shy black bear, a bold bobcat, and a tiny fawn lying perfectly still while his mother foraged.

The bugs were not as bad as they'd expected, due to the highly acidic water, and they found they could drink the water without getting sick. And so a couple of weeks drifted by, day by day. They made quick forays into the towns and tourist centers for food, bug repellant, and other necessities.

Except for the occasional campers gliding through with all their modern gear, Okefenokee seemed untouched by their modern society. They could imagine it being just the same many, many centuries ago, when aboriginal Americans canoed through it. And they wished they *were* aboriginals so they could live in there forever, holding each other close at night.

But they could not hide in Okefenokee forever, or even much longer. They didn't like stealing from people, their pilfering was probably being noticed, and the authorities must have located them. Eventually, they would probably send rangers in airboats to bring them out.

But removal of their microchips required medical help, and they couldn't just walk up to a medical and ask. And if they got too far from the swamp, they were sure to be picked up by police.

CHAPTER 17

◆ ◆ ◆

True marriage love is possible only between those of like mind,
therefore it is only possible between those of the same sex.

—IOLANDA VOORHEES, *SPEECHES*, 2073

MAY 13, 2218, FAIR CITY, PENNSYLVANIA:

MADDY WAS BEATING MARLEY AT chess, as usual. Marley thought she was doomed until Maddy made a really dumb move that allowed Marley to take her queen.

"Maddy, I know something's wrong," Marley said. "You're not even thinking about what you're doing."

Maddy looked at her thoughtfully, and there was pain in her eyes. "I really, really want to tell you something, Marley," she said. "But I'm afraid."

"Why?" said Marley, alarmed. "You know I don't tell secrets. You can tell me anything. You've always told me everything, haven't you? I don't care if it's weird or different or wrong. I'll love you no matter what."

Maddy smiled. "Really? No matter what?"

"Of course. Haven't you told me everything for a year now? Have I ever betrayed you?"

"Of course you haven't. Of course I'd trust you with anything. It isn't that. It's that ... I think you'll be hurt. It's something I've wanted to tell you, but I couldn't."

Marley's words came out in a rush. "You know I'm crushing hard on you, and you don't feel the same way. It's okay, really, you can tell me. We can just be friends if you want. I'm okay with that …"

"No, no, shut up, Marley," Maddy interrupted, shaking her head. "It's not that. Not really. I mean, I'm totally crushing on you, too. It's just that it can't work. It can't work because I have to leave."

"Why?" Marley's eyes were suddenly wide with alarm. "Y'all are moving? Why?"

"Not the family, Mar. Just me. Just me, because …" Marley had never seen such a pleading, fearful look. She could feel Maddy gathering all her courage to say what she had to say.

"Because I'm really a boy," Maddy whispered, barely audible.

Marley just stared at her—no, at *him*—while her mind tried to grasp this, and refused, and tried again. She—no, *he*—clearly wasn't joking. Marley was dumbfounded. Her best friend for the past year was a *boy*? The girl she thought was a forever love and a soul mate, was a *boy*? A thousand thoughts raced around in her head, so fast she couldn't speak.

How could she do this to me? How could she not tell me? How could I be so close to a boy and not know it? I thought I was in love with a girl. I can't be in love with a boy. How could I mistake a boy for a girl? Boys are totally different. Boys are aggressive and dirty. How could I not tell? I thought I was finally attracted to a girl. In love with a girl. I thought I was okay. Maddy isn't Maddy. She's some-one else. She's a boy. He's a boy. I don't even know this fucking boy. It was all a farce. It was a lie from the very beginning. This whole year, she's been lying to me every single moment. How could she do that? How could I not see it? The person I thought was my best friend doesn't even exist. The person I loved doesn't exist.

Tears welled up and spilled over.

"How could you?" Marley struggled to say at last. "How could you be around me for a whole year and not tell me that? How *could* you? I thought we were as close as two people could be." The confusion and betrayal and the sense that the Maddy she knew had never existed wrangled inside her. It felt as if her best friend had just died, and at the same time, she'd hurt, betrayed, and wronged her in the worst way. Maddy had tricked her into falling in love with a *boy*. When she was just beginning to think she was normal. Maybe she was not normal at all. Maybe she would never be normal.

Anger rose up in a rush, energizing her whole body as a furious sob broke from her. "You've been lying to me this whole time. As long as we've known each other, it was all a friggin lie—every minute, every second we were together. How *dare* you get so close to me, you lying bastard."

Adrenaline flooded her brain, demanding release. She upset the chessboard, scattering the pieces. She picked up the small table they'd been playing on and threw it across the room. As Maddy reached out to restrain her, she swung and slapped his face with all her strength, uttering a strangled scream. Maddy grabbed her hands and wrestled her onto the bed, holding her down with his body as she struggled, and putting a hand over her mouth to stop the angry words pouring out of her.

"Hush, hush. Marley, please. Mama Sue will come up here if you don't hush. I wasn't allowed to tell—didn't dare to tell anyone, Marley, not one person *ever*, not even you, not even my little sisters. It's too dangerous for all of us if anyone knows. Please, Mar, *please*. I never meant to hurt you. I just wanted so much to be close to you. I just couldn't stay away from you. There was no good time to tell you. I wanted to so many times. You can't imagine what it was like. I had to trust you first. And then I was afraid to hurt you, and afraid that you'd hate me. And I love you so much, Marley."

Marley could have hurt him badly and escaped, but even in the heat of her anger, she realized that she didn't want to. She struggled against him less vigorously as the adrenaline rush abated, and she allowed his words to soothe her as she lay there, under him, trembling and breathing raggedly, her mind still swirling. *Gods, he's strong.*

And for the first time since Maddy uttered those dreadful words, Marley's mind had calmed just enough to wonder what all this was like for *him*.

'I'm totally crushing on you too … I love you so much.'

"You can let me up now," said Marley. "I won't hit you again. I just want to talk." She could feel her own heart beating hard, and she fought against the damning realization that she was now much more sexually aroused than angry, and she did not particularly *want* him to get off of her. But Maddy released her, and she sat up and wiped the tears from her face. "Let's sit in bed like we always do," she said.

So they sat close together on the bed in her little room. It was strange that Maddy's body beside her looked and felt the same as always, except the charge that she felt—like an electric current where his body touched hers—was now much stronger.

"Do you remember, about a year ago, Mar?" said Maddy. "When you first started coming to my house, we talked about Natural women who don't want to give up their boy babies?"

"Yes, I remember," said Marley.

Maddy continued, "But we didn't talk about how some mothers actually *don't* give them up, and how one of those baby boys was me."

"But you said that the authorities are right there to take the baby as soon as it's born," Marley said.

"Yes, they are, if they know," said Maddy. "The authorities watch us pretty closely. They think our lifestyle is a gateway to outright subversion. But Mama Lara is a medical. She's part of a really close, secret network of medicals, some of them Naturals and some not. They do secret early sex screenings, so the mother knows if she's having a boy before the authorities do. Then they can help her fake all the records and tests that come after. Some girl baby's fingerprints, footprints, and DNA are part of my official identity. Unless me or that girl gets in trouble with the law, it's not likely to be noticed."

"But why would anyone want to raise a boy?" Marley asked. She'd always thought that little boys pissed all over the place, and wanted to fight with everyone. Had Maddy been like that?

"Mama Lara says she loved me from the moment I was conceived," said Maddy simply. "She didn't want to abort me or give me up. She knew of others who had kept boys." He paused, letting Marley process the information.

"I'm the only boy in my circle," he went on. "But I talk to some others, online, anonymously. You'll never hear anyone talk about hiding boys, even inside the circles. If not for those anonymous, encrypted chat rooms, I would have thought I was the only one, ever. I don't even know where the others live. But we help each other deal with it. Some of the boys start hormone treatment before puberty, and just grow into their female identity and go through life like that. But a lot of them sneak away when they're about my age."

"Why couldn't you do that, Maddy?" said Marley, feeling some hope. "The first thing. Why couldn't you stay here as a woman? I mean, you've passed so well as a girl all this time. You wouldn't have to leave, then."

He shook his head. "I can't," he said. "I mean, physically, maybe I could. My voice is changing, and I'm getting too tall, and maybe I could stop all that with hormones. But I just can't, mentally. I can't hide anymore, pretending to be something I'm not. I want to be somewhere that I can grow up to be a man."

"But yunies live in the city," said Marley, thinking. "Couldn't you pass for one of them?"

He shook his head. "It doesn't work legally, officially. A girl can't legally grow up to be a yunie. The authorities keep track of yunies too much, they have their place in the system. And if you want to work, or buy things, you have to be in the system. No, I would have to pass as a woman my whole life—no one could ever know that my mother kept and raised a boy. She could lose everything. All her money for sure, her medical license for sure, and possibly my sisters. I can't risk all that, and live my life in fear for myself and for them. The authorities have to believe that I'm a runaway girl, or at least not be able to prove otherwise."

Marley absorbed this. "So what's your plan?" she asked.

"There's a thing they call the Underground Railroad. Remember how centuries ago, white people kept black people as slaves? There was an Underground Railroad then. It wasn't really a railroad, but a bunch of places that the slaves could hide until they got to a place where they were free. This is the same kind of thing."

"But where does it end up?"

"There's an island in the Pacific Ocean. Men are free to live there without being amended. And men and women are allowed to live together and love each other."

"But how can that possibly work? Isn't it dangerous there? With all those fertile men?"

"I don't think so, Mar. I think we've been taught a lot of stuff that's not true. Both of us, all of us have. All the stuff they tell us about men and boys, girls like you just believe it, because people you trust tell you it's all scientific, and you never actually meet real boys or fertile men. But I've grown up hearing all this stuff, and they're talking about *me*. And it just doesn't compute. I'm no more violent or aggressive or dirty than a girl. And supposedly puberty makes it all so much worse? But it hasn't. I'm just growing fast and thinking about sex—the same stuff that happens to girls. I don't want to fight and hit people. I'm a lot less competitive than a lot of girls we know."

In fact, I just attacked you and you didn't even hit back, Marley thought, but didn't choose to say it out loud.

"Anyway," Maddy continued, "I don't have a choice. If I stay here, I'll ruin the lives of all the people I love as well as my own. I have to get away, and let them pretend that I ran away and just disappeared or died."

"So you can't *ever* come back?" Marley asked, tears welling up in her dark eyes.

"No, never," he said, hugging her close against him. Marley snuggled against Maddy, as she had so many times before with her bestest friend. She felt disoriented. This boy next to her *was* her best friend, the same person that he was yesterday. And, as shocking as it was, as disturbing as it was to change her concept of him from girl to boy, she had to admit that her attraction to him had only become more intense. Those exciting, illicit feelings aroused by the boy porn were infusing the feelings she'd already had for Maddy. She wondered if some part of her had known all along. Some part of her had responded to the boy under the girl disguise.

Her anger dissipated as they talked, and her feelings of betrayal subsided somewhat as he explained his life to her. He had been raised to keep this secret from his first dawning awareness of gender, as a matter of survival. His psyche had grown around that secret, and his presentation as a girl was so ingrained and habitual he didn't even think about it. And he loved her.

What if boys weren't really nasty, and wasn't really bad to love a boy? How could it be bad to be what you are? And how could it be bad to love someone?

But, but, but. All the things Marley thought she knew kept popping up in her mind, like those ancient Weebles that would not stay down. Fertile men are dangerous. Women cannot live with men. Men cannot love women. But her feelings for Maddy felt right and good and irresistible.

If boys are so very different from girls, then how could Maddy pass as a girl all these years? And even now, growing up, he's gentler and kinder than a lot of girls I know. Maybe those things we were taught are not always true.

"I want to go with you," Marley said suddenly. "I *have* to go with you."

"Oh, Marley." Maddy looked right into her eyes. "It's too dangerous. I couldn't put you in danger like that. You can stay here and have a nice, proper life."

"It wouldn't *be* a nice life without you," said Marley. "And I can't let you go on a dangerous journey without me. I would die a thousand times, wondering and worrying about you. And I just want to be with you more than anything else."

"Even though I'm a boy?"

Marley was silent for a long minute, working up her own courage.

"Maddy, can I tell *you* a secret, too?"

Maddy actually laughed. "I guess it's your turn, yeah."

"I didn't tell you because I thought you'd be disgusted. But I have hetero feelings. For a long time now. I—I watch boy porn ... and I like it."

"You *like* boys?"

Marley nodded. "I've been trying not to watch it, and not think about it. I tried hormone treatment and counseling all last winter to make me want girls, but it didn't work. Well, I thought maybe it was working because I was attracted to *you*. But the boys would never stay out of my head. I would try not to think about them, and think about the girl I loved instead."

"Was that *me*?"

"Yes," Marley exclaimed. "I never, ever felt this way about a girl before, Maddy. I'm sure I can't live without you and I'll love you forever. But girls aren't supposed to feel that for boys. The boy stuff is just hetero lust, isn't it?"

"I don't know what it is. But I feel the same way about you."

As Maddy looked into her eyes, Marley was mesmerized, as always, by the gold-flecked hazel, and those long lashes, the most beautiful eyes she had ever seen. "You *like* that I'm a boy?" Maddy asked wonderingly, as if it was more than he ever could have wished for.

"I don't know," Marley said, and tears flowed again. It was agonizingly confusing. "I just don't want you to go away. I don't want to lose you. And now I just want you more than ever, even though it's wrong to want you now. You should be with a boy, and I should be with a girl."

They lapsed into silence, thinking their own thoughts.

"Maddy?"

"What?"

"How do you know you're not normal? You've never met another boy."

"I've talked to some online. And I've seen boy porn, too. I feel crazy lonely sometimes for other boys, just to hang with. But *you*—I've wanted to kiss you since I first saw you."

"Really?"

"Really."

"So why didn't you? I've wanted to kiss you, too."

"I know. It's been hard for me not to. It felt wrong to let you kiss a boy without knowing. And I was afraid you'd want to do more, and, you know, get under my clothes."

"Do you want to kiss me now?" Marley asked.

"Yes."

For moments, they looked into each other's eyes, feeling strange and shy. Then their lips met gently, tentatively, and Marley felt a thrill rush into her belly, making her weak. Her eyes closed, and her lips parted, and the kiss deepened.

This, she thought, *is what kissing is supposed to feel like.*

CHAPTER 18

◆ ◆ ◆

All babies will now be produced at the Reproduction Centers,
and only the girls will be given to their mothers to raise. Male
babies will be raised in the camps. We will be done with this
angst about taking boys from their mothers at puberty.

–Iolanda Voorhees, 2067

2212, Colchester, New York:

"Ariel, I think I have something for you," said Vanessa's best Natural friend
one day when they met for lunch in a café. Imanda lived in a circle that was
effectively closed to anyone who wasn't born in it. But she had friends in other
circles and had been keeping her ears open to help her friend Ariel find a spot.
The year was 2212, and Vanessa was now 24.

"It's the circle right next to the reservoir," said Imanda. "They've been
Natural-friendly for ages—twenty or thirty years, maybe. Everyone there is
liberal and accepting, even if they don't embrace the lifestyle themselves. They
want it to be 100% Natural eventually, and they're willing to take in some
people newer to the lifestyle."

Vanessa could hardly believe her luck as she set up her things and decorated her new home. In a circle of 26 housing units, 18 were occupied by
Naturals, and there were 23 girls (if they *were* girls) under the age of twenty
living there. Vanessa hid her hand-held DNA reader in the extra space behind

a drawer in her desk. She didn't want to carry it around with her. There were two yunie couples in the circle, which meant that simply scanning the community areas for male DNA wouldn't do any good, even when she found herself alone in those areas, which was rare.

Two of the women there were her friends already, and she set out to make friends with more. Interior decorating was a good way to get into people's homes. And she was always eager to help mothers care for their girls. Some of them accepted gratefully, but she could not get that close to all of them. Even within the closeness of the circle, she sensed some caution with regard to the newcomer.

On a few occasions, she took her pocket DNA reader with her into a home, and tried to pick up DNA when she used the bathroom. But the readings were confused. They showed a wide range of DNA, or a garbled mess. These Naturals must be using something to confuse the readings—cleaning products, a laundry additive, lotions, hair products—she didn't know what, but something was destroying and confusing the shed DNA in their homes.

Online at home, under her real name, she worked for the passage of a law that would allow authorities to make unannounced home visits to any homes with children. The Naturals were fighting it, of course. She inwardly rejoiced when the law passed, and began to be enforced on the Naturals.

Of course they were all arguing hotly online that this was a violation of their rights and the enforcement was discriminatory and intolerant of their way of life. This was what they had predicted, and others had called them paranoid. The Web buzzed with argument, some people wanting the law repealed, and others wanting it even stronger.

Modgirl: Natural girls should submit to unclothed inspections without warning, for their own protection. How do we know they're not being abused when they're all covered up and kept at home? There's so much potential for abuse. Society has to be vigilant.

Starlight: What about the girls' rights? They haven't grown up with casual nudity. Forcing them to undress for strangers will cause them a lot of emotional distress. You're abusing them to look for abuse.

Naturalwoman45: It's not a crime to be different. What happened to tolerance?

Modgirl: Naturals are totally tolerated. But because there is the potential to hide abuse, society has a duty to look for it. We're not saying people are guilty. But normal people have public bathing and their girls go to school. This law is just putting the Naturals on the same level.

Naturalwoman45: But there's no reason to think they're being abused except that it's possible. There used to be a thing called "probable cause."

Modgirl: Yeah, back in the 21st century. A stupid men's idea. All that did was hobble the authorities so they couldn't investigate suspicious things, and lots of people got away with doing bad things. Are you one of those back-to-the-Dark-Ages people?

Naturalwoman45: I just think women have a right to their privacy if they're not doing anything wrong.

Starlight: Girls have rights in our society. Surprise home visits are enough. Forcing girls to take their clothes off when they don't want to ... that's like rape. Is that how you want our authorities treating our girls?

Van79: Does anyone really believe those girls want to dress like that? Who would want to wear all those clothes all the time? And stay home from school? And not go to the baths? I think their whole way of life is abusive to the girls.

Starlight: Cops can ask girls for a private interview, and take DNA with the girl's permission. No need to take clothes off.

◆ ◆ ◆

Vanessa personally hated the modest clothing, and hated that she couldn't go to a public bath. The girls in the circle seemed content with it, at least until they started going outside of the circle to school. Then some of them wanted to be like normal girls. Vanessa sympathized, but was careful not to express it. Inside the circle, she expressed nothing but unmitigated enthusiasm for the Natural way of life.

After the Mandatory Unannounced Home Visit law was enacted, Vanessa called in a tip, and uniformed cops came to investigate one of the homes in her circle. Vanessa had recommended that they interview the children away from the mothers, and take DNA samples. As she had suspected, the younger child was male.

Two days later, Vanessa received a text from one of the moms: *Please come over. Police here.* She felt a pang of guilt as she responded to this woman who thought she was calling a supportive friend. She suppressed the pang. *She broke the law, and she deserves whatever happens.* Vanessa would play her part.

An emotional scene was playing out in the cozy circle home. The cops had arrived without warning, demanding to see the five-year-old child. They had stripped the child naked in the living room to confirm to everyone present that he was in fact a boy. They had re-clothed him in a baggy khaki outfit. When Vanessa arrived, they were snipping off his hair very close to his head, as if they were so offended by his looking like a girl that they couldn't let it go on for one more minute. The boy and his eight-year-old sister were sobbing with confusion and fright, while the mothers suppressed their own panic and tried to comfort their children.

"How can you do this to her?" one mother demanded. "She's an innocent child. Can't you see how scared she is?"

"Back off," the officer said unsympathetically. "And stop saying *'she'* like you don't know he's a boy. This is totally and completely your fault. You've done this to your child by keeping him where he doesn't belong. We're required by law to remedy the situation before more harm is done, and all this emotional distress is *on you.*"

Several friends from the circle had gathered around in support, and seemed almost unable to believe this was really happening. They all knew the system, and the risks of going against it, but they had never experienced this side of authority.

Vanessa appeared as distressed as any of them, especially when they took hold of the boy's hands to take him away. "*Please,*" she said dramatically. "Let the boy hug his mamas one last time before you take him."

The officers allowed this. And then they pulled the boy away, through the door, out to their car, and the mothers dissolved into hysterical screaming and weeping. *Over a boy,* Vanessa thought, feeling a wave of disgust that she did not show. And yet, yesterday that boy was just another happy child playing in the circle. The drab clothes and clipped head seemed to transform him into a lesser being.

Back home on her computer, Vanessa discussed the case with her coworkers.

> *Van79:* I recommend that the girl be transferred to another couple in this circle. Her mothers should lose their parental rights, and all their Ameros, of course. But we don't want the girl traumatized by authority any more than she has been.

◆ ◆ ◆

A week after the boy was discovered in Vanessa's circle, two 13-year-old girls ran away from home. Vanessa had not even suspected these girls and had not asked for any investigation of their families. But she was quite sure that these girls had no problems at home. Other than being boys, there was no conceivable reason for them to run away. Vanessa reported her suspicions immediately after the moms reported their girls missing. But by then, the girls had vanished without a trace.

The circle community rallied around the families with comfort and support. But there was a quality to the families' grief that didn't sit right with Vanessa, and only confirmed her suspicions. Compared to the emotional response of the women whose boy was taken away, they seemed to accept the disappearance of their children just a bit too easily. Their demands that the police do everything to find the girls struck her as an act.

Vanessa asked for DNA sweeps on the homes of the two families, and this was done. The next morning, both families had disappeared, and again, there was no trail to follow. The DNA results were confused, but did contain some male DNA. Vanessa was quite sure that two hidden boys and their criminal mothers had slipped through her fingers, right there in the circle where she was living.

Vanessa carefully questioned her friends in the circle, but she could not get anything useful. They all told the same story: the teens ran away, and the moms and other kids went to look for them, and no one knew where any of them had gone.

"So the moms must have had some idea where the girls went," she said to her neighbor, who was very close to the families. "Otherwise, how would they know where to start looking? Is it possible those girls were actually boys?"

"Not that I ever noticed," said the neighbor. Vanessa saw a guarded look in everyone's eyes. She was confident they did not suspect her, but they weren't talking—not even to each other. But Vanessa had to try a little harder. She lowered her voice to a whisper. "Do you think they got on the Underground Railroad and went to the Island?" she asked.

"I don't know that either," said the neighbor.

"What if I wanted to go there, too? I'd have no idea who to ask."

"You don't ask anyone," the neighbor said, and there was a look in her eyes that warned Vanessa not to push it. "From what I've heard, anyway, which isn't much. But what I've heard is that they find you."

CHAPTER 19

◆ ◆ ◆

Girls were never safe growing up with boys.

–Iolanda Voorhees, 2073

MAY 14, 2218, FAIR CITY, PENNSYLVANIA:

MARLEY WOKE UP, DRESSED, ATE breakfast, and took the walkway to school like any other day. But inside her head, the world had changed. Her best friend was a boy. She was in love with a boy. She sat through her classes, but could not concentrate on what she was supposed to be learning. Suddenly none of it mattered. She messaged Maddy, and they left early together, going back to Marley's house.

"So what are we going to do, Mad?" Marley asked after about half an hour of kissing.

"Are you really sure you want to come with me?"

"It frightens the heck out of me, but yes."

"My moms have arranged for me to leave next Friday," said Maddy. "The story is that I said I was going to stay at Tamara's, so they won't be expected to miss me until I was supposed to come back. They'll be distraught that I'm missing, and cooperate with the authorities and all that, but I'll be pretty well away by then."

"I'll tell Mama Sue that I'm staying with you for a few days, then. I'll send her a message before she misses me. We can send messages, right?"

"Yes. Untraceable, from web cafés."

"Are you scared too, Maddy?"

"Yes, of course."

They cuddled close, holding tight to each other.

"Will it be less scary if we're together?"

"Yes, but now I'm scared for *you*. Oh, Marley." He squeezed her so hard it hurt a little. "It feels wrong and selfish, but I'm so glad you're coming with me. I would have been so lonely and sad, leaving you and going all alone."

After a pause, he said, "On Friday, they'll tell us the first place to go. We'll never know more than the next step ahead. They've taken lots of people safely to the Island this way."

"Will we ever see our families and friends again?" Marley asked.

"I don't know. I don't think so."

"What if we get caught?"

"We won't get caught," said Maddy.

"We'd be put in a lifer camp, wouldn't we?"

"Yes. But the Railroad people are good. We won't get caught."

"I don't want to think about it," said Marley. "I just want to *go*."

They fell into silence, holding each other.

MAY 14, 2218, BETHANY, GEORGIA:

On a warm May night, Kevin and Gerald went on a foraging expedition to the outskirts of a small town called Bethany, named after the 21st century movie star from Georgia. The boys targeted a large, well kept, fairly isolated house. There was no car outside, and no lights on inside. They walked around the home stealthily, trying doors and windows. The French doors into the kitchen were unlocked, so they crept in and listened for sounds of occupants. Hearing nothing, they set to work raiding the cupboards and refrigerator.

Suddenly a piercing shriek made both boys jump and turn around to see a little girl of about twelve, in a white nightgown, with an enormous mass of dark curls falling around her face, her eyes and mouth wide open. Seconds later, Kevin was holding her and covering her mouth with his hand, as gently as he could manage.

"We're not going to hurt you," he whispered earnestly into her ear. "I promise. We just need some food. We thought no one was home. We're so sorry we scared you. I want to let you go. Will you be quiet?"

She nodded, and Kevin took his hand off her mouth. Her eyes were round as saucers. "Are you *boys*?" she whispered.

"Yes. We're boys. Is your family here with you?"

"No, I'm all alone," she said honestly, forgetting everything she'd been taught to say in a situation like this. In her crime-free world, the lessons were not driven in very hard. "My moms went out and left me with the baby."

"Well, we really don't want to hurt you, do you believe that?"

"Yes," she said. She was recovering her composure.

"We're runaways," said Kevin. "We don't like to steal, but we have no other way to eat. We thought this looked like a home that could spare a bit of food."

"Oh, it is," said the girl. "We have plenty of food. Just go ahead and take what you want." She waved them away from her, indicating that they should go back to the cupboards and continue with their pillaging. She sat at the kitchen table, watching them.

"You don't look dangerous," she said presently. "Boys are supposed to be dangerous."

"Is that what people tell you?" Gerald asked.

"Yes. Dangerous and violent. They have to be kept away from people, until they're fixed up. After they're fixed up, they don't do bad things to women and girls." She paused for a moment, still regarding them thoughtfully. "So I guess you've been fixed up, then? Is that why you don't want to hurt me?"

"No," Gerald said. "We haven't been fixed up. And we don't want to be. But we're not dangerous. We've never wanted to hurt people. Not girls or boys or anyone. You've been taught a bunch of lies. We were taught a lot of lies, too. It's the people in charge who are really dangerous. When boys are 'fixed up' as you call it, it hurts them. It takes something very precious away from them. It's a really *bad* thing to do. They tell us those lies to keep boys and girls away from each other, because they don't want boys and girls to like each other."

"They say bad things happen when boys and girls are together," said the girl. "It makes everyone unhappy, and then society falls apart."

"Well, we think that's all made up," said Gerald. "I mean, I don't really *want* to be around girls that much. I've never actually met a girl until right now. But us two, we love each other. We just want to be together, and they weren't going to let us stay together. They wanted me to make babies for women, and they wanted him to get fixed up, and live in another place. But we wanted to be together, so we ran away."

"Wow," said the girl. "That's really mean that they won't let you stay together. I'd really like to help you. But I don't know what my moms would think of that. They've always told me that boys are dirty and dangerous. They'll be home in about an hour, though. Maybe they would like you if they met you."

Gerald and Kevin exchanged looks. "I don't think we can risk that," said Gerald. "Please don't tell them about us. They might tell the authorities. We're in danger whenever we come into town."

"What we really need is a medical," said Kevin, who'd filled up their bags and sat down next to Gerald at the table.

"You're sick?"

"No. Not sick. We have some … things inside of us that tell the police where we are. We have to get them taken out so they can't find us."

"Oh," she said, and pondered this. "Well, I have a medical who I like a lot," she said. "She always says I can tell her anything."

"Do you think she would help us, or would she turn us in?" Kevin asked. "That's why we're stuck. We can't just go up to a medical's office and ask. And I don't think any woman will want to help us."

"Well, I'm a woman, and I want to help you," the girl said, a little proudly. "How about if I ask her? I always go to see her in the summer, unless I get sick, which isn't very often."

"Could you pretend to be sick so you could see the medical?" asked Gerald. "Like, tomorrow, maybe? And then ask her if she would help some boys?"

"I could do that. And then I could phone you."

"We don't have phones," said Kevin. "We could come and see you again when your moms aren't home. We need a way to know that they're not home."

"Could you give us a signal to look for?" Gerald asked. "Like a flag in the window, or leave a toy outside?"

The girl thought about this. "I'll put my teddy bear outside the back door when they go out," she said. "They go out pretty often, but not always for a long time."

"We'll hide back there in the woods and watch carefully," said Kevin.

"You should probably get going now," said the girl, a little anxiously. "They'll probably be home soon. My name is Natasha."

"You're an awesome person, Natasha," said Kevin. He reached across the table and grasped her hands. "You're the first girl I've ever met, and I really like you. I'm really sorry that we scared you. I'm Kevin."

"And I'm Gerry," said Gerald. "I think you're awesome, too."

Natasha grinned.

CHAPTER 20

◆ ◆ ◆

I cry when I think of Bonito. I loved him so desperately,
fearing that he was the last man I would ever see. And now I
wonder if he will ever see the son who bears his name. I hope
little Bonito will grow up as kind and brave as his father.
I'm full of fear for all of us, but especially for this precious
little boy. I have no idea what the future holds for him.

—MARLENA MADISON, UNPUBLISHED JOURNALS, 2063

MAY 16, 2218, FAIR CITY, PENNSYLVANIA:

RAIN WAS FALLING FOR THE third dreary, gloomy day in a row. Walkway covers were up, keeping them dry, but Marley missed the sun and sky. She had a small bag packed with some extra clothes. She rolled up a few soft, form-fitting items. Summer clothes did not take up much space. She packed essential makeup and toiletries, a water bottle, and a container of high-energy nut snacks.

Mama Sue was painting an old end table that she was upcycling. She had cleared enough floor space to put down newspapers to catch the dripping paint. Speckles of sea-green decorated her graying hair, and she had rubbed some on her cheek. Marley watched her, and a lump rose in her throat. So many unsaid things would never be said now, or ever.

"Pretty color," said Marley, squatting down on the floor nearby.

"Thanks," said Mama Sue. "I'm putting marbles all over the top. See?" She indicated bags of swirly green marbles.

"That'll look awesome, Mama Sue." *Out with it, Marley. Don't let this get weird*, she thought. "I'll be staying at Maddy's for four days next week. We're working on a big project together. We don't have plans, right?" The lies felt horrible coming out of her mouth.

"No plans," said Mama Sue. "They don't mind having you?"

"Nope," said Marley.

MAY 19, 2218, FAIR CITY, PENNSYLVANIA:

Marley sat cross-legged on the attic floor. Mama Sue was away at work, and Marley was looking for a memento to take with her. Mama Sue had packed away all of Mama Jo's things. The only picture of her was the one on Marley's dressing table.

I guess it's too painful for her to look at Mama Jo's face, Marley thought, putting down a jewelry box and picking up a photo album. Dust made her sneeze—the dust collection system could not keep up with this amount of hoarded stuff. She found a picture of Mama Jo and Mama Sue with her, their newborn baby. They were looking into each other's eyes over Marley's curly, dark little head. Precious.

An old album labeled "Jo's family" had photos going all the way back to the war. Like many families, they had lost everything from before the war, and treasured what came after. The album was fashioned like an old, leather-bound book, and opened like a book. But inside the covers, the device offered Marley thumbnails and slideshows.

Gama Osanna's great-grandmother Marlena looked back at Marley with haunted eyes—eyes that had seen the horror of World War III. Then Marley saw a happy photo of Marlena with her little brown baby, Bonito. Then one of Marlena, Bonito, and baby Esperanza. Then Espie and baby Mahima on the beach in North Carolina, beginning a long tradition of mamas and babies on the beach where Marley had spent so many summers. Marley looked long at the image of beautiful Mama Jo holding her little baby self.

Marley, when she had a baby girl, would be far away in the Pacific Ocean. There would be no Carolina beach photo. Marley would break this long tradition because she was a *man-lover*. She would probably never see her quirky Gama San and sweet Gama Yim again. A lump rose in her throat, tears threatened, and she felt doubt and shame. She closed the album quickly.

A scrapbook album labeled "Our Life Together" was a real book, with photos printed on paper, and all the embellishments that Mama Sue had loved to play with. Wedding pics showed Mama Jo in a frothy white gown, and Mama Sue in deep fuchsia, with smiling attendants and bouquets of fuchsia and yellow flowers. There were lots of pics of Mama Jo. Apparently Mama Sue was the photographer of the couple. Artsy pics. Artsy nudes. Sexy nudes. With her light skin and dark hair, Jo was stunning captured in black and white. Mama Sue was an artist in all kinds of media. That was one reason she kept everything.

But lovely Mama Jo was a scientist. There was a picture of her graduation, in her cap and gown, and her Master's in Food Chemistry, carefully framed on the page.

Marley found older photos of Mama Sue sitting in small airplanes and helicopters, or standing next to them. Mama Sue could fly anything, apparently. She was mad for flying when she was young. There were pics of both of them: couple selfies taken in various cockpits, and a few taken of them by other people. Pics of all the places they flew together. Mama Sue had never flown Marley anywhere that she could remember. It was hard to believe that her frumpy Mama Sue had been this cool person.

Marley's birth document from the Rep Center had a page of its own. Her legal name—Marley Joselanna Nyimbo Osanna Iolanda Mahima Esperanza Marlena Madison Jessica Donna—traced her egg-maternal line back into the 20th century, where it disappeared into the old patriarchal system of surnames, and women's names were lost.

A person's name is like Pi, Marley thought. *As many places as you can remember, or as many places as you need.* In everyday life, she'd never used more than "Marley Joselanna Nyimbo." Almost everyone had an "Iolanda" in there somewhere.

The next page was the first picture of Marley, and then lots and lots and lots more baby pics. Baby eating. Baby bathing. Baby sleeping. Baby in a hundred adorable outfits. Baby's first steps. Toddler running, climbing, dancing. The pics were all nicely arranged on the pages, with carefully chosen background paper, and tiny baby shoes and flowers and little extinct African animals.

And then a letter. Just stuffed in there, not framed. And blank pages after that. Marley unfolded the letter.

> Dearest Susan,
>
> I am going away with Jack. I hope that you can forgive me some day.
>
> I know that this kind of love is wrong, and you know how hard I've tried to conquer it. But I cannot fight it any longer. I have to accept that it's a part of me I cannot change. If I stay, I will only continue to make you miserable. I am so, so sorry that I did not know myself better when I married you.
>
> I am leaving Marley with you because you love her so much, and I could not bear to take both of us away from you. And the road we must take is too dangerous for a little one. I hope that sometimes you will look at her and remember me with love.
>
> With great love and sorrow,
> Joselanna

By all the fucking gods, Marley thought. *Mama Jo left us on purpose. Mama Jo left us for a man. What dangerous road did Mama Jo take? The same "road" that I'm about to take with Maddy? And she died on it?*

Marley felt a little light-headed. Maddy had said they must make the authorities believe they were dead. *Was Mama Jo's death just a story like ours will be? Could my egg-mama still be alive?*

Grief surged up inside Marley. Grief for the loss that she didn't even remember, and for the emptiness of the life that followed in its wake. *Mama Jo left me behind, and Mama Sue was stuck with me.* A couple of tears dropped on the page before Marley closed the book.

But under that book, she found the perfect treasure to take with her. It was a large, gold-plated, engraved locket with small photos inside of Mama Sue and Mama Jo, looking as happy as could be. *When they were happy together, and they both wanted me.* She slipped the chain over her head and hid the locket under her shirt.

◆ ◆ ◆

Down in her room again, Marley looked around at all the vestiges of her childhood that she was leaving behind. *I wanted to leave all these kid things behind,* she thought. *But not so suddenly, all at once.* As long as she could remember, she had gone to sleep cradled in this undersea motif of waves, bright fishes, and green plants. She mustn't think about it or she would cry again.

She saved everything on her home device to her drive in the sky, where she could find it later with her passwords. She imagined her computer forlorn on her desk. She would have to leave her wrist device behind too, but not here. Nothing traceable could come with her.

What would she say to Mama Sue in parting tomorrow morning? She had felt so impatient to get away, but now it was all feeling very real and scary. She mustn't say anything odd or suspicious to Mama Sue. She mustn't cry. Should she leave a note? No, that would be dangerous. Could she get a message to her somehow when she was long gone? She had to leave Mama Sue with a story that would make her feel okay about it—she owed her that. But what story?

I'll tell her I found the letter. I think Mama Jo is still alive. I've gone off to look for her. It's a good reason to run off, and it takes the focus off Maddy. I just dragged my bestest along with me. But no. It would be stupid to just take off, looking. I'll say that Mama Jo wrote to me. That she told me where she was and I'm going there. But what if she really is dead, and Mama Sue knows it?

But Marley had a very strong hunch that Mama Sue didn't know. Of course Mama Sue wouldn't want Marley or anyone else to know the truth—that Jo had abandoned both of them to run away with a man.

◆ ◆ ◆

"It's a good cover story," Maddy agreed when they met in the afternoon. "Mama Lara and Denissa have to put on a good show of looking for me, co-operating with the authorities and all that. They're not so likely to dig for the truth about me if they think you just dragged me along. And your Mama Sue hasn't committed a crime."

Marley felt sad and anxious, but there was no way she was turning back now. She was filled with a sense of adventure. Her safe, predictable, restricted world would be unbearable now without Maddy. She wanted to be with Maddy no matter what. And she wanted to see that fantastic island where it was okay for girls to love boys. She wanted that very much.

CHAPTER 21

◆ ◆ ◆

There is no question that the Enlightened Society has achieved
peace and prosperity by controlling male aggression and
competition, and has achieved a high level of contentment with
the enhancement of same-sex attraction. But we need to stop
denying that there is a heterosexual minority that is shut out
of this contentment, and that treatment cannot change this
orientation. We must find ways for these people to be happy, too.

—Subversive Voices website, 2212

MAY 20, 2218, FAIR CITY, PENNSYLVANIA:

As it happened, Mama Sue was out having coffee with a friend Friday morning when Marley left the house for the last time.

It's probably better, Marley thought. *I would have cried, and given myself
away.*

Marley left a short note:

Mama Sue - Love you lots and lots. See you
Tuesday. Marley.

She had sent a delayed message to Mama Sue's inbox that would not show up
until Tuesday:

106

Dear Mama Sue,

I got a message from Mama Jo. She is not dead, like you told me. She is living with a man way out in the country, in another state. I have gone to find her, and my best friend Maddy is going with me. I will try to send you messages so you know we are safe. Try not to worry. I am sure you will be happier without me.

Love, Marley.

She took the walkways to Maddy's circle. The sadness was palpable in Maddy's home. Maddy snuggled on the couch with Mama Lara, whose whole face was wet, and Denissa was on the other side of Lara with her arm around her shoulders. They were just holding each other quietly in a tableau of grief. The smaller girls were somber, and their eyes were red, too. Everything had been said that could be said, and now they were just holding each other close for as long as they could.

Denissa gave Marley a long hug. "Dear Marley," she said. "I know it's wrong, and I feel so guilty, but I'm so *glad* you're going with our Maddy. I'm so glad he won't be alone. And we'll miss you very much, too."

◆ ◆ ◆

After a final round of hugs, Marley and Maddy slung their small bags onto their shoulders and left the house. They took the walkway to the garage where Maddy's mother kept her car, looking around at the home city that they would probably never see again. Maddy used his mother's card to get into the garage and start the car. The car would be tracked by GPS, but there was nothing suspicious or illegal about a couple of girls going on a trip in a mother's car. The car settled into place, and the ride became soft and smooth. Maddy set their destination, and pushed the steering wheel back into the dashboard. He slid the front seat back.

"Ever seen one of these before?" Maddy asked, handing Marley a large, thick book.

"A book?" said Marley.

"No, silly. A *map* book."

"Oh. No, I haven't. How quaint," said Marley. They opened the book and looked at it together.

"This is how we'll have to find our way around after we get off mag roads and leave this car behind," Maddy said. "You have to study the maps in the book to figure out where you are, and figure out how to get where you want to go, and then drive there by hand. If you forget what to do next, you have to stop the car and study the map again."

"No wonder people didn't travel much," said Marley. "What an aggravation it must have been. Can you imagine having to steer the car all the time? That would get old after about ten miles."

"I think we're going to find out what that's like," said Maddy. "But we can study the route now, so we'll know what to do when we get off."

Mag road 76 took them about a hundred miles into the middle of Pennsylvania and put them off in a small country town. Maddy switched to hand control, pulling the seat forward and the steering wheel out. Marley followed along in the map book and reminded him where to make turns. They passed fields of early spring vegetables, sprawling greenhouses, and long, low barns with manure smells wafting from them.

"There it is," said Marley. "Paul's Vegetable Stand."

Maddy pulled into the wide space in front of a low building with an open front displaying bins of fresh fruits and vegetables. Following instructions, Maddy drove the car under a carport and parked next to another car. The two of them got out and walked up to the produce stand.

"We're looking for free oranges," Maddy said to the yunie behind the counter.

"I see," said the yunie. He shouted over his shoulder, "Karlo, they're here." A short, dark-skinned man came out of the back, wiping his hands on a cloth. "Very good. Hi, kids," he said brusquely. "Take these vegetables and come with me."

They walked back to the carport together, Maddy carrying the bag of vegetables. "We do all this under the roof," Karlo said. "Eyes in the sky, understand?" Marley and Maddy nodded, feeling surreal. Karlo handed Maddy a card. "This goes to this car here," he said. "It's an untraceable car, okay? No GPS at all. No brain. Got to use your own brains to get where you're going, okay?"

The teenagers nodded.

"Give me your map book," said Karlo. Maddy got it out of the car. "Here's your destination for tonight," said Karlo, pointing. "Don't make any marks on this map. Just remember. I'll need the card to your mama's car, and you'll need to leave your phones in there, too. I'll be driving that car farther out and then losing it, understand? You two and the car will disappear together."

"Yes," they both whispered.

The man's tone softened. "You are very young kids," he said. "Are you sure you want to go on? You can't go back after this, you know."

"Yes, we know," said Marley.

"We want to go on," said Maddy. "We have to go on."

"You are a boy and a girl, yes?" he asked. "And you love each other?"

"Yes," they both said at once.

"I wish you happiness, then," he said with a smile. "You will find other such Romeos and Juliets where you are going. Be very careful. It is a long way with many dangers. Have you ever driven an old car, or driven on these old roads?"

Marley and Maddy both shook their heads.

"Well, then," said Karlo. "I should show you a few things before you take off." He talked to his partner on the phone, and the other man came out and drove away in Mama Lara's car with their phones. "I'll go pick him up later," Karlo said. "But if anyone's spying, it looks like you two just bought vegetables and left. Now I'll take you two out for a spin. It's a little different from driving a city car, and we don't want you to have any trouble."

He showed them how to strap in and turn on the car, and Marley drove first. She thought it felt like a tank, or a boat—so big and heavy. The road felt rough, and she had to keep her hands tightly on the wheel, and watch out for holes. But she was getting the hang of it. She pulled over and let Maddy take a turn. They drove back to Paul's Vegetable Stand and parked under the carport.

"This is a pretty new motor, and fully charged," Karlo said. "I don't expect any problems. I just want to show you a few things just in case. We don't want to use phones, and these roads can be rough." He showed them how to run diagnostics on the car, and where the extra oil was. "Follow the route I've shown you exactly, and if you're over an hour late, we'll come looking. If you do break down, get away from the car, stay out of sight, and watch for us. Police might come to check it out, and even take it away. Keep 'Buddy' here with you. If police take away the car, leave Buddy next to the road so we can find you."

Marley could not help laughing when Karlo reached into the car trunk and pulled out Buddy, a large, dilapidated neon green teddy bear. People would think that he fell out of a passing car, and no one bothered to come back for him—or that he was thrown out of a car and left deliberately.

"Well, off you go, then," said Karlo. "Good luck to you kids. It should take you three hours to get there. If you're not there in four, I'll come looking for you. Hopefully I won't see you again, and I wish you all the best."

"How can we ever thank you?" Marley asked, giving him a hug.

"You can get there safe, and be happy," Karlo said.

CHAPTER 22

◆ ◆ ◆

Marriage between men and women never worked well, because
men and women have different minds. Women strove to make
men more like them, to connect with them in life and love.
This striving often ended in abuse, infidelity, and divorce—
sometimes even murder. The mating instinct was mistaken for
love, but the mating instinct forms only a fleeting bond.

—Iolanda Voorhees, *Scientific Principles of Human Society*, 2068

2214, Colchester, New York:

VANESSA WAS EXTREMELY PROVOKED BY the runaway girls who were probably
boys. Living right under her nose all that time. She vented her frustration on
her closest colleagues online.

> *Van79:* The Underground Railroad exists. I'm absolutely fuck-
> ing sure of it. How else could young teens completely dis-
> appear like that?
> *Sika34:* The kids were probably kidnapped and the car stolen.
> The Underground Railroad is a subversive fairy tale. It's all
> wishing and hoping. Criminals aren't nearly smart or coor-
> dinated enough to actually *do* that. I mean seriously, that
> Island they talk about? A man-made island in the Pacific

where they have some kind of hetero-friendly utopia? You can't really think that exists. There is *zero* evidence of it.

ForceForGood: They believe it exists, though. That's why they act the way you saw. But it's all a fantasy. Criminals are out there preying on these kids, and the family members, too. The gods only know what they do with them. It's a horrible shame. These hidden boys think they're running off to a hetero utopia when they're really going to horrible abuse and death. That's why the MUHV law needs to be stronger. We need to just go in there, run a quick DNA on all the kids, and take the boys out before they have a chance to run.

Van79: I'm all for that. It's just amazing how well some of them pass for girls. I had no idea about those two. Makes me feel like a fool.

Sika34: Subversives take them and train them in terrorism. They tell them about the Island, maybe—but then they tell them that they should stay here and fight for men's rights or heteros' rights or the Old Way, or something. They never stop believing in the Island, but they never get there.

Bar56: I've been watching this for many years. Fifty years ago, there really was an ocean liner in the Pacific that was a hetero haven until it was outlawed, and the government claimed it was destroyed. But maybe it wasn't. Or maybe they made another one. I think the Railroad may still be taking people to a place like that. I think you all may be underestimating these people.

Van79: Well, I want to find out. It's my new ambition. I don't feel like I'm accomplishing enough where I am, and I don't think there is anything more to find in that circle now. I want to see if I can get on the Railroad myself. Will you help me do that?

A superior colleague called Barilla agreed, and worked to get Vanessa a new undercover assignment.

Barilla had been working for a few years on computer programs to identify Railroad activity. The program analyzed purchasing records for items used to make false ID cards: synthetic papers, laminating pouches, laminators, encoders, and hologram paint. Items used to change people's hair were also tracked. One person buying items in both categories was worth investigating. But most Railroaders were not that stupid.

Heteros were known to hide in mixed-sex neighborhoods, and especially mixed-sex buildings and circles, and hidden heteros were automatic suspects for Railroad activity. The program scrutinized purchasing in those neighborhoods.

Anonymous tips from neighbors could be fruitful. Nosy neighbors might notice a guest leaving with a different hair color or in a different car. But to advertise the need for these tips would draw attention to the fact that people were escaping the Enlightened Society in large enough numbers to concern the government. That fact was not for public consumption.

Barilla agreed completely with Vanessa that infiltration was the best strategy, and got Vanessa another undercover assignment. Vanessa told her friends in the Natural circle that she was having an online romance with a woman in Florida, and she was going to move there. She would communicate with them for a while, and then taper it off. They would never know that they'd been infiltrated.

◆ ◆ ◆

In 2214, Vanessa changed her name again, to "Ruby," changed her hair to dark and curly, and moved into one of Barilla's suspect neighborhoods in Oswego.

Again, she spent the better part of a year building acquaintances, friendships, and trust in her community and online. But this time she threw out subtle hints that she was a closeted hetero. Her decorating profession got her into people's homes. She offered advice and services to her new friends and neighbors free of charge, and people grew accustomed to her looking critically around their homes. This was always followed by some good decorating or organizing advice. But Vanessa was also looking for evidence and listening for leads. She steered conversations and invited confidences. She pursued acquaintances and intensified friendships that looked promising.

CHAPTER 23

◆ ◆ ◆

I met the dearest young woman a week ago, the day after my 100th birthday party. A young hetero called Akiko, traveling around the country looking for a place to feel comfortable. It's heartbreaking to see so much anger and shame in beautiful young eyes.

—MARLENA MADISON, UNPUBLISHED JOURNALS, 2142

MAY 20, 2218, PENNSYLVANIA:

MARLEY HAD NEVER SEEN THE night so dark, or so many stars in the sky. She'd never been this far out from a city. She'd been tracing their way on the map with the help of a small flashlight while Maddy drove the car. They'd pulled over and changed places three times now. They were both getting a better feel for driving this heavy car by hand on the rough roads. But Marley was tired and ready to stop for the night.

"It's on this stretch of road, Mad," said Marley, after instructing Maddy to turn right at a dark, deserted intersection. "I'm just looking for numbers now. I just saw 202. And there's 206. We're going the right way. Oh, just look at the stars, Maddy."

"I'll look at them when I stop the car," said Maddy wearily.

"Does driving make your neck hurt? I could rub your neck," Marley suggested.

"Yeah, it does. But don't stop watching for numbers. You can massage me all you want later."

"There is it, Mad," Marley exclaimed. "Number 246."

At last they were pulling into the driveway of their destination. A teal and white sign, hanging on wooden posts, advertised a Bed & Breakfast. The house was large and white with teal shutters and elaborate gingerbread trim. The roses climbing all over the main house were not blooming yet, but the gardens sported a profusion of daffodils, hyacinths, and tulips.

Maddy and Marley parked the car, walked up to the front door hand in hand, and Marley softly tapped the ornate iron doorknocker. A very old, white-haired lady opened the door with a warmer smile than Marley thought they deserved at such a late hour.

"We're here to see Mrs. Freeman," she said.

"Oh, come in, you darlings," said the old lady. "We've been expecting you, and just beginning to worry." She ushered them into a huge kitchen, and pressed them to sit down at the table. "Are you kids hungry?" she asked.

"A little bit," said Marley. "There were sandwiches in the vegetable basket."

But Maddy said, "I'm starving."

"Of course you are," she said kindly. "Just one moment."

She stepped over to the wall, and picked up an intercom. "Romeo and Juliet have arrived safe and sound," she said. She picked up a phone and sent a text message. "Telling Karlo you got here," she said. As she opened the refrigerator and brought out platters of tea sandwiches and scones, two more old ladies joined them around the kitchen table.

Akiko, Isoki, and Mizuki were sisters, all in their nineties, all born in this house. Isoki had raised daughters and granddaughters there, and the bed and breakfast business had been going for almost fifty years.

"I hope you like this English tea sort of thing," said Akiko. "It's our specialty. But the tea is herbal, so you won't be kept awake." The teens nodded—their mouths were full.

The ladies sat around making small talk while Marley and Maddy wolfed down a couple dozen little sandwiches—the cucumber and salmon ones were

Marley's favorite—and scones heaped with clotted cream and homemade preserves.

"When you're done here," said Akiko, "we'll just settle you in your rooms, and we'll talk tomorrow."

They were offered adjoining rooms, but wanted only one, and were asleep minutes after climbing into the soft bed together.

◆ ◆ ◆

CHAPTER 24

Women need not worry over our treatment of men; they are
as happy as they can be. Breeders are held in high esteem, and
yunies are released from the burden of male hormones.

–IOLANDA VOORHEES, 2094

MAY 20, 2218, BETHANY, GEORGIA:

KEVIN AND GERALD CHECKED NATASHA'S house every day for a week, until one evening the teddy bear appeared outside the back door. Then they knocked at the back door and she let them in.

"My medical can't help you, but she knows someone who can," said Natasha. "My medical can drive you to the other one's office. You need to come back at 9:00 tomorrow night."

The boys were fearful. "What if the medical is planning to turn us in?" said Gerald.

"I don't think she is," said Natasha. "I told you I'm a good judge of people, right? I had a good feeling about you two almost right away—not *quite* right away—even though everything I've heard about boys is bad."

Maybe she's just never met a bad person, Kevin thought. *Maybe she was just lucky that we didn't want to hurt her.* But he wanted to believe her. What choice did they have, anyway?

"We're never going to get out of the swamp if we don't trust someone, Gerry," he said.

"I know," said Gerald. "I think we're gonna have to trust your judgment, Natasha. And your medical's."

"Okay, then," said the little girl, looking very serious, and spreading her tourist map of Okefenokee out on the table, smoothing it with her small hands. "She said you should meet her at the canoe drop-off, right here." She pointed to one of the places where pickup trucks drove canoes and canoeists to the water. "She has a white car with a red stripe on it."

She got them some food, and they sat with her for a little while, eating cookies and drinking milk.

"I won't ever see you boys again, will I?" she said. "I won't ever know if you got through okay." Her big dark eyes were sad. Suddenly she got up and ran away. She came back with two little rings in her hand. "I want you to both have something of mine," she said. "I'm a very lucky person. I'm always winning things. I want you to keep these on all the time."

The boys solemnly put the rings on their fingers. Kevin was able to slide his all the way onto his left pinkie, but Gerald could only get his halfway on.

"We'll never forget you, sweetie," said Kevin. The boys enveloped the girl in a big sandwich hug before they left.

◆ ◆ ◆

The next night, they climbed into the back of the small, white, red-striped car, and hunkered down so they wouldn't be seen. Natasha's medical drove them past a few small towns to the home office of a surgical colleague. This medical greeted the boys and ushered them into her surgical room. She did all the work herself, and, just an hour after they arrived, the boys were bandaged and the microchips were destroyed.

"Will those things lead the cops to your house?" Kevin asked anxiously.

"Only, I think, if they happened to check your location while you were actually here," the medical said. "We can't be 100% sure they didn't, but I think it's pretty unlikely. You've been gone for weeks. They're probably just checking once a day or so to see where you are."

"But what if they did?"

"Well, that would be very bad luck. If I think I'm going to be arrested, I will have to disappear, too," the medical said. "It's a risk we take when we help people like this."

"But *why* do you want to help us?" Gerald asked. "We were always told that women hated boys, and wanted them to stay locked up in their camps."

"Well, I don't hate boys," said the medical. "I'm helping because it's the right thing to do. Not all of us believe all that Voorhees Second Enlightenment stuff. Males are 30% of the population and have no civil rights. They're treated like slaves or animals. That's just wrong."

"But why would you care what happens to men and boys?" Gerald asked.

"I care what happens to *humans*," she said. "Everyone deserves freedom and a chance at happiness. I can't enjoy my life fully knowing others are oppressed and doing nothing about it."

She gave them water and pills to take. "When this anesthetic wears off, you'll be in pain for a while," she said. "You need to take these every four hours for a few days. Now, let's talk about what you're going to do. You boys were very lucky to get this far. I admire your courage. What you did was amazing, really. But you're a little short on planning, I think. What did you intend to do from here?"

"We really didn't have a plan," Gerald admitted sheepishly. "We figured out how to get out of the camp, and thought we'd figure out what to do next after we got out."

"Did you want to hide somewhere on the continent? Or were you trying to get to the Island?"

"The Island?" said Kevin.

"You don't even *know* about the Island?"

The boys shook their heads.

"Okay then," she said, taking a breath. "Let's get in the car and I'll tell you all about it while we get you away from here."

◆ ◆ ◆

The medical drove them to the home of two female friends, and the boys stayed hidden indoors until they were fully recovered. The only women Kevin and Gerry had ever known had administered and guarded the camp in a very hands-off way that minimized contact with boys. In Kevin's rare and intimidating encounters with them, these women had regarded him coldly, as if he were a loathsome sort of animal. It was strange and wonderful for him to get to know grown-up women who were sympathetic to the plight of boys and regarded them as equal humans.

The boys appreciated the soft beds and regular meals of home-cooked food, and the friendly, sympathetic conversations that opened up a whole new world to them as their surgical wounds healed. Kevin was tremendously relieved to be in the hands of caring adults who knew what they were doing.

When the boys had healed enough to make travelling more comfortable, the women hid them in the back of a small van and drove for hours. They disembarked in front of a large old house surrounded by woods, with no other houses in sight.

Two male couples lived on the forty-acre estate, which had been a Railroad link for the past ten years. Two of them were yunies, and two were intact. These men told the boys an intriguing tale of an underground medical at their Young Men's Camp who gave them yunie tattoos without actually doing the surgery, and then counseled them on how to pass for yunies at the camp and out in society.

Three other boys were staying there as well, having been smuggled out of a camp not far away in Georgia about two weeks earlier. Jackson was thirteen, Axel and Benjamin were only twelve. They'd been together all their lives, and had been dorm brothers at their camp. A subversive camp father had arranged their escape, chip removal, and transport.

"Wow, I wish we'd had someone like him in our camp," said Gerald after the younger boys shared their story. The younger boys listened with awe as Gerald described his escape with Kevin.

The generous forest cover of oak, hickory, and pine on the property protected the boys from satellite surveillance, and they spent many hours outside in the shade as the Georgia summer heated up. Sometimes hikers wandered through, but a silent perimeter alarm signaled the boys' wrist phones so they could hide, move away, or go back inside, and the hikers were none the wiser.

The boys enjoyed the freedom to let their hair grow. Tight black curls were forming on the heads of Axel and Benjamin. Gerry was now sporting blond curls, which Kevin found adorable and couldn't stop playing with. Kevin's own deep chestnut hair was growing in glossy and straight, and Jackson's thick black hair was growing straight up.

CHAPTER 25

◆ ◆ ◆

Women are struggling to survive, traumatized by the recent past
and afraid for the future. Voorhees is highly charismatic, and her
ideas are giving them hope and making sense of things. There's
this "never again" feeling … this feeling that if we don't do things
in a drastically different way, the human race will go extinct.
So yeah. Sexual segregation would be drastically different.

—MARLENA MADISON, UNPUBLISHED JOURNALS, 2063

MAY 21, 2218, PENNSYLVANIA:

WHEN MARLEY OPENED HER EYES Saturday morning, she knew exactly
where she was. She stretched, luxuriating in the smoothness of the satin sheets
against her bare skin and the sweetness of waking up with Maddy beside her.
He wore a long nightshirt that he had refused to take off. She snuggled up
against him and kissed his face until he woke up and kissed her back. They lay
together talking until one of the elderly sisters called them down for breakfast
on the intercom.

After a sumptuous breakfast of eggs, toast, sausages, and grapefruit, the
ladies took Marley and Maddy to a room where they operated a small hair
salon. Isoki washed Marley's hair, and then Akiko went to work on it.

"I'm thinking straighter, shorter, and blonde," Akiko said. "It will make
you look like a different person."

"Okay," said Marley. It hadn't occurred to her to change her looks, but she felt she was in the hands of experts. The old ladies had been moving people along the Railroad for fifty years, long before Marley was born.

"How do you feel after your first night away?" Akiko asked, applying curl relaxer.

"Conflicted and confused," said Marley. "It feels totally right to be with Maddy. It feels totally right to love him. But it's pretty scary, running away like this, going to some strange place really far away, and not even knowing how we're getting there. And not knowing what I believe anymore. That's pretty weird, too."

"I understand," said Akiko. "I ran away when I was young, too. Back in the forties. I traveled all over the country, trying to find some place to belong. I was hetero, and I hated myself for it—could barely admit it, even to myself. In my travels, I met a very old lady who was about twenty when the war started. She told me what things were like before the war, Voorhees, and the Enlightened Society. What she told me changed my life."

"That's amazing," Marley exclaimed. "You actually talked to someone who was alive in World War III?"

"I did indeed," said the old woman.

Akiko snipped off a few inches of Marley's hair, and pulled the relaxer down to the new tips. "It helps when you realize that Enlightened Society theory is a religion," she said. "Voorhees scoffed at religion, and went on and on about science—but that was just a way to make 21st century people believe in it. The science wasn't really there behind it, she just convinced people that it was. Now it's a big, self-perpetuating lie because so many people truly believe that it's based on real science. So, even though you're very young, don't be afraid to question, and measure what you've been told against your own experience."

Mizuki was curling Maddy's hair and coloring it a deep dark brown. She waxed Maddy's chin, upper lip, and eyebrows, which made Marley cringe. Maddy had been doing this himself for some time now, and he was amused by Marley's discomfort. Marley hadn't given hair removal a thought since she went to the MediSalon with Lallaina a few years ago.

"Why didn't you go to the MediSalon and have all that removed?" she asked him. "Like a girl would."

"Think about it, silly," said Maddy. "They would've wondered why I didn't take all my clothes off and have my whole body done."

"Oh," said Marley. "Of course. And Naturals are too *modest* for that sort of thing." She rolled her eyes, and Maddy laughed. Marley wished she could take back all the times she'd ribbed Maddy about his modesty, thinking it was just a silly piece of the Natural culture that he ought to let go of. He had forgiven her ignorance and understood her intentions all along, but now she felt obliged to make fun of herself.

◆ ◆ ◆

"Wow, I do look like a different person," Marley exclaimed, looking in the mirror after her hair was rinsed out and dried. "And so do you."

In a secret basement room, Isoki photographed their new looks and made them new identity cards from a database of created identities kept by the Underground Railroad. They spent some time studying their new identities and calling each other by their new names, Hayley and Alissa. Then they studied the route to their next destination in Ohio.

"I wish we didn't have to leave here," Marley said, as they snuggled into bed that night. "I think it's the best place in the world."

MAY 22, 2218, PENNSYLVANIA:

Sunday morning, Marley and Maddy, now Alissa and Hayley, got an early start in a different GPS-free car. They took a winding route on local roads through the hills, woods, and farms of Pennsylvania and into Ohio. The weather was cloudy and sunny by turns. Trees were showing hints of green, and dogwoods and crabapples bloomed pink and white along the edges of the woods. It was late evening when they arrived at a somewhat dilapidated motel in a small town in the southwest corner of Ohio.

They asked for a Mr. Frederick, and were shown to a shabby but clean enough room. The man gave them a cursory, "We'll talk in the morning," and left them alone.

They set their small bags on one of the beds, and Marley turned on a lamp.

"They could use a decorator here," said Maddy.

"Really," Marley agreed. "These colors are *sick*. I think they used paint from the free rack that nobody wanted. And those bedspreads are just wrong."

Somehow this depressing décor made her feel small and young in an uncaring world.

CHAPTER 26

◆ ◆ ◆

I went to the Reproduction Center to get pregnant again. Yes, the world is in a terrible state, and we're barely surviving. But I want the human race to continue. I was told that I was not allowed to have a natural pregnancy, because they cannot take the risk of me having a boy. So they took eggs from me, and I will go back in nine months to get my baby girl. I have already decided to call her Esperanza, to remind me that there is hope for the future.

—MARLENA MADISON, UNPUBLISHED JOURNALS, 2066

MAY 23, 2218, OHIO:

MONDAY MORNING, MR. FREDERICK GAVE them a modern rental car, registered to the fictitious mother of Marley's fictitious identity. This would allow them to take mag roads to their destinations in Indiana and Illinois. This underground man was handling them expertly, as the others had done, but without the warmth.

I guess I need to grow up, Marley thought. *Not everyone in this big world is going to pamper me or ask me how I'm feeling.*

"Yay for modern transportation," she exclaimed gratefully as she programmed the car for their destination in Indiana. She'd never fully appreciated it before. Now she reveled in the luxury of lounging in the car with her feet up, effortlessly passing through city centers where buildings towered high, and they could see people on walkways through the clear air, villages nestled among the flowering trees in their spring glory, meadows of narcissus and greening grass, and farms with grazing cows.

"Oh, look, Maddy, Shetland ponies," Marley cried. On another farm they saw little dwarf goats, and on another, llamas.

The mag road put them off in their destination village, and Maddy hand-drove along lanes between attached rows of red brick homes nestled among tall oaks and ashes, just beginning to green. They found the row they were looking for, and a slender woman with almond-shaped eyes opened the front door.

"We're Hayley and Alissa," said Marley.

"I'm Lee," said the woman. "Do come in." She wore a long, simple black dress that echoed the straight black hair falling freely well past her waist. Marley stepped inside, and her eyes swept over an elegant home with furnishings of superb quality. Lee ushered them to a sitting area where another woman and two yunies rose to greet them.

"This is my wife, Anna," said Lee. "Brendan and Austin live next door." Then she showed them into a spacious washroom to freshen up. The painted ceramic tiles made the fixtures appear to be standing in a woodland clearing, surrounded by curling tendrils of ferns with leafy branches above and natural stone underfoot. Marley breathed in sharply.

"Tiles like this cost 200 Ameros each, at least," she said. "Gods, I do hope I get to take a bath here."

Back in the main room, food beckoned to them from the glass top of a Victorian sideboard hundreds of years old. Marley piled a plate with stuffed mushrooms, salmon, and fresh cut fruit while Lee poured drinks for them.

As they settled on the couches to eat, it became obvious to Marley that the love connections here did not agree with the marriage documents. These were two hetero couples living under a cover of normal marriages and separate homes. *What a clever arrangement*, she thought. *Everything is legal, but their lovers are right next door.*

After they'd eaten, the adults quizzed Marley and Maddy on their new identities, looking for hesitation and contradiction.

"If you're ever stopped," said Lee, "speak as little as possible, and think carefully before you speak. Take out your ID before you open your mouth. This will remind you not to blurt out your real name."

"Okay," said Marley. She felt a twinge of dread. She didn't like to be reminded of the reality that they could be stopped and questioned. "Do lots of people come through here?" she asked. "How do you know who to trust?"

"The Railroad is basically just a network of trusted friends," said Anna. "We know the person who sent you here, and we know the people we're sending you to. Teens are very unlikely to be infiltrators. We don't want to know more than we need to, in case we're ever caught. The tricky part is finding the people who need us without giving ourselves away."

"Right," said Marley. "Because those people are all hiding what they are, sometimes from themselves, even. Now that I'm accepting myself, I'm beginning to wonder about other people, like the friend who showed me boy porn. Maybe *both* of us were pretending to think it was disgusting. Maybe both of us were turned on by it. Maybe she's a hetero, too, and neither of us dared to admit it to the other, even though we were close friends. All the teachers, medicals, and counselors say that hetero feelings are just an immature phase. But it didn't go away for me when I did what they said to do."

"It doesn't go away, Alissa," said her hostess. "What they don't teach you is that before artificial wombs and Reproduction Centers, heteros were the overwhelming majority, because that's what happens naturally. Now the Rep Centers treat all the embryos with hormones to make them come out normal. It doesn't always work—it *often* doesn't work. And then people are shamed and persecuted to cover up how often it doesn't work. But Alissa, believe me, there is nothing at all *wrong* with you."

MAY 24, 2218, INDIANA:

Tuesday morning, they set off again in the same car they drove the day before. At a web café in a small town, Maddy showed Marley how to access her information in the sky without revealing where she was. It was afternoon—Marley's email would have landed in Mama Sue's mail, and there was already an answer for Marley. She opened it with trepidation.

> Dear Marley,
>
> I did not want to tell you that your egg-mama abandoned both of us and ran away with a man. I thought it would hurt you too much. But now you know. She loved you very much. She loved both of us. But she didn't want to endanger you, or leave me all alone.
>
> Of course I am not happier without you. What a silly thing to say. But I hope that meeting Jo brings you some peace and some answers. Love you always. Stay safe, and come home soon.
>
> Mama Sue

Marley sent a reply:

> Dear Mama Sue:
>
> We are not there yet. But Maddy and I are safe and well. I cannot write often, but will write again when I can. Please don't worry.
>
> Marley

They spent another hour on the mag road after that, and exited again in the small town of Beaudelaire. They found a roadside garage near the exit, and stopped there to wait as instructed. They waited, comfortable but impatient, in the car until a dark green van pulled up. They looked inquiringly at the driver.

"Alissa? Hayley?" he said.

"Yes, that's us."

The van doors opened, and they climbed into the back together. The man drove away without speaking another word. Something about him suppressed their impulses to talk, to him or each other.

The taciturn man took long, winding country roads for about an hour, into farmland where houses were miles apart from each other. He turned into a driveway and stopped at a long metal gate guarded by two rough-looking men. One of them came over and talked to their driver, raising his arm and resting it on the van. Marley saw a holstered gun—or a stunner, maybe—under his shirt. She'd never seen either of those things in real life before. City authorities didn't even carry stunners, let alone lethal guns. Its presence frightened her.

Brief words were exchanged, and the men opened the gate. The driver proceeded about half a mile farther to a long, low, unkempt building, where they disembarked with their small bags. Walking apprehensively through that door, Marley got her biggest shock since she found out that her best friend was not a girl. The room was simply crawling with *real, live, undisguised boys.*

CHAPTER 27

◆ ◆ ◆

The sexual needs of men and women are incompatible. Men
abhor commitment; only the act of mating interests and pleasures
them. Women seek love and connection, and sex for them is about
bonding. Women have been continually raped to service the desires
of men, while men have been vexed by the bonds of marriage.

–IOLANDA VOORHEES, 2084

MAY 24, 2218, ROSES' FARM, ILLINOIS:

MARLEY CLUNG TO MADDY, AND felt him clinging to her as well. She realized
that this was as weird—perhaps weirder—for Maddy as it was for her. The
room grew suddenly quiet as the boys stopped jabbering and shouting at each
other, all heads turned, all eyes stared at the newcomers, and more than one
mouth fell open. These were not boys like Maddy, raised in a world of women
and yunies. These were boys' camp boys—short-haired, plainly dressed, and
rowdy. Maddy and Marley were frozen in place, hanging onto each other in
the doorway. A frowsy, fortyish woman, as innocent of makeup as the boys
were, hurried over to them, wiping her hands on a dishtowel.

"Oh, my," she said, with a kind but amused sparkle in her eye. "I think I
see a bit of culture shock going on here. I'm so sorry you couldn't be warned,
you poor dears. But I assure you, it's going both ways. These boys have never
seen girls before, either." She swept her hand to indicate those present.

"I'm not a girl," said Maddy firmly, almost defiantly. Marley had never heard his voice sound so low, and she felt him straighten up to his full height beside her. She could feel the keen embarrassment and confusion emanating through his body. He was meeting his own kind, his own age, for the first time in his life, and he didn't know how to be a boy. Marley forgot her own discomfort for a moment and tried to imagine how he felt.

"Oh, of course not. I'm sorry," said the woman matter-of-factly. "I'm called Mrs. Rose. Let me introduce you to the boys. Of course you won't remember all the names right away. Your name, dear?" she said, looking at Marley.

"M-Alissa," said Marley, and she looked quickly up at Maddy, hoping he wouldn't screw up, too.

"Hayley," said Maddy softly.

"Hayley," the woman repeated, knowing full well that Hayley wasn't his name at all. "But here, of course, we can call you by a boy's name, can't we? How about ... Hay*len*?"

"Halen," said Maddy, and just a hint of a smile crept onto his shell-shocked face. "I like that."

"I like it, too," said Marley.

"Boys—Melissa and Halen," Mrs. Rose announced. "Can you all say your names, please?"

As she pointed at them, they called out, "James," "Robert," "Peter," "Michael," "Stuart," "Kyle," and "Tyrone." Only seven of them. It had seemed like twenty when they opened the door.

"And Darlene," said Mrs. Rose, indicating a young woman who had just appeared in the doorway from the back rooms. She was no taller than Marley, with a slighter build, porcelain skin, and chin-length, straight black hair. She had the chic and sophisticated look of a city woman.

Darlene and Marley exchanged smiles, and Marley was sure they would be friends.

A man had come up behind the frowsy woman during the introductions. Now he reached out and shook Maddy's hand. "Welcome, son," he said warmly. Then he gave Maddy a crushing, manly hug. "C'mon back here with me. Let's get you out of that fucking dress." He was pulling Maddy away with an arm around his shoulders. He nodded at Marley. "Welcome, little woman," he said. "Mrs. Rose will take care of you, won't you, dear?" He turned towards the woman and gave her a quick kiss on the mouth.

Gods, Marley thought. *They just kiss right in front of people.*

When Maddy returned, his dark, curly hair (which Marley was just getting used to) was pulled back in a braid, but he was wearing shorts and a muscle shirt like most of the other boys, and most of the makeup had been removed from his face. He looked uncomfortable, obviously not used to showing so much of his skin. He smiled shyly at Marley, and she went over and hugged him hard.

"Hi, Halen," she said. "I like the new look." But a little part of her also felt shy and scared. Different hair, different name, different clothes, and a different, new look in those hazel eyes. Was the Maddy she had come to love still in there?

The boys gathered around Marley and Maddy, asking them question after question, and staring at Marley with frank fascination. "Please don't stare at Melissa, boys," Mrs. Rose admonished, but it did no good at all.

Marley realized, with some amusement, that these boys regarded Maddy—now Halen—not as a weirdo, but as some kind of celebrity, like someone who had lived in a land where candy grew on trees. And Marley *was* that candy. They all regarded Marley with frank but reverent curiosity.

Mrs. Rose invited Marley to help her in the kitchen, and with Marley gone, the boys went outside to play. "I wondered if you might have questions for me," Mrs. Rose explained. "We get very few city girls here—mostly camp boys—so I'm curious about your life, too."

"Are all these boys heteros?" Marley asked.

Mrs. Rose thought for a moment. "I believe five of them are hetero, and two are normal, though I don't ask," she said. "The Da's who choose which ones to sneak out tend to choose heteros over normals. And they almost always choose boys who are about to be castrated. But I want to hear *your* story."

Marley found herself spilling the whole tale, as well as many of the questions and doubts that plagued her. "What about violence and war?" she asked.

"Hasn't our society solved those problems and made the world safe? Isn't what we're doing here threatening our whole civilization?"

"*We* don't think so," said Mrs. Rose. "We certainly don't want violent crime, or to have wars happening again. But there is violence in this society that you've been taught not to notice or think of as violence. Castrating boys is a horrible act of violence. The violence of it is hidden by the fact that the boys are taught to believe that it's right and necessary, and inevitable. In fact, they're taught that remaining whole is a *sacrifice*, and that breeders are honored for that sacrifice. Girls and women too—they're deprived of fathers, husbands, and brothers, but they don't know what they're missing. The lack of awareness doesn't make it okay."

Marley frowned, thinking. She'd never heard anyone pining for a brother or a father. She loved the uncles in her circle, though. Would having a father be like having an uncle living in your house?

Things that Marley had always believed were now unraveling inside her brain. In theory, she was chopping vegetables. But her knife had been still for many minutes, and Mrs. Rose did not remind her of her task.

"But the great wars, World Wars II and III, with the bombs that could blow up the world many times over—wasn't all that done by men?" she asked. "Maybe what we have now isn't perfect, but isn't it better than doing that again?"

"I guess almost *anything* is better than people blowing up the world," said Mrs. Rose. "But the problem is, Melissa, that the history you've been taught is all twisted. I know that's hard to believe. Who am I to contradict all that authoritative history, right? But we believe that all those lessons were written to indoctrinate children to conform to this way of life.

"Some of us believe that war is caused by authority and power, not by men per se. Men wouldn't go to war if they weren't indoctrinated or forced to go. Yes, men are stronger. And often more aggressive or competitive. But that doesn't make them all abusive or warlike. I grew up on the Island with boys and men, Melissa. They're just as human and loving as we are—like your Halen.

"And what about you?" she looked directly at Marley and smiled. "If this is a perfect society, then why does a girl like you have to run away to be with a boy you love? Should boys and girls not be allowed to love each other? Should mothers be forced to give up or hide their baby boys?"

"Is it even *possible* to have a society that makes everyone happy?" Marley asked.

"Ah, that's a very good question. But I don't think a society 'makes' people happy—at best, maybe, society can refrain from getting in the way. I think the best we can do is leave each other in freedom. So each person can pursue what they want for themselves." For a minute or two, they worked in silence, Marley suddenly remembering that she was supposed to be chopping, and picking up another tomato.

"Maybe that's enough talk for now," said Mrs. Rose. "Would you like to go out and see what the boys are doing? Dinner will be ready in about twenty minutes."

So Marley went out. The boys were playing football. She watched their young bodies running, throwing, catching, and crashing into each other. They were laughing and whooping. And Maddy was right in there, throwing, catching, and yelling with the others. He looked so happy, so free.

He is finally allowed to be what he really is, she thought. And tears stung her eyes. She had never seen his body like this. In the shorts and muscle shirt, she could see the slender muscularity that had always been hidden under his excessive clothing. Maddy noticed her watching, and stopped to look at her. The happy smile on his face made her melt inside. It was a melting that started in her chest and trickled down through her body. While he was distracted, the freckly redhead called Stuart bowled him over and stole the ball. Maddy went down laughing.

"Marl-*issa*," he yelled up from the ground. "Come and play with us."

Play with the boys? She could play with the boys? She suddenly had the feeling that she and these boys were in an uncharted social wilderness. What was right? What was wrong? Did any of them know? Marley just followed her heart and ran out to join the game.

◆ ◆ ◆

After a simple, plentiful, and noisy dinner, Mr. and Mrs. Rose shooed all the kids into the dormitory to sleep. Mrs. Rose pulled Marley aside. "I have a bed for you in another room," she said.

Marley's eyes went round. "But I don't want my own room," she said. "I like to sleep with Mad—with Halen." Sensitive to the older woman's expression, she suddenly felt confused, doubtful, and ashamed. *Man-lover.* All the shame and filth of that slur flooded her mind. Her eyes dropped, and a pink flush came to her golden-brown cheeks.

"Melissa, no," said Mrs. Rose quickly. "What you feel isn't wrong or bad. It's just that it would be disastrous for you to get pregnant right now."

"*Pregnant?*"

"Yes."

"From sleeping with a boy?"

"Well, yes. Not sleeping. But having sex with a boy."

"Well, he wouldn't do that animal mating thing to me," said Marley with indignant revulsion.

Mrs. Rose seemed slightly taken aback. "Well, you could discover that you *want* to," she said delicately. "Or that he wants to. And you're both fertile."

"I am not one of those crazy porn women who's into mating," said Marley firmly. "And Halen doesn't want to do that, either. Why would he? We don't want to make a baby, and we would never do it *that* way." The idea of babies growing inside of women's bodies still horrified her. "I'm not a Natural, you know."

"Melissa, you don't understand boys."

"I thought you said men were good people, amended or not. Now you're telling me Halen would go animalistic on me and force me to have a baby? He's my best friend."

"I know, Melissa," she sighed. "They *are* good people. There's just so much you don't know, so much you couldn't know, growing up in a society of women. When fertile men and women live together, they have ways—" She stopped and thought for a moment. "Oh, wait, do you have an implant? Do you have monthly cycles?"

"I don't bleed, if that's what you mean. We get that stopped as soon as it starts."

"I'm sorry," said Mrs. Rose. "I grew up on the Island, and as I said, I haven't met a lot of city girls. I forgot that you would have had that done, even without boys around. But I still don't think you should sleep in there with all of them. How about if you and Halen sleep in your own room?"

"OK, I guess," Marley relented.

◆ ◆ ◆

But Halen wanted to sleep in the dormitory with the boys. At this news, Marley curled up on the bed and began to cry.

"You like them," she sobbed. "You love your own kind, like you're supposed to, and I'm a freak. You want to kiss them. You're normal."

"Oh, Marley, no." Distressed that he'd upset her, Halen hugged her and tried to wipe away the tears. "It's not like that at all. You don't know how weird this all is for me. I don't want to *kiss* them. I want to kiss *you*. But I want to talk to them. Because they're like me. And I've never been with people like me before. It's like I'm finding out who I really am, and what I really am, and what it's like to be a boy and have everyone know it. But Marley, the only one here I want to kiss is you."

And he showed her by doing it. And doing it again, and again. When he finally left Marley alone in her room, her body raged with intense feelings, and her mind was in turmoil as everything she had known about life turned upside down and fell apart.

CHAPTER 28

◆ ◆ ◆

The romance novels that entertained women for centuries,
glorifying their lust for rich and powerful men, will be
looked upon with utter disgust by future generations.

—IOLANDA VOORHEES, 2076

FALL 2215, OSWEGO, NEW YORK:

ON A BRISK FALL DAY in 2215, when the trees of New York state were just breaking out in bright yellows and reds, Vanessa stopped in at her friend Larrine's for coffee. She'd asked Larrine if she could come and talk. Now she stirred her coffee nervously, and put in several spoonfuls of sugar.

"Stop with the sugar, Ruby dear," said Larrine, laughing. "Just relax and tell me what you're so worried about."

"I broke it off with that woman I was telling you about," Vanessa said. "The one from Ohio." She sighed, and went silent, as if thinking about what to say. "It just didn't feel right. It *never* feels right. I really want to get married and have girls, but I'm afraid it won't ever work for me." She stirred her coffee as if all that sugar would never dissolve.

"Larrine," she said. "I've never told *anyone* this. You must promise me you won't tell a soul."

"Of course I won't," said Larrine.

"I think I'm just not attracted to women. I think I may be attracted to men."

"Oh, honey," said Larrine sympathetically, putting her hand over her friend's. "I'm *so* glad you told me. You know I don't judge people about that. You can't help it, you know. It's just the way you're born."

"I knew you wouldn't judge," said Vanessa, showing relief nevertheless. "And it's so hard keeping it inside, with everyone I know. I hate these feelings so much. I don't want to be this way. It gets in the way of what I want so much—marriage and family. I want that, but I don't want to be fake with someone, you know? I've tried to suppress it and change it, and I just can't."

Larrine seemed to be considering carefully what to say. "We've been friends for a while," she said finally. "You know I don't think acting on hetero feelings is morally wrong. I think it's wrong to marry someone when you're not going to be happy with her. You know, don't you, that some people have secret arrangements where they can live hetero and look normal to the outside world?"

"Really? I mean, I've wondered sometimes, about some people ... some couples."

"I know some people doing that. It's dangerous, of course, especially if you have a child. If you're caught, the man will be sent away, and you'll lose everything. And if you're caught again, they'll send *you* to a camp, too—a women's work camp. But sometimes people love each other enough to take that risk."

"I think I would, if I were in love with someone," said Vanessa. "But I hardly know any men. I've been trying so hard to have relationships with women. And all the yunies I know—all these years they've been too old for me. But I'm 27 now, so 30 doesn't look so old any more. But oh, Larrine, I'm so glad I told you. Just to really be myself with someone feels so good."

"Yes, it feels good to be who you really are," said Larrine.

They had many conversations after that. As their bond strengthened and their trust deepened, Larrine told Vanessa about the Island, and her participation in the Underground Railroad. Though Larrine was normal, and had no desire to go there herself, she was passionate about helping oppressed heteros find their way to freedom.

"I want to help, too," said Vanessa. "I think I may want to go. But not yet. But I want to help other people like me."

Larrine was getting guests about once a month, and she worried that the frequency could raise flags. Diverting some to Ruby would be good.

"I can't give you the addresses of the people I know," said Larrine. "I know you, but they don't, and that's how we do things. For now, you can host people, and I will give them their next destination after they leave your place."

Vanessa did not object. She could be patient. Larrine's friends used fictitious names online, and she could communicate with them. She would gradually gain the trust of more people, as she had gained Larrine's trust.

CHAPTER 29

◆ ◆ ◆

In boys, the male nature has not yet been tamed. Nor has it
been put to use in the service of humanity. Boys should be
shorn and plainly dressed to reflect their unredeemed status.

—ROSANNA IOLANDA, *PRESIDENTIAL ADDRESS*, 2132

MAY 26, 2218, ROSES' FARM, ILLINOIS:

MARLEY SAT IN FRONT OF the small mirror in her room, showing Tyrone how she put on makeup, though she hadn't brought a lot of it with her. Tyrone was fascinated with the process, the tools, the products, and the results, and wanted to try them on himself. She explained that the soft lines around her eyes were permanent, but she could make them more dramatic. About once a week she applied a product that thickened and darkened her lashes. And then there was the fun stuff: the colors and glitters.

Darlene was the first person Tyrone had ever seen with makeup on, and he had been intrigued, but too shy to ask her about it. Marley was the second person.

"Almost everyone in the city—all the girls and yunies and women—wear makeup," said Marley. "Almost everyone has some colored hair and tattoos. One of my yunie uncles is so glittery and decorated, I wouldn't recognize him without it. Some people aren't into it that much. But you never see frizzy hair like Mrs. Rose has, or whiskers like Mr. Rose, or people just plain and shorn like you boys are."

"I'd never even heard of makeup," said Tyrone. "And the hair. Your hair is so pretty, and smooth, and *long*. Can I touch it?"

"Sure," Marley laughed. Tyrone ran his fingers studiously through her blonde tresses.

"They used to show us vids of yunies in the city," said Tyrone. "They wanted us to see what life was like there. Some boys—like me—couldn't wait to get out of those camps and grow our hair and wear awesome clothes. Most of the boys don't care, and the Papas don't know why it's like that."

Marley pondered this while she applied glitter to Tyrone's eyelids and cheeks. "Maybe," she said, "the authorities don't want you to be able to pass as girls. If a boy escapes from a camp, he's really easy to spot, right? So camp boys have to hide in trucks and vans. But Halen just rode in a car with me."

"Lucky *hetnukkie*," said Tyrone.

"Hetnukkie?" Marley laughed.

"It's an insult," Tyrone explained. "And yeah, our trips were boring as hell. We were finally outside the camp, but we couldn't see a *stinging* thing. Could you make *me* look like a girl?"

"I think I could," said Marley. "You'd need a wig, or hair extensions. Halen says long hair is safer for hidden boys, especially older boys. But lots of girls have short hair. Like, James, Rob, and Peter have as much now as some girls. But it can't just be a grown-out mess. It needs to look stylish, you know? Colored and cut in a cute way. Temporary tats are easy. And Halen knows all about getting rid of facial hair—most of you don't have much anyway."

◆ ◆ ◆

Hours later, Tyrone and Marley gathered all the boys in the dormitory.

"I talked to Mrs. Rose about passing you boys as girls," said Marley. "She said the reason they don't do that is mostly because of how you all talk and act. You all have weird accents and camp slang that could give you away if you got stopped and questioned. So we need to teach you how to talk and act like girls."

"I'm up for that," said Robert. "Girl lessons."

Others nodded in agreement, and daily lessons in city girl language and mannerisms commenced. Often the lessons disintegrated into bouts of hysterical laughter.

"You really say, 'Fuck me with a carrot' just to say hello?" asked Robert.

"Pretty much, yeah," said Marley. "To other girls."

"But why a carrot? Why not a cucumber?" asked James.

"Or a big zucchini?" said Tyrone.

"I'll fuck you with *my* big zucchini," Peter shouted.

"You can't say *that*," Marley exclaimed.

"Like you have a big zucchini, Peter," said James. "More like a string bean."

Darlene brought out some of her own glitters and perfumes for them to play with, and Halen kept notes on all the camp slang that sounded strange to city-bred ears.

CHAPTER 30

◆ ◆ ◆

Subversives take advantage of the ephemeral hetero feelings of
young girls to lure them away from home and subject them to sexual
torture, after which they murder them. Hidden boys escaping
from Natural communities also suffer this fate. The subversives
augment their ranks with boys stolen from boys' camps.

–Topics in Law Enforcement, Fourth Edition, 2208

Summer 2217, Oswego, New York:

After about nine months of taking guests from Larrine, Vanessa was
getting calls directly from a contact called Janine. And she was contacting
Scarlett, Jamba, or Sunni directly to see where she could send her guests next.
She was well in now.

"I've been getting a fair number of people," Vanessa told Barilla. "It's increased since I started helping, and I'm getting people once or occasionally
twice a month, usually for one night, but sometimes longer. Sometimes I
color their hair. They can get new ID's at Sunni's, and change cars on the
way to Scarlett's. I don't know the real names of these Underground women,
but I know where the destinations are now. I've had a bunch of young ones
come through here. They all look like girls, but sometimes they admit to being boys. I could tip off the cops every so often, and make it look like random

stops. But if I do that too often, I could be cut out of the system. I've got such a good cover now, I wonder if I should go after bigger fish."

"I don't think we should risk having you cut out," said Barilla. "We don't want to waste our investment on a handful of escapees. What about going farther in?"

"Like, maybe it's time for me to go all the way to the Island?" said Vanessa excitedly. "Once there, I could tell you everywhere I stopped. I'm still not convinced the Island actually exists. But people keep coming through here, telling me they're going there. I want to find out where they're going."

"Unless they're all going to their deaths," said Barilla. "But I don't really believe that theory. I think they're getting off the continent somehow. If you went as far as you can, we could get a lot of information, and maybe some major hubs and important people. But let's not rush it. You're establishing yourself as a trusted member of the Underground, and that's an investment. Eventually it's going to pay off big."

CHAPTER 31

◆ ◆ ◆

We have got things right, and we must keep them right. From this day forward, not one word of subversive speech will be tolerated.

–Aspera Vas Cortine, *Presidential Address*, 2107

May 2218, Roses' farm, Illinois:

"Are you ready to try a trot?" Tyrone asked Marley. He had helped her aboard a gentle palomino, and they'd made one round of the loop through the woods at a walk. "They like to run on this uphill slope."

The Roses kept six horses for teaching Railroad guests to ride. But Kyle and Tyrone, who had grown up in a horse-breeding camp, had taken over the riding lessons during their stay.

Marley clicked her tongue and leaned forward a little in her saddle. She felt the horse's gait shift, and then—wow, trotting was pretty rough, and a little scary. She thought she'd be bounced right out of the saddle, and she grabbed the saddle horn to keep her balance.

"Just keep going," Tyrone encouraged her. "It gets better." They walked and trotted the loop several times. Marley found her balance, and the third time around, she rode the bounces without holding on.

◆ ◆ ◆

Coming in after a horseback ride on a sunny day, Marley and Halen headed for the basement game room, which the Roses stocked with games that imparted useful skills and knowledge. They found Kyle strapped into a simulator chair, concentrating hard as he practiced hand-controlled driving on a high level where traffic and potholes came thick and fast. James was on the weapons simulator, learning to use stunners, pistols, and rifles.

Wilderness Survival was Marley's favorite game. The Desert Biome was the hardest, but Marley now knew how to get water from a prickly pear, collect dew, and avoid eating barrel cacti. At the higher levels of the game, scorpions and venomous snakes were hiding everywhere. Mr. Rose had assured her that desert survival was not on the agenda for their journey, but that survival skills had, on a few occasions, allowed people to evade authorities.

Prairie, woodland, and wetland biomes were more familiar, and easier to live through, especially in the spring and fall seasons. Marley learned that she could eat chickweed, purslane, lamb's quarters, and dandelions—all weeds she'd pulled out of the circle gardens every summer.

Darlene and Marley weeded the vegetable garden together, and made a salad from the tender spring weeds. They had to douse it liberally with the boys' favorite dressings to get them to eat it.

JUNE 1, 2218, ROSES' FARM, ILLINOIS:

Marley was preparing potatoes for baking—scrubbing, drying, rubbing them with oil and salt, and poking them with a fork so they wouldn't explode in the oven. A horsefly that desperately wanted to be on the other side of the windowpane was distracting her.

Mrs. Rose was continually busy with some phase of preparing food for this horde of people, and Marley liked helping and chatting with her. This older woman with her frowsy hair, her kind, unadorned face, and her simple country ways, was inexplicably a kindred spirit.

"There's something that bothers me," Marley said.

"What is that, dear?"

"Well, I don't want to offend you," said Marley.

"Don't worry about it," Mrs. Rose said. "Almost nothing offends me."

"Well, the whole subversive thing feels so yucky to me," said Marley. "I didn't really think, when I ran off with Halen, that I was becoming a subversive. He had to leave, and I just had to go with him. But I don't want to destroy our society. I've always thought our society was great, and subversives were just idiots who didn't understand that all the old problems would come back if they got their way. I've seen some vids online of stupid, ignorant men who want to destroy things."

"So you've been naughty and looked at subversive websites?" said Mrs. Rose, smiling.

"Well, yes, of course," Marley laughed. "We all do, at some point, I think."

"Of course you do," she said. "What vids did you see?"

"They were on a site called *Man Power*," Marley said. "Everyone's heard of it. There's a scruffy-looking guy who spouts off about blowing up Rep Centers and schools, saying everything modern is from the *devil*. I mean really. The *devil*? It seems like everyone's seen that vid, and it's always there—like the authorities can't figure out how to shut it down."

"I've seen that website, too, Melissa," said Mrs. Rose. "And you know what? I think it doesn't get shut down because the government actually runs it. I mean, I'm 98% sure the government runs it. I know that sounds kind of crazy. But, A: it never gets shut down, B: it's way more popular than it deserves to be, and C: I've never met anyone in the Underground who is anything like the people in those vids."

"But, see, that does sound really wacko," said Marley. "Why on earth would the government run that website? It's totally anti-authority."

"I think it's part of their propaganda," said Mrs. Rose. "They're taking *some* of the truth and wrapping it in a repulsive package so people won't want to believe it. And they bundle up some true things with some really obvious lies so you won't believe any of it. So if you hear the true things elsewhere, you'll just think they're subversive bullshit."

"Wow, really?" said Marley, frowning as she chopped onions carefully with a knife, the way Mrs. Rose had showed her. "I guess it worked on me, then. Because I've been kind of cringing, you know, waiting to meet *that guy* at some point in my travels, and really not wanting to meet that guy or have anything in common with him."

Mrs. Rose laughed. "Don't worry, sweetie. You're not going to meet *that guy*. I've been in the Underground all my life, and I've never met anyone like that guy. I mean, yeah, some people might look a little rough to your eyes, raised where you were. Some of us aren't as sophisticated and stylish as city people. But nobody thinks science is from the devil. Hell, nobody even believes in the devil."

Mrs. Rose scraped the chopped onions from their cutting boards into the soup. "Damn these onions," she said. "I can't cut them without crying, can you?"

"I've never chopped onions with a knife before," said Marley. "At home, we had an appliance for that. There's a gadget for everything in the circle kitchen."

Mrs. Rose opened the oven and starting placing the potatoes on the rack. "Nobody wants to blow things up, for godssakes," she said, continuing her previous thought. "We just want to live and let live."

"So the authorities just want us to think of subversives that way?" said Marley. "So we won't want to be one? But on my way here, I met some very chic and sophisticated people in the underground. Rich, educated professionals. Business people."

"Yes," said Mrs. Rose. "There are all kinds of people in the Underground. Heteros are being oppressed in all walks of life. Subversives aren't just a bunch of wackos who hate civilization. There's a lot of subversive literature that might open people's minds if they actually looked at it. Because they really *have* been lied to, about a lot of things, for a very long time. The authorities work harder to suppress the good stuff. The stupid stuff actually helps them, and I'm quite sure they create most of it."

CHAPTER 32

◆ ◆ ◆

Our Honored Breeders carry the burden of male fertility
for all of us. Let them grow as big and strong as they please.
Let them brawl and be promiscuous. It is their privilege to
be supremely and perfectly masculine. Subversive voices
whine about the oppression of men, stubbornly refusing to
see that these men live happily in their freedom from the
relentless demands and restrictions of wives and children.

—Iolanda Voorhees, 2095

JUNE 8, 2218, ROSES' FARM, ILLINOIS:

MARLEY WAS FEELING RESTLESS AS the second week at the Roses' farm came
to a close. She tried to be patient, knowing that the adults were working on
arranging the next part of their journey.

Cuddled next to Halen one night in their little room, she was awakened by
hushed voices, doors opening and closing, and footsteps on the bare wooden
floor. Who had come in the middle of the night? More boys? A girl, maybe?
She heard Mrs. Rose making noises in the kitchen. Too intrigued to go back
to sleep, she got up to see if she could help.

"Melissa," said Mrs. Rose. "Why are you up?"

"I heard you. I can't sleep. Can I help?"

"Yes. Just put this stew in the heater, would you? And bring out four bowls when it's hot. Thanks. And don't try to make conversation. These boys don't want to talk."

Slightly disappointed, Marley brought out the bowls of stew on a tray, and set them down in front of the new boys. Three pairs of dark eyes regarded her silently, three bodies huddled close together on the bench at the table. There was a man, too. A tall, dark man with a Mexican look. Marley held her tongue, set down the bowls, and went back to bed.

The new boys were given their own room to sleep in. They were very quiet, and did not want to make friends. Their arrival prompted a lot of hushed discussion among the four adults, discussion that stopped abruptly when Marley entered the room. The screen disappeared from the kids' den. The adults said it was broken, but Marley did not believe them. There was something they didn't want the kids to know. Worry, tension, and mystery crackled in the air.

JUNE 9, 2218, ROSES' FARM, ILLINOIS:

Mr. and Mrs. Rose wanted Marley and Halen to travel to the next destination in a car with Darlene and the new man while the rest of the boys traveled by truck and train. But Marley and Halen wanted to go with the boys.

"We're planning on hiding them," said Mrs. Rose. "But there's always a chance they'll be seen. And with just boys, we have a chance of talking our way out of it. Some people could believe we're just transferring boys or taking them on a field trip. But there's no explanation for boys and girls together."

"Halen and I could cut our hair and dress like boys."

"We don't want to cut Halen's hair. He may need to be a girl again."

"What if we cut it to their shoulders, braided it, and hid it under caps?" said Mr. Rose. "The other boys' hair is all a bit grown out, too. They would blend in well enough."

"But what about Marley's body? Boy clothes won't hide her shape."

Mrs. Rose whipped up an undergarment for Marley on her sewing machine. A tight band minimized her breasts, and padding around her waist hid the curve of her hips. In a T-shirt and shorts, with her hair contained under a cap, she passed nicely as a slightly pudgy boy. The other boys split their sides laughing when they saw her, and "Little Fat Boy" became her new nickname. Marley imitated the boys' accents and used their slang. Halen said, "Finally, there *is* a boy I want to kiss."

But underneath the fun, they all knew that their situation was deadly serious. Apparently something horrible had happened in Tennessee, and the countryside around the farm teemed with alert, angry authorities. Marley knew that the adults were trying to shield them from the news reports, but standing outside the room where the adults were gathered, she overheard news reporters speaking of a terrorist cult that stole boys from camps and brainwashed them into committing murderous violence.

"These people are extremely sick and scary," said a newscaster ominously. "They want to take our society back to the dark ages when women were the slaves of men, and men were the slaves of the most powerful and virile. These people *hate* science, peace, freedom, and the technology that makes our lives decent. And most of all, they hate normal women."

Mr. Rose noticed Marley and waved her into the room. "We don't want all you kids seeing or talking about this," he said. "You'll hear about it eventually, but now is not the time. Can you trust me on that?"

Marley nodded.

"That newscaster is talking about the Underground—about us," Mr. Rose said to Marley. "They want people to be afraid of us. I know the authorities in the city are sweet and kind to girls. But they're different out here where the men and boys are. They're different once you're on the Railroad, trying to escape the system. If they ever catch you, you mustn't trust them or believe anything they say.

"They want girls to grow up thinking it's a free country, but it's not. Ask those Honored Breeders if it's a free country. Their camps are 'high security,' which means they'll be shot and killed if they try to get out of them. If everyone were free, this enlightened system would fall apart in a month."

"But if everyone were free," said Marley, "Wouldn't those big, angry breeder men go around killing and raping people?"

"A few of them might," Mr. Rose admitted. "Gods only know what they do to them in there. They don't even look like normal men anymore. But the thing is, the vast majority of fertile men are not killers or rapists. What this society does is convict every baby boy the moment he's born, and treat him like a criminal all his life. Do you think that's fair or good?"

"No," Marley said, realizing that she'd never once been encouraged to see things from a male point of view.

I want to be with Halen, she thought. *But I feel safer with those big, scary men kept securely behind fences. So am I subversive or not?*

CHAPTER 33

◆ ◆ ◆

Let males be males. Let the boys fight with sticks, and
piss where they please. They are what they are. But it's
the height of folly to mix them up with girls.

—Iolanda Voorhees, 2100.

May 11, 2218, Oswego, New York:

Vanessa was excited about her next adventure as the spring of 2218 came
into full bloom. She got a call from Janine asking if she could host a young
woman. The young city woman came to her house the usual way. But before
she left in the morning, Vanessa emailed Scarlett. "I've been getting some
really funny looks from a neighbor today. She was close to my house for no
reason, and I think she was spying on me and my guest," she wrote. "I have a
very bad feeling about this. I want to get myself out of here now. I want to go
all the way to the Island."

Scarlett wrote back with directions. After directing her guest to her next
destination, Vanessa drove to a car dealership where she traded her car for one
that was GPS-free. At the next destination, she got a new identity and a new
hair color. Then Scarlett wrote: "We need you to pick up two passengers and
drive them to your next destination." She gave directions, but no more information than Vanessa needed.

May 13, 2218, New York:

The destination was a small, rural hospital, not far from a boys' camp. Vanessa took a long, narrow road around the perimeter of the campus, and into the visitor's parking garage, then up three levels, and parked, as directed, across from the elevators. She waited. She ate the sandwich she'd bought on the road, and tipped the driver's seat back so she could relax. Dusk turned to darkness. She had a view of an ugly flat roof with heating and cooling units on it. She pulled out her device, sent some messages, and played a game. People came off the elevator and hurried to their cars. Cars drove away—down, down, down to the road.

She studied her new ID, and a new, unfamiliar woman looked back at her from the card. Not Ruby, not Ariel, not Vanessa. Her black hair—chin-length, straight, with a few wisps of bangs—contrasted sharply with her pale skin.

Late at night, three men came out of the elevator, two pushing wheel-chairs. Their greetings were polite but terse. Gently, they loaded two groggy, heavily sedated boys into the back seat of her car, and covered them up well with blankets. They gave her a destination about an hour away. Wide awake and glad to be doing something, she followed the other car out of the garage and away from the hospital. Then she had to concentrate hard as she drove along the winding old roads of rural New York, where nighttime was much darker than she was used to.

At the house, two yunies came out and carried the sleeping boys inside.

◆ ◆ ◆

In the morning, Vanessa went into the kitchen to find the boys eating the breakfast that the yunies had made for them. They were apparently very hungry. Vanessa watched them, fascinated and revolted. The only boys she'd ever seen in real life had been passing as girls, except for the little one she'd seen for a few minutes with all his hair cut off. It was disconcerting to sit down to breakfast next to a couple of real, obvious boys who weren't hiding what they were. They wore shorts and T-shirts in shades of khaki and brown. They had hardly any hair. They were busy stuffing their mouths with pancakes and sausages, talking as they ate, and wiping their mouths on their arms.

"Are you the woman who drove us?" asked the freckled one with red hair.

"Yes," she said.

"Nice to meet you," said the boy. "I'm Stuart."

"I'm Michael," said the other.

"I'm Darlene," said Vanessa.

CHAPTER 34

◆ ◆ ◆

Yunies have been set free from that ancient, selfish
mania for passing on their own genes no matter how
flawed. Now every man contributes what is best in
him—his genetic endowment or his talent.

—IOLANDA VOORHEES, SPEECHES, 2073

JUNE 13, 2218, ROSES' FARM, ILLINOIS:

FINALLY THE DAY CAME TO move from the Roses' farm to their next destination. A big, white, enclosed truck was loaded with bales of hay, and all the kids were hidden in a space inside the load. The hay was poky, but it smelled sweet and good. With a few blankets laid over it, the hay was pretty comfy. Marley and the boys huddled together in nervous excitement. The Roses' place had been an oasis of good food, fresh air, and a stolen sense of freedom. Now they were venturing out again into a hostile world.

Darlene had already left, driving a car. The tall, dark man who had arrived with the new boys was completely concealed in the back. She would be able to take a mag road for much of the distance. A man Marley had not met before was driving the hay truck.

The ride to the train station was long and bumpy on the old roads. They arrived at about 9:00, shortly after sunset. The truck backed up to the door of the freight car in which they would travel most of the way. The men opened the back of the truck, and unloaded hay bales, stacking them to build two walls of hay between the truck and the freight car door. When the walls were high enough, the kids scurried between them into the freight car, and sat in a quiet huddle while the men finished their work.

Next the men built a wall of bales high enough for the teens to hide behind, in case anyone came along and looked inside. Then they proceeded to make the wall thicker and thicker with additional bales. They worked with few words, and an occasional grunt of effort as they swung the heavy bales into place. The bales were arranged so the kids had a rough stairway from their hiding place to the top of the load. In case of fire, Marley and the boys could escape through the top hatch, or slide down to the side door. Finally the freight car was full, and metal screeched against metal as the door was pulled closed, leaving the teens in darkness. They spread their sleeping bags on the bales to make a comfortable nest. Halen had an untraceable wrist phone for emergency communication. He gave them all a little light while their eyes adjusted to the darkness. Marley hugged her knees, breathing in the sweet smell of timothy hay. The dim light fell on a circle of pale, apprehensive faces.

The freighter would take about six hours to reach their unloading point in South Dakota. They had a cooler with food and water. A portable potty—really just a bucket with a wooden seat—had been hidden behind the hay at the other end of the car. To use it, they would have to climb up the hay-bale stairway, crawl over the top of the load, and climb down at the other end.

The train began to move, very slowly. Then faster and faster. Well out of the depot, the kids began talking again, and opened the cooler to see what Mrs. Rose had packed for them to eat. There were various wraps filled with meats, cheeses, and vegetables, and tubs of mixed fruits and raw vegetables. There were homemade cookies and bottles of water. They tucked into the food as the freighter hummed along the smooth track.

The three new boys sat together in one corner of their dark cubbyhole. They were always together, and always quiet, the two younger boys huddled close on either side of the oldest one. The youngest, in fact, had drifted off into a sedated sleep while everyone was eating. They had kept to themselves in the week they'd been at the Roses' farm. The youngest one had not spoken a word to anyone, and never left the oldest one's side, even to use the bathroom. Marley had overheard adults whispering about this in concerned tones. She thought it was time to try to open them up.

"Why don't we tell our stories for these new guys?" she suggested. "Me and Halen can start if you want."

The boys nodded eagerly. So Marley and Halen told about how they had found each other at school and decided to run away together. The other boys had heard it all before. But Marley noticed the new boys paying close attention.

"What color was your hair before?" asked the black-haired one, Jackson.

"Very dark brown, with turquoise streaks," said Marley.

"Do a lot of girls in the city like boys?"

"I don't know," said Marley. "I thought I was the only one. Now I think there must be lots of girls like me. But everyone is hiding it."

Then Stuart told them about the boys' camp in New York where he and Michael had been dorm brothers.

"Back in May," he said, "we both had to go to the hospital for surgeries. Our favorite Papa went with us. Right before we went into surgery, he told us what he was going to do, and why. There's this Underground network at the hospital. The medicals said that we both died in surgery, and they sent our microchips and ashes back to the camp with our Papa. Except of course, they weren't *our* ashes."

"We were pretty drugged up, so there's a lot we don't remember after the operations. We ended up in a car with Darlene, but I don't even remember that part. But she brought us all the way from the hospital to Roses' place."

"What kind of surgeries did you have?" Jackson asked.

"I had a hernia, and Mike had some heart valve thing," said Stuart. "Our Papa told us that we wouldn't be picked for breeders because those things were wrong with us. I didn't really care, though. I always thought I'd rather leave the camp and live with women. But he said, if you *like* women, you can't let on, or they'll do something to you so you don't want them anymore. If you really want to be around women, they think you're a dirty hetero. So that's kind of a suck, isn't it?"

"Yeah, it is," said Halen.

"Me and Kyle got smuggled out with some of the horses that were going to an Underground ranch," said Tyrone. "We had a Papa who helped us, too. But James, you should tell yours. Your story is *cosmic*." Tyrone was using city slang that Marley had taught him.

"Sure," said James. The new boys listened attentively as he recounted the story of his escape with Robert and Peter.

"I wonder who, and when, and how they buried those pipes that you went through," Marley said after he finished. "I guess we'll never know. But I wonder about those boys you thought were dead. I wonder if they're on the Island."

"I don't dare to hope," said Peter. "One of the boys last summer was a good friend. I cried for weeks. I wonder if anyone is crying for us now."

They all went quiet, pondering this sobering thought.

Marley broke the silence. "Kevin," she said gently to the oldest of the new boys. "Why don't you tell us your story?"

Kevin acquiesced, and began to speak softly in the darkness, just loud enough for them all to hear over the humming train. Marley listened with rapt attention as he described his daring escape with Gerald and their weeks of hiding in Okefenokee. She wanted to hug and kiss Natasha, and the women who put their own freedom at risk to help boys escape to freedom. She pictured the five boys together on the property in Georgia, relaxing in a hidden oasis under the trees while the adults made a plan to move them to their next destination.

CHAPTER 35

◆ ◆ ◆

The anarchists are correct in saying that authority
is dangerous in the hands of men. But in the hands
of women, authority is gentle and caring.

–IOLANDA VOORHEES, 2085

JUNE 4, 2218, GEORGIA / TENNESSEE:

ONE DAY A TALL, STOCKY man called Richard Gonzalez, from Mexico City in
the state of South Mexico, arrived at the woodsy estate with a small moving
truck. The truck was fully loaded with furniture and goods, except for a cubbyhole behind a partition at the front. The five boys knew they were in for a
long, cramped, boring ride. They couldn't see out of their hiding place, and
they entertained each other as best they could. Kevin told funny stories about
the boys, teachers, and fathers back at Osceola, and he seemed to have an end-
less supply of jokes. Benjamin got queasy, and at one of their stops, Richard
gave him some pills that helped. The boys managed to lie down in the small
space, partially on top of each other, and as the hours of travel slipped by,
eventually they all dozed off.

Kevin dreamed of sirens before he realized that he was actually hearing them. The truck was stopping, and then he heard voices. A harsh, angry
female voice rose to a high pitch, alternating with the voice of their driver.
Then he heard the loud pop of a stunner. Richard's voice stopped and the

female voice said something he couldn't make out. They heard the back of the truck opening, and light flooded in over the partition. All the other boys were awake now, wide-eyed and holding their breath.

"Anyone in there?" the female voice shouted, banging on the side of the truck with a heavy nightstick. The boys were silent as death. They waited, frozen, while the woman outside presumably listened for any noise.

"Don't hear nothin', Abbott," said another female voice. "He seemed okay to me. Driving a truck don't mean he's guilty."

"Let's just make sure," said the first voice. A minute later, there was a clunk and a hissing noise. The back of the truck began to fill with a gas that stung the boys' eyes. They all held their breath as long as they could, but finally they had to breathe in. The gas filled their lungs with fire, and they felt like they were going to die. They could think of nothing but escaping the burning gas, and they all scrambled over the partition and the strapped-in furniture to get to the blessed relief of untainted air. Their eyes stung and streamed with tears. The membranes of their mouths and noses burned. Wiping their streaming eyes, they saw three women in black police uniforms, aiming stunners right at them.

"Boys," the one called Abbott spat out, staring at them with furious hatred. "We've caught ourselves a bunch of nasty, stinking, sneaking boys. What do you think of that, girls? Pays to be persistent, don't it?"

Abbott's baleful eyes bored into them as she addressed the five boys. "I despise runaways," she said. "Our country gives you everything: food, shelter, schooling, toys. Acres and acres of our best land to play on. And all you care about is keeping your nasty little nuts and wreaking havoc and raping nice girls.

"See if they got microchips," she addressed the woman next to her.

"We got no reading from the car," said the third woman. "Want me to scan them?"

"Yeah," said Abbott. The other woman grabbed a microchip scanner from the car and came close to the boys. This one didn't look hateful. She looked nervous and uncomfortable. Fearful, even.

Who's she afraid of? Kevin wondered. *Us? Or Abbott?*

The woman came close and scanned the boys' bodies, then backed away and took out her stunner again.

"Nothing," she said.

"So they've had them removed," Abbott sneered. "Sneaky little vermin. Getting help from those Underground criminals, are you? What did they tell you? They're going to take you someplace where you can fuck all the girls you want?" She laughed derisively. "Stupid boys. It doesn't pay to listen to criminals. But you couldn't just take what you were given and do as you were told, could you? Ungrateful, pissy little animals. We should just exterminate everything with a dick and save ourselves a lot of trouble."

"Abbott ..." said the third woman.

"What?" Abbott snapped back. "You don't want me to hurt their feelings, or what? These creatures don't have feelings. They're barely human." Her expression changed to fiendish delight. "Let's play with them," she said to her companions.

"Take your clothes off," she snapped at the boys. "I want to see those precious parts of yours. *Now*," she yelled.

When the boys hesitated, she holstered her stunner and drew her pistol. Kevin saw the other two women exchange a glance. They were not happy with this.

"I'm not playing around, now," Abbott said, in a quieter voice, aiming the lethal gun at each of them in turn. "Clothes off, or I start blowing off heads."

As the boys stripped naked, she said thoughtfully, "You know what would be funny, girls? If that stunned bastard in the front seat woke up and had to explain why there were a bunch of dead, naked boys in his truck. I bet he'd be willing to trade some good underground information for his sorry little life."

"We can charge him with kidnapping and trafficking boys," said the woman on Abbott's left. "That should get us plenty."

"Not as much as if we charged him with murder."

"But, Abbott—"

"Shut up. I'm in charge here," Abbott snarled hotly. Then she laughed again. "Look at them, with their pathetic, ugly little parts. I've always wanted to kill me some of these vermin. Should I shoot all their little dicks off first, though?"

The comprehension that she really meant to kill them coalesced suddenly in Kevin's mind. The idea was so foreign to him, so far outside everything he'd been taught about the Enlightened Society, that until this moment, he'd been quite sure that she was just trying to scare the piss out of them, and doing a very good job of it. But the sudden look of horror on the other women's faces banished that, and he knew.

His body tensed like a spring. He heard her say, "Let's start with the littlest," her aim shifted to Axel's crotch, and the deafening report of the pistol boxed Kevin's ears as he lunged for the gun half a second too late. Axel dropped to the ground, screaming in agony. Kevin and Gerald crashed into Abbott simultaneously, bowling her over backward onto the ground. The other two women closed in, beating the boys' bodies and heads with nightsticks. Stunned by the head blows, Kevin lost his grip on Abbott, and was paralyzed, almost senseless, for a few long seconds. He heard another shot, and Axel's screaming stopped abruptly. He scrambled up, dizzy and disoriented, just in time to see Abbott, back on her feet, firing her pistol at Gerald's head as he lay unconscious on the ground.

A bomb of blind rage exploded inside Kevin's brain. Only faintly aware of his own actions, he rushed at Abbott, grabbed her by the hair, wrested the gun from her hand, and fired it point blank into her face. He'd never even held a real gun before—the noise was deafening, the kick startled him, and the slide smashed back, cutting his hand. He barely managed to keep his grip on it. Time slowed as he recovered, spun around, and saw Jackson and Benjamin grappling with the other two women, whose guns had gone astray on the ground. Kevin knocked Jackson clear and put a bullet into the woman's head, then two strides took him to the other grappling pair. He dropped down onto the other woman, shoving Benjamin away to get a clear shot at the one who had scanned them. She looked up into his face for a moment with an expression of horror before he fired into her face. Half deafened, and still raging, Kevin went to Abbott's corpse and emptied the rest of the clip into her head and body, beat her face in with the empty gun, then stood up and kicked her body with his bare feet, feeling no pain at all.

For long seconds that felt like eternity, Kevin vented his rage on the dead body, until suddenly the rage was spent, and a cold rationality took over. Jackson and Benjamin had vomited profusely on the road, and now cowered together near the lifeless form of Axel, watching Kevin with huge round eyes.

"Get our friends into the truck," Kevin ordered. They lifted Axel and Gerald into the back of the truck, smearing blood on their bare skin. Kevin held Gerry's hand for a moment. He felt absolutely nothing. He noticed Natasha's ring halfway down Gerry's pinkie finger. He wondered, crazily, if Natasha's luck would have worked better if the ring had fit all the way on.

"Get your clothes on," said Kevin, and the boys silently obeyed. Kevin picked up the clothes of the dead boys and put them in the truck. Then he closed the back and put his own clothes on. He wiped off the empty gun and left it there with the dead women. He took a stunner and a pistol that had not been fired and put them in the front of the truck.

"We're all going up front," said Kevin. The two younger boys followed his lead without speaking. They pulled their heavy, unconscious driver to the passenger's side, and the two boys scrunched in around the big man while Kevin got behind the wheel and figured out the controls of the truck. He started it up and drove away.

He'd never driven a truck before. Never fired a pistol before. Never killed a human being. Never bashed in a skull with a pistol butt.

◆ ◆ ◆

Kevin still felt absolutely nothing; his mind was as clear and keen as an eagle's eyes. The patrol car they'd left behind had told him they were in the state of Tennessee, and the signs said Old Route 40. But he had no idea where to go from there. He just knew he had to get as far away from those dead women as he could, as fast as he could without drawing attention or losing control, and wait for Richard to wake up.

Kevin took the first exit off the highway onto smaller roads. About half an hour later, Richard regained consciousness, and knew immediately that things were very wrong.

"Do you remember being pulled over by police officers?" Kevin asked. "Three of them. Three women. They stunned you. Then they gassed us out of the back of the truck. They were going to kill us all. They killed Gerald and Axel. We—I killed them."

"Jesus Fucking Christ. All three?"

"All three. I've been driving since then, taking different roads going north."

"Pull over and let me drive," said Richard. "We don't want anyone to see a boy at the wheel." They stopped and changed places. Richard went to the back for a few minutes. Kevin heard the back door open and close again. Richard climbed back into the driver's seat, looking sick and stunned. "I had to see for myself," he said shortly. He made a call on his wrist phone. What he said sounded like small talk, and Kevin understood that it was a coded message. In some other life, the code would have interested him. "We've got to drive for an hour now," he said to the boys.

◆ ◆ ◆

Richard drove into the foothills and up to an abandoned campground on a high bluff above a deep lake—a forlorn place of rotting wooden buildings and tall weeds in what had once been open spaces for group activities. "This place couldn't compete with the beaches at the other end of the lake," Richard said, not that anyone was interested. "Went out of business years ago."

He parked the truck facing the steep bank going down to the lake. The man and the boys stood behind the truck for a few moments, holding hands, heads bowed, thinking private thoughts, paying their last respects to their friends. Then Richard let off the brake. They all pushed the truck to get it rolling, and it rolled slowly down the slope, picking up a little speed as it went, and toppled over the edge. It splashed heavily into the water, and slowly sank into the lake, taking little Axel and Kevin's beloved Gerald to their final resting place, with Natasha's tiny ring.

◆ ◆ ◆

Mercifully, Richard and the boys did not have to wait there long. A car had been dispatched to take them to the nearest safe house for the night. A man and a woman lived there, and received them with solemn faces and few words. They ministered to the boys—preparing baths, bringing them new clothes, offering food, which the boys did not touch, and giving them pills to sedate them so they could sleep. As the younger boys succumbed to their medication on either side of him, Kevin knew that he had changed irrevocably from the boy he was that morning. Instead of a loving partner and friends, he now had two little brothers for whom he felt a fierce, defensive love devoid of tenderness. He had looked into the face of evil, and become a merciless killer. Kevin drifted into sleep and dreamed of pistols firing and blood pooling on the pavement around a beloved blond head. Again and again, he saw a woman's eyes looking up at him in terror.

CHAPTER 36

◆ ◆ ◆

Because boys' violent nature has not yet been amended,
they are susceptible to subversive propaganda. And they
have great love for destruction and explosives.

—Report of Subversion Task Force, 2149

June 8, Roses' farm, Illinois:

A few days later, Kevin, Jackson, and Benjamin were driven to the Roses' farm in Illinois. The younger two were sedated for the trip, but Kevin refused it. He watched Mr. Rose move the screen from the kids' den into the room off the kitchen, and after the adults were in bed, Kevin left the other two in a drugged sleep and turned on the news.

"Three of our brave, dedicated officers were brutally slain in the line of duty Saturday in Tennessee," said a talking head who looked like a doll. "Their bodies were found on the road near their police cars. All three were shot in the head, and one was brutally beaten. Officials say that terrorists who traffic boys have been linked to the area, and the officers were stopping trucks on the old highways for random searches. The suspect is this man, Richard Gonzalez, whose ID was found on one of the officers. He should be considered armed and dangerous." A picture of Richard went up behind the speaker.

JUNE 14, 2218, ON THE TRAIN TO SOUTH DAKOTA:

A long silence followed Kevin's story. In the darkness, the others could not see Marley's tears, and she could not see theirs. She suppressed sobs with difficulty. Halen felt her shaking, and held her more tightly. Everyone remained quiet, and eventually they all drifted off to sleep.

They were awakened hours later by the train stopping. The loading process was reversed, except that now the men were loading hay and kids into two smaller trucks instead of one. The men opened the door and unloaded bales, making a passageway for the kids to the first truck. Then they packed them in and loaded up the second truck. One of the men pulled Kevin aside and spoke to him before they shut the doors. When both trucks were loaded, they pulled away. They were in South Dakota now, headed for a ranch. Marley and the boys nested in the hay and tried to go back to sleep.

Again, Marley was awakened by the cessation of motion. She hoped they had arrived at their destination. Halen's wrist phone blinked faintly, and he answered it. He relayed the message to the others who were awake.

"Inspectors," he whispered. "Keep perfectly quiet, but don't worry. They have it under control." The phone showed that the time was 5:40 a.m., and the darkness was not so deep now.

They heard the back door open, and voices came to their ears over the hay. A flashlight beam briefly lit up the space between the hay and the truck roof. Marley heard a voice say, "Let's just gas it and see if anyone's in there."

"Oh, *man*, can you not do that?" she heard the driver say, "I got that on my last run, and the damn cattle won't eat the hay after that. I won't get paid for the load. I'll unload the whole truck for you if you want."

Then Marley heard the sound of hay bales being unloaded. Thumping feet, thumping bales, grunts of men. She didn't dare peek over the top to see how close they were getting. But before their hiding place was breached, the inspectors were apparently satisfied, or else they got bored of watching, or tired of helping, she couldn't see which. Marley heard some quiet conversation, and then the men were loading the bales back in. She sat down, very quietly, and tried to still her pounding heart.

After many long minutes, she heard the truck door close again. The drivers got back in the front, and the truck moved again. Halen got another call from the man in the passenger's seat. "Well, that went off superbly," Marley heard the voice through the phone. "Reggie was perfect. Just so you know, we have a bunch of guys with stun guns in the other truck. We weren't taking chances on this trip. All you boys okay back there?"

"Yes," Halen said, "we're okay."

"How's the little fat one?" There was a slight chuckle in the voice.

"She's okay," said Halen. He'd been holding her close the whole time.

As the truck lurched along, Marley scooted over next to Benjamin, who was huddled against Kevin as always.

"Are you guys okay?" she asked.

"As much as we can be," said Kevin. "Ben here was sedated, and slept through it, thankfully. I knew about the guys in the other truck. They told me about them before we left. Sorry I didn't mention it before they told us to be quiet. Still, I'm … a bit rattled."

◆ ◆ ◆

The sun was well up and everyone inside the truck was awake when they stopped again, and they all felt the truck turning and backing up. Two men opened the doors, and the teens looked into the hayloft of a big barn.

"You'll be going through the barn and under a covered walkway to the house because of satellite surveillance," said one of the men as he helped them down from the truck. The men took them through the hayloft, down a narrow set of stairs to the lower level, and then along the walkway into the sprawling house. Marley had a sinking feeling that they would not be allowed outside to explore the beautiful, wide-open prairie land that she saw from the walkway. Despite her inadequate and interrupted sleep, she felt wide awake now in this new place with the sun shining.

A breakfast had been laid out for them in a large, communal dining room. They served themselves from a buffet, and sat down on benches at rough wooden tables. A tall, muscular man in his fifties, with about two days' growth on his face, stood up and introduced himself. Marley had never seen a man so carelessly groomed and roughly dressed, or so well-muscled. She was reminded of Fake Subversive Guy.

Is he that guy? she wondered. *The one Mrs. Rose said I'd never meet?*

"I'm Addams," he announced in a loud, gruff voice. "I run this place. My job here is to keep you safe and teach you some useful things for as long as you're here. All I care about is getting you out of this country safe and sound. I have some rules, and I'll kick your little butts if you break them. I don't care if you fucking hate me as long as you're safe on my watch. So listen up."

Marley suppressed a smile. *But I like this man*, she thought.

"You can go outside two at a time," Addams continued. "You *must* wear cowboy hats whenever you go out. That way, if anyone's watching via satellite, they won't notice any increase in the number of people here, and they won't be able to make out your faces. We want all of you to ride horses every day, in case you need to travel by horseback at some point. There's a lot of other stuff to do here to amuse yourselves and learn some useful things when you have to be indoors. And also, there will be absolutely *no* fighting or teen drama crap. All right now, enjoy your breakfast. When you're done, you can meet everyone else."

CHAPTER 37

◆ ◆ ◆

The tales of blissful life in the hetero haven were
nothing but subversive propaganda.

After taking control of the ocean liner from the gang of
men in charge, we found battered women and children.
We heard stories of women dying in childbirth.

All adult occupants were taken to work camps, and
children were taken to boys' camps or adoptive
homes. The ship was destroyed and sunk.

—REPORT OF PACIFIC HETERO HAVEN TASK FORCE, 2171

JUNE 14, 2218, ADDAMS' RANCH, SOUTH DAKOTA:

ADDAMS SAT DOWN TO FINISH the plate of breakfast he'd just started when the
kids showed up. Richard Gonzalez, sitting next to him, had arrived during the
night, and they'd been quietly discussing the happening in Tennessee. In the
decades that Addams had worked in the Underground, he'd seen a lot of things
go wrong. He always tried to learn whatever there was to learn. And then he
stuffed the bad memories into a box in his brain and locked them up tight.

Now he studied the new arrivals as he ate his eggs and sausage. Mrs. Rose,
in her encrypted message, had said that she was sending ten camp boys and a

city boy and girl. Which ones were they? Some boys had removed their caps, revealing various amounts of grown-out hair. But two of them had longer hair braided close to their heads. Addams watched curiously as the taller one fussed with something under the pudgy one's shirt, and pulled out an undergarment that he placed beside him on the bench. So that cute pudgy one was the girl.

His eyes paused on three boys sitting close together, and he recognized the looks of boys who had survived horror. The grim, hard look. The fearful look.

Damn that hateful woman to hell, he thought.

Addams always came at the young ones gruff and forceful from the start. They had to have some fear of him, some fear of breaking the rules that had so far kept his ranch off the authorities' radar. And he didn't want them getting too close to him. He'd loved and lost too many over the years. He couldn't afford to love any more.

The two youngest men on the ranch, Jordan and Jaden, had finished their breakfast and were conversing with the kids now: getting to know them, getting close, like Addams used to do. Those boys had wormed their way into his heart six years ago. They were fourteen then, freshly smuggled out of a camp in Wisconsin. They'd fallen in love with the ranch and everything Addams was doing. After a year on the Island, they'd insisted on coming back to work with him. They felt like sons now. No, he couldn't afford to get his feelings tangled up with any more of these kids. His job was to move them on safely.

He stood up again. "Listen up," he barked, and the room became quiet immediately. "We have a range where you will learn to use weapons. But you will not touch anything there until you've had instruction from an adult. Do you all understand?" He looked around the room, meeting each one's eyes. "And you will not go near any horses until an adult has assessed your ability. You can play all you want in the game room and media room."

When he spoke, the girl watched him intently, with curious, perceptive eyes.

He would have to watch out for that one.

2168-2188, PACIFIC OCEAN OFF CALIFORNIA:

When Addams arrived in the world by natural birth in the year 2168, he was named Armastus. He was the first baby born on the ocean liner Libertad, floating ten miles off the coast of California, and all 672 heteros on board joined in the celebration. Over the past six months, heteros had been arriving. They were making a haven for themselves, away from the morals and laws of the Enlightened Society, out from under the surveillance of government and the nosiness of neighbors. More babies soon followed—babies named Upendo, Cinta, Eros, Laska, Liberty, and Azadi. Love and liberty were celebrated with every birth.

The next year, a second ocean liner was added, giving the growing population more room to develop their own ecosystem and economy. Most residents believed that the authorities of Canusaco would ignore their venture, happy to be rid of them. But as word of this viable hetero haven spread through the continental population, authorities discussed how to respond to this gross and blatant display of immorality just off their shores. A thriving hetero community was a slap in the face of the Enlightened Society.

Armastus was two years old when the third ocean liner and several barges were added. Construction of a pontoon island was also well under way. Residents were producing electricity from the sun, wind, and waves, and raising vegetables with hydroponics. Cows and chickens had been brought to live on one of the barges. The population had burgeoned past 2,000, and over 200 Island natives had been born to hetero parents. At this point, the authorities cracked down, and a decree was passed. Travel to the Island was now a crime, and controls were tightened all along the coastline. Tugboats were chained to pontoon islands, and the floating archipelago moved many miles farther out into the ocean. Island voices online went silent, and the Underground began to form.

◆ ◆ ◆

Armastus and the Island grew up together, far out in the sunny Pacific. Underground connections were established in Hawaii as well as on the continent. Pontoon islands grew larger and more numerous, some of them devoted to banana and coconut trees, and some to cotton. Islanders raised tropical fruits, avocados, macadamia and kukui nuts, and coffee. They cultivated seaweed and ate a lot of fish.

As a boy, Armastus lived for those rare, exciting days when a fishing vessel came in, bringing escapees as well as things from the mainland that Islanders could not make or grow. Then children gorged themselves on fresh peaches, plums, cherries, and apples. Sometimes a helicopter would fly out to a ship and bring people back. As Armastus soaked up their stories, a desire began to grow in him to go to the mainland and help people escape. He learned about the Underground, the Railroad, and the encrypted websites that kept Islanders in touch with Underground people on the mainland. Authorities were now claiming that the Island had been depopulated and sunk.

"I expected them to keep ignoring us, waiting for us to fall into chaos and violence as their beliefs would predict," Armastus' mother told her young son as he breakfasted on taro pancakes with lilikoi butter. "We thought that would give us time to show people that this kind of society can work, instead of just arguing and theorizing about it anonymously online. But they didn't give us time. Now only a handful of subversives know that we're here, and almost nobody listens to them."

◆ ◆ ◆

Refugees continued to trickle in. They were mostly hetero yunies and women, but also some fertile men who told stories of escaping amendment, and a few brave young girls. Yunies in some of the boys' camps had begun smuggling out boys. Many of the women, yunies, and girls could travel far and fast before going underground on the west coast. But boys had to be smuggled there slowly, sometimes clear across the continent.

When Armastus was twenty, he felt it was time for him to leave his island home and help people escape the Enlightened Society.

"But it's so dangerous there, Ari," said his mother. Her many happy years on the sunny islands were evidenced in the smile lines etched into her brown face. But her eyes were fearful. "You don't know the culture over there," she said. "And you'll never pass as a yunie. You're much too tall and muscular. They'll spot you right away."

"I'm planning to work out in the ranch country, Mama," said Armastus. "The Railroad needs more destinations in those states, where there aren't so many people. Often people have to drive hundreds of miles on bad roads to get to the next place. And out there, people don't care so much if a yunie takes a lot of hormones. Strong men are more appreciated in the ranch country."

"You've done some homework on this, haven't you?" said his mother, only slightly appeased.

"Yes, I have," said Armastus. "I want to get my own place someday, and build an oasis out there for the boys that people are smuggling out of the camps."

◆ ◆ ◆

On the mainland, Armastus found employment on various ranches with cattle, horses, and bison, and he definitely liked horses best. He drove countless miles with boys, girls, women, and yunies hidden in loads of hay or feed. He bought homes well situated for hiding people.

In 2203, he assumed management of a ranch in South Dakota, purchased with laundered Underground funds. He'd had several different names on the continent, and here Armastus became Addams the horse rancher, and began to build his oasis.

CHAPTER 38

◆ ◆ ◆

We have located and destroyed all the weapon hoards
of the anarchist communities. Lethal weapons
have no place in the Enlightened Society.

–IOLANDA VOORHEES, 2064

JUNE 14, 2218, ADDAMS' RANCH, SOUTH DAKOTA:

MARLEY MET MOST OF THE other adults on the ranch over the course of the day. There were three women—Dahlia, Maya, and Samika—and one man—Carlos—who were born and raised on the Island with Addams, though they were all much younger. Dahlia had become Addams' lover after insisting that he needed some women on the ranch. Maya, Samika, and Carlos were a threesome of bisexuals, which Marley found fascinating.

Koster, a tall 30-year-old, sat next to Marley at lunch.

"Fun to have a girl here," he said. "We get mostly camp boys, often women and couples from the cities, but not often girls your age."

"Were you born on the Island?" Marley asked.

"Nope. Greg and me are twins. Our moms are Naturals. They live in San Francisco. They arranged for us to go to the Island when we were ten, before things got too scary with puberty and all. A couple summers ago, we came here to work with Addams. And then Greg and Tray over there—" he moved his hands together suddenly, while making an indescribable noise, "just got together like raspberries and cream. Just look at them. You can't separate them with a crowbar."

Marley giggled at the mental image of Koster trying to separate raspberries and cream with a crowbar. Tray and Greg were eating lunch at the other table, very close together.

"Aw, they're a cute couple," said Marley. "So where's Tray from?"

"Ian and Trayden came from a boys' camp in Missouri. They were on the Island for a while, and came here the summer before me and Greg."

"Who are those young ones?" Marley asked.

"Oh, Jordan and Jaden," said Koster. "We call them the Jays. Same deal, but they came back here right away. They're like Addams' sons."

◆ ◆ ◆

Dahlia took Marley to the small room where she would be sleeping, which opened off the same long hallway as all the adults' bedrooms.

"I hope it's okay for you," Dahlia said. "Not up to city standards, I'm afraid."

"Oh, it's absolutely charming," said Marley. The whole wing was a simply built addition made of pine lumber, but this room had been painted creamy white. The multi-colored, round braided rug appeared to be made of various leftover scraps of fabric, and bright, flowery curtains adorned the window. The comforter on the simple metal-frame bed was of the same floral fabric, and a bunch of silk roses stood in a vase on a wooden chest of drawers.

"This whole place is pretty ranchy," Dahlia laughed, looking pleased. "But we keep a couple of rooms nicer for city women and girls like you and Darlene. I love playing with fabric and paint, actually—but it's hard to find time for it. Took me a year to get that rug done."

"You'd get along with my Mama Sue," said Marley. "She's always refurbishing or making something."

Halen showed her the boys' bunkhouse, but assured her that he would be sleeping in her room. The bunkhouse was painted the same cream color, but a repaint was long overdue. Two rows of metal bed frames were made up simply with unmatched pillowcases and blankets for chilly nights. The boys had crates under the beds to stow things if they had any things to stow. Three beds had been pushed together so that Jackson and Kevin could easily reach Benjamin, who had frequent nightmares and sometimes woke up screaming. But Marley was happy that the three of them wanted to be with the other boys, and that the uncomfortable mystery surrounding them was gone.

Benjamin still did not speak, and became agitated if Kevin wandered out of his sight. Kevin was cold and unaffectionate but uncomplaining, and took care to stay close to him at all times. Jackson stayed close to them too, but he was opening up, even laughing sometimes. Marley sensed a strong, unsinkable quality in that boy.

◆ ◆ ◆

Marley and Halen talked about Kevin that night as they cuddled in bed.

"That poor kid," said Halen. "He's a friggin' hero. But what happened really messed with his head. Jackson says he was really funny and friendly when they first met. I hope he can get over it." Halen hugged Marley so tightly that she grunted a little. "I never would have let you come with me if I'd known it was so dangerous," he said.

"What do you mean, *let* me?" said Marley. "I wasn't gonna let you go without me. I'm just happy that we're together, Mad—Halen."

"Mad Halen," he said, loosening Marley's braided hair with his fingers. "Mad Halen and the Little Fat Boy."

"Halen?" Marley said.

"What?"

"I feel so bad for the way I've thought about boys and men all my life."

"You shouldn't. How could you know any better?"

"I guess I couldn't. But I feel like I should have. Those cop women ... I just never would have imagined that women could act like that, ever. I knew some mean moms and some mean girls. Just ... what made people decide that all women were better than all men?"

"Beats me. I know *you're* better than a man, though." He was teasing her, and kissing her. "Much, much, better."

JUNE 2218, ADDAMS' RANCH, SOUTH DAKOTA:

The second day at the ranch, Marley, Kyle, and Peter watched attentively while Dahlia crafted a new ID for Richard, renaming him George Black. She stressed to them the importance of using his new name at all times. He was in a lot of danger now, with his ID photo all over the news. He could not risk being seen at all outside of Underground circles, and he certainly couldn't drive anymore. But a man had to have an ID. All men were required to show ID when asked, and could be arrested on the spot if they didn't have one. With a false one, he could at least get away from a cop who didn't recognize him.

The kids worked out a riding schedule for the day, and those who weren't riding discovered the game room, shooting range, gym, and library.

"You're probably going to be here for two or three weeks," Addams announced the second night at dinner. "It's very dangerous out there right now, with federal authorities on high alert. We don't want to risk your safety by being impatient. We've never been on their radar here—we're just another horse ranch. We drink beer with local cops and their grunts, and we keep our ears open. There's a lot of pressure on the locals right now to watch and report whatever they see.

"So we need to just hunker down and stay out of sight until the feds and locals aren't in such a tizzy. We've got plenty of space, and lots of things to do and stuff for you to learn that could be useful in a pinch when you're on your way again. I hope you can all be patient and have a good time here."

◆ ◆ ◆

Carlos and Addams taught them various martial arts and self-defense techniques in a big indoor gym. Marley learned to punch and kick and grapple. She learned nastier techniques involving eyeballs and testicles that could not be practiced on real people. Addams lectured and quizzed them about all kinds of situations, sometimes timing them and yelling at them like a drill sergeant while they tried to think, training them to think fast and do the right thing under stress.

◆ ◆ ◆

Several days passed before Marley got up the nerve to check out the shooting range. Kevin was there, shooting, with Benjamin sitting quietly next to him.

"Hey, Mel," Kevin said, setting down a rifle and pulling off his hearing protectors. "You wanna try?"

"I'll just watch you. Koster will be here in a minute."

"Oh yeah. The rules," said Kevin. "Well, grab some earphones and watch. Some of these are loud even with mufflers on."

Marley put her elbows on the table and focused her eyes down range. The three-sided room was lined with sound-absorbing material, with sound-absorbing walls down range, too. Cardboard targets and self-healing targets moved on wires, controlled by a computer.

The muffled shots were not as bad as Marley expected, but she was startled by the barrage of golden shells that came at her as Kevin fired ten times in rapid succession.

"Hey, you're shooting *me*."

"I forgot about that," said Kevin, cracking the ghost of a smile. "Maybe you should be on the other side of me."

But then Koster appeared to give Marley her basic instruction. He went over range safety and sound precautions, and showed her stunners, pistols, and rifles.

"Of course all these weapons are illegal," he said. "I'm sure you know that the Enlightened Society doesn't allow anyone but the police to own stunners, let alone lethal weapons. Everything here came from old anarchist stashes from before World War III, or were stolen from the police.

"We carry stunners a lot," he continued. "You may actually have to use a stunner. We rarely use lethal weapons, but the police do, so it's good to know how they work. Of course there's disagreement, but most Undergrounders want to use the least amount of force necessary to preserve our lives and freedom. Stunners are best for that."

He set a target at ten feet, and Marley fired at the bull's eye with a stunner.

"That's not bad at all," said Koster, eyeing the grouping, and moving the target to 15 feet. "Stunners are short-range weapons. This is about your maximum distance to get a hit and knock someone out. Don't even try if they're farther away. You'll just waste shots."

Then Koster gave her a target shaped like a human. "Try aiming for the torso," he said. She did, and got all her shots on the torso. "If you think you got a hit, and it doesn't work, the person is probably wearing body armor. So try for the thighs. Never a head shot. You'll probably miss, and if you do hit them in the head, there's a good chance of killing them."

Marley took five shots below the waist of the target, and got three hits.

Then Koster showed her a pistol. How to see if it was empty, put on the silencer, load it, and always keep it aimed away from people.

"Don't put your finger on the trigger until you're about to shoot. Let out your breath, and squeeze the trigger. Good. Don't anticipate the kick. Breathe and squeeze."

Marley found the pistol scary. It was small and close and kicked so strongly in her hands. Rifles were better. Shooting at far-away targets through the sights was fun. She visited the range every couple of days after that, and frequently found Kevin and Halen there, competing to be the best marksman in the group.

◆ ◆ ◆

Chores were a constant. A few cleaning bots roamed the house, sucking in large amounts of dust and dirt. Marley frequently found them beeping and blinking for someone to empty them. Clothes had to be continually put through the washer/dryer and taken back to the right rooms. Food preparation was always underway in the kitchen. The covered walkway to the barn allowed the teens to go over there any time to clean stalls or feed the horses that were being kept there for them to ride.

CHAPTER 39

◆ ◆ ◆

A woman desires a beautiful, clean environment. Men care
little about their surroundings. They are more suited to a
simple life with few possessions and much outdoor activity.

—IOLANDA VOORHEES, 2093

JUNE 2218, ADDAMS' RANCH, SOUTH DAKOTA:

VANESSA FOUND THE RANCH UTTERLY dismal. She'd thought the Roses' house was bad until she saw this monstrosity. The haphazardly built mess of additions was completely graceless and devoid of decoration. Some of the wooden walls weren't even painted. Doors and windows were constantly open—dust and dirt wafted in, and god-knows-what from the adjacent barn was tracked over bare plywood floors by scores of dirty shoes and boots. Cats and dogs ran in and out as they pleased. One morning she came down to find Carlos bottle-feeding a foal, wrapped in blankets by a roaring fire. A *horse* … in the kitchen.

The original ranch house was the center of the sprawling complex of additions, most of them not quite finished. Addams and his crew couldn't be bothered with trims, thresholds, or finished floors. They had thrown down rugs that were now worn and stained.

And the resident crowd were all more or less unkempt. They trimmed one another's hair, quickly and badly, and very little shaving was evident. There was no trace of makeup or hair color on anyone. How could they stand to look at each other all day?

The camp boys were like wild animals, bathing only when told to, and completely innocent of table manners. The only one here who took any care for her appearance was Melissa, and Vanessa was having a hard time pretending to like that girl. She prided herself on her ability to fit into any group, make friends, and get people to like and trust her. But she had not expected the culture shock that hit her out here.

Melissa. In Vanessa's mind, the girl represented all of the people who were willing to destroy the Enlightened Society for their own petty desires. This girl had her boy, and her desires were all that mattered to her, civilization and history be damned. And she was only fifteen. She hadn't even had the decency to struggle against her heterosexuality for a decade or two before giving in to it. In her sex-crazed little mind, feeling it made it right. And to top it off, city-raised Melissa had taken to this dirty, graceless culture like a cat to a cardboard box.

◆ ◆ ◆

Vanessa asked Jaden to saddle the paint pony for her so she could go for a ride. She had avoided the horses at Roses' farm, and had hoped to avoid horses entirely. But here, the adults talked about moving the kids on horseback as if that was a normal thing to do. She was still afraid of the larger horses that tried to knock her over with their big heads, or stomp on her feet, but with Jaden's help and encouragement, she had screwed up the courage to get on this pony. She'd ridden it around the ring, and gone out onto the prairie road with Jaden. He was always eager to assist her, and Vanessa noted the signs of a crush. She wondered how she could make use of his feelings.

"I want to see if I can manage by myself today," she said. "Without following someone else."

"Well, that's brave," said Jaden, smiling. "But you'll do just fine. Pipo is quite lazy. He won't break into a trot unless you really insist on it."

"I won't," said Vanessa. "I'm quite sure I would fall off if he did."

Vanessa donned her cowboy hat and guided the pony out into the ring next to the barn. She walked him around the ring once before opening the gate and steering him onto the ranch road. She passed close by the grove of cottonwoods where the underground tunnel came out from the basement. The trap door was covered with growing grass, and she couldn't see where it was. She put in her earpiece and made an untraceable satellite phone call to Barilla as the pony plodded along.

"This is definitely a big hub," said Vanessa. "They've been using this place for fifteen years with no one suspecting a thing. They have a stockpile of weapons and they know how to use them. They have an underground tunnel from inside the house to a cottonwood grove 100 feet away. There are eleven adults here—some Islanders, some escapees—but they're all long-term, dedicated Undergrounders. And twelve kids now, eleven boys and a girl. And Richard Gonzalez, who's now going by George Black. I drove him here myself."

"Wow, that's a good haul," said Barilla. "I knew we'd get something good if we got you farther in there. I think we definitely need to scoop up some of these people, especially the cop-killer. We'll get kudos for that."

"Well, let me know what you're planning," said Vanessa. "I'd like to continue on with some of them if that works, and you can scoop up the rest."

"We'll let you know," said Barilla.

CHAPTER 40

◆ ◆ ◆

A number of secret camps have been found in remote, less
populated areas where subversives were training stolen boys
to wreak havoc on our civilization. Giving help or quarter
to any escaped boy is a serious crime. Citizens should call
authorities immediately if they see a boy outside of a camp.

–Topics in Law Enforcement, Fourth Edition, 2208

June 2218, Addams' ranch, South Dakota:

MARLEY GRABBED HER COWBOY HAT and met Halen in the barn, where he
had their favorite horses at the grooming station. She took out a currycomb
and set to work on a golden bay called Charlie. When Tyrone and Peter returned from their ride, Marley and Halen were ready to go. Marley reached
for the saddle horn and swung herself up onto the tall beast, who stomped and
swished his tail with eagerness.

Marley could never get enough time outdoors in this beautiful country, so
different from what she had known. She could see for miles and miles across
open, gently rolling prairie to distant clumps of trees. The sky was so much
bigger than in Pennsylvania—so big that she could see weather coming from
miles away. To the west were barely visible mountains, their lofty peaks just
breaking the horizon. She loved how the clouds swept across the sky, and

changed sunny skies to wind and rain in half an hour, and then cleared up again just as fast.

Comfortable now in her saddle, with that sense of balance and oneness with her mount that she had so envied in Tyrone a few weeks ago, Marley gave Charlie his head and raced with Halen down the smooth, dusty dirt road.

Marley had set herself the task of learning the names of all 89 horses on the ranch—the brood mares and stallions, the wobbly new foals, and the naughty yearlings. She helped Carlos bottle-feed the preemie foal he'd taken by cesarean section from a dead mare. He'd been trying to induce other mares to nurse him, but had not been successful so far.

◆ ◆ ◆

Carlos and Maya had a somewhat haphazard collection of native South Dakota flora growing near the ranch buildings. Occasional stabs at planned landscaping were evident, but some of their collections had just rooted themselves where they sat and grown too big to move.

"Hobbies always get pushed aside for chores," Maya laughed. "Still, it's rather lovely the way it is, don't you think?"

Vegetables were more carefully raised in an irrigated garden, fenced in against rabbits and deer. Three people in the garden was not a remarkable number, so Marley could spend all the time she wanted out there, wearing a large hat to protect her from the sun and satellites.

"We have a campsite way off in the wooded hills over that way," said Carlos, indicating a northerly direction. "That's where we'd run to if the feds got wind of our Railroad activity here. There's no trail to it, and the location is never programmed into a GPS. We just all know how to get there. And we have food stored there, too, if a quick escape is needed."

"But what if we don't know the way?" asked Marley.

"Well, we'd take you there, of course. It's possible you could find it using the compass and pedometer on your saddle if you knew the markers by heart. But if you missed a marker, you'd couldn't get back on track without a GPS.

And we don't want people using the GPS to get there. The route was carefully planned with dogs and satellites in mind.

"There's a mag road a few miles north of the campsite, and we're thinking of getting you all to the mag road by way of the campsite."

"I want to learn the markers," said Marley.

After getting an okay from Addams, Carlos began teaching Marley the markers as they worked in the garden together, and Marley recited them to herself every day.

◆ ◆ ◆

After another long, active day of riding, gardening, and doing chores, Marley tossed her clothing onto the braided rug in her little room, closed the flowery curtain, turned off the light, and slipped naked under the light bedcover with Halen. Despite the summer heat, he still slept in his nightshirt, and did not want the light on. His persistent aversion to being seen perplexed Marley, and she was trying to be patient with it. The moon was hiding tonight, and the country darkness was total.

"You're happy to see me. I can tell," she teased, her hands finding their way under the nightshirt.

"I can't see you at all, but I'm happy to feel you," he said. "And taste you."

And then his mouth captured hers in a deep kiss, and the talking was over.

◆ ◆ ◆

The adults watched the news and listened to the police radios in a room adjoining the kitchen/dining area, which was the hub of the house. There was an understanding about keeping Jackson and Benjamin away from there. But other kids often listened in.

The outrage over the three officers killed in Tennessee was still palpable on the airwaves.

"Wanton murder."

"Cold-blooded killings."

"Terrorists."

On the news, Marley saw the woman who had first come across the scene, and the officer who had responded to her frantic call. There were smiling photos of the slain officers, and the ID photo of Richard Gonzalez, whom they now called George.

"It was the most horrible thing I've ever seen," said the woman, shaking her head, visibly upset by the memory.

"Officer Abbott's face was unrecognizable," said the officer sitting next to her. "I've never seen someone so horrifically beaten. The man who did this is a monster—the worst of the worst."

It's all wrong, Marley thought. *It wasn't wanton, wasn't cold-blooded, and there were no terrorists. And George didn't kill them. That Abbott woman was the terrorist—she was the cold-blooded killer. Do the authorities even want to know what really happened?*

DNA collected at the scene linked the murders to missing boys from Florida and Georgia, as well as the unknown man in the photo, the news story went on.

"This man is thought to be a subversive ringleader, luring boys from their camps and training them to be terrorists against our Enlightened Society here in North America," said an earnest blonde woman with perfect hair and a perfect face. "Authorities are hot on his trail, and a break in the case is expected soon," she assured the public.

None of that is true, Marley thought. *There are no terrorists. Only people trying to escape. Are they really hot on George's trail? Or are they just saying so?*

Marley was afraid for George, and for all of them.

◆ ◆ ◆

Authorities had ramped up the checkpoints on the old roads, especially for trucks and vans. Koster came back from an errand off the ranch, reporting that his truck had been searched.

"The officers who stopped me were ones I hang out and drink beer with," Koster said. "They were really apologetic about it. They said the feds are putting pressure on them, giving them quotas for checkpoints and searches. They said personally, they think the cop-killer is probably off the continent by now, but they have to meet their quotas."

CHAPTER 41

◆ ◆ ◆

It is offensive for a boy to adopt civilized dress and habits. Yunies
earn this privilege through amendment and long education, but
it is dangerous to blur the difference between boys and girls.
Furthermore, shorn heads and camp slang make boys easier
to find if they escape. It's impossible for them to blend in.

–IOLANDA VOORHEES, 2097

JUNE 2218, ADDAMS' RANCH, SOUTH DAKOTA:
ADDAMS WAS DOING HIS BEST to avoid the adorable girl with the perceptive
eyes. But she was so darn friendly, and highly inquisitive about everyone on
the ranch and everything they did there. And now she had cornered him yet
again, while he was emptying new bags of feed into containers in the feed
room. She was giving him a long spiel about passing camp boys as girls.

That's crazy, he thought. *These boys could never pull it off, with their rough
manners and the way they talk.*

But the girl went on and on, telling him what they'd been doing at the
Roses' farm, and Addams began to think about it.

"It just might work," he said. "If they had a city native like you to coach
them. They would need time to absorb it and practice it, though. If they were
stopped and questioned, wigs and makeup wouldn't do shit if they didn't talk
right."

"Well, it seems like they often stay in one place for a pretty long time. They could use that time to practice that stuff and grow a bit of hair. We could do hair extensions instead of wigs—that way a cop couldn't just whip it off."

We're having more trouble with trucks and vans being searched, Addams thought. *And it's risky to do things the same way too often. We've never had trouble with boys hidden in cars, but they could start searching cars at some point.*

"If the boys could pass as girls, we wouldn't have to hide them," he said out loud. "A woman could take three or four at a time."

"Yes," she exclaimed. She was so lit up—her big, pretty eyes sparkling with enthusiasm. "Maybe that's my niche," she said. "Maybe I'll come back here and work with you, like the Jays did, but doing hair and makeup and girl lessons."

She is absolutely right, Addams thought. *She would be extremely useful here. But goddamnit, I want her safe on the Island, loving her boy without a care in the world.*

He shrugged, and said gruffly, "Welcome to the Underground, girl."

CHAPTER 42

◆ ◆ ◆

Backwardness is endemic to rural areas. Satellite
surveillance will help us keep a closer eye on those
areas where enforcers are spread more thinly.

—IOLANDA VOORHEES, 2098

JUNE 2218, ADDAMS' RANCH, SOUTH DAKOTA:
MARLEY SAT IN A CIRCLE with her friends, breathing hard after a rigorous martial-arts workout. She'd thrown a lot of her friends on the floor, they had thrown her, she'd kicked and punched the crap out of an uncomplaining dummy, and they'd played "avoid being shot" with paint guns until they were all exhausted. Now Addams brought out handcuffs and showed them how to escape from them. He gave them small adhesive pouches containing plastic cuff keys, which would be missed if they were swiped with a metal detector. The key had a round grip and two different key shapes for both kinds of standard cuffs. When traveling, they would stick a pouch to their skin somewhere under their clothes. Addams and Carlos worked with the kids until they were all proficient at escaping cuffs.

After the handcuff lessons, it was Marley and Halen's turn to go riding. They saddled up and rode to the front gate to visit Greg and Trayden, who were on perimeter duty. Marley dismounted and went into the gate house, which she had not yet seen. Tray was inside, fixing things and occasionally glancing at a row of security cameras. The gatehouse had become a mending station for tack, clothing, and anything small enough to take there to work on.

"Addams insists on us doing this, even though nothing bad has ever happened here," said Tray. "People got bored to death and made it into a fixing station. We play a lot of games here, too. And we love visitors."

◆ ◆ ◆

The adults had decided to move the kids two at a time on horseback to the wilderness campsite about five miles away. From there they would ride two or three at a time to the nearest mag road exit, where Underground women would pick them up in small cars. The horses would be taken back to the ranch in trailers. The women would take mag roads into Montana, avoiding the plague of checkpoints on the old roads.

Dahlia and Samika rode to the campsite to set things up, taking George along to stay there, and then taking Kyle and Tyrone, who were both expert riders, to learn the route. The boys would take turns bringing the other kids two at a time. Marley had now committed the markers to memory, and taught them to Halen. She wanted to try getting there on their own.

"That's very impressive," said Dahlia. "But we can't let you try that. You're too likely to miss one thing and get hopelessly lost. But you can try leading the way with Kyle or Tyrone as a backup."

Marley and Halen helped Robert and Jackson saddle up to ride away with Kyle. Tyrone showed up later in the day, and the next morning, they were saying goodbye to Kevin and Benjamin. Marley groomed horses for them in the barn. Halen, Dahlia, and Addams came out to help saddle and bridle them. Marley gave Kevin a long hug, trying to squeeze her love into the sad, grim boy. He felt lumpy and hard with a stunner in a shoulder holster and a pistol in a hip holster. Then Kevin swung up onto his own horse and put on his cowboy hat. Marley thought he looked like a gunslinger from the 19th century.

JULY 1, 2218, ADDAMS' RANCH, SOUTH DAKOTA:

Dinner and bedtime were quiet with so many boys gone. Vanessa snuck away and talked to Barilla. "George Black is at the campsite, and I can't give you that location until I get there," she said. "I'll go with the last batch of kids. You can have the local feds round up the adults here, and then come to the campsite. But I want to escape with at least some of the kids. Make sure they know not to blow my cover, or shoot me."

"Got it. I'm coordinating with the local feds now. Your contact is Kara63. She will message you when they're ready to move."

CHAPTER 43

◆ ◆ ◆

In the Enlightened Society, all weapons of war are obsolete.

–Iolanda Voorhees, 2073

July 3, 2218, Addams' ranch, South Dakota:

THE EARLY MORNING PROMISED ANOTHER baking hot day under a cloudless sky. People at Addams' ranch were awake and active, getting things done before the heat came.

Marley stood on the front porch, gazing through the screen at the green expanse of prairie between her and the front gate. Michael and Stuart had gone off riding that direction. She'd just finished some cleaning chores, and was thinking about putting on her hat and going out in the garden to harvest some vegetables for lunch. Kyle would be showing up some time today to take her and Halen to the campsite. Mike and Stuart would go the next day, and then Darlene would go with Ian and Greg, who would guide them all to roadside meet-ups and bring all the horses back. Marley felt excited but sad. Over the past weeks, the ranch had come to feel like home, and the people like family.

She put her device in her pocket. She could just make out Michael and Stuart riding back. As they got closer, she could see they were going at a full gallop straight back toward the house. She was just thinking, *They shouldn't be riding that fast on the rough*, when Addams' voice barked over the intercom:

"All hands to barn—saddle horses—stat."

Something was wrong. Suddenly fearful, she bolted through the house to the barn. Addams, Jaden, and Jordan were flinging saddles onto horses and cinching them up. Halen was there seconds later.

"Melissa, bridles for all these," Addams shouted. Heart thumping, Marley quickly grabbed the correct bridles off their hooks, and ran over with them. Five horses were ready when Michael and Stuart galloped in and tumbled off their sweating ponies.

"Tanks," they both gasped, eyes wide with fear. "We saw tanks."

Addams shouted on the barn intercom. "All hands to barn. All hands to barn. Darlene! Darlene to the barn. Where the fuck is Darlene? Asleep? Game room?" he shouted at Jaden and Jordan, who were hoisting the younger boys like potato sacks onto fresh horses. Marley was already up on Charlie, and Halen was on a speckled paint.

"You four, move out," Addams shouted at the mounted teens. "Gallop on the flat, slow down when you're out of sight. Get to the campsite. Don't look back, don't *come* back. Go."

This last word was punctuated by a slap to Charlie's rump, and Marley was glad she'd grabbed a good handful of his mane as the horse almost leapt out the barn door.

The smooth dirt road went straight away across flat pastureland for a good distance before curving between low hills and disappearing from view. Marley, Halen, Mike, and Stuart urged their horses to a full gallop, and Charlie took the lead. The wide openness that Marley loved so much made her feel small and exposed now. They slowed to a canter as the road curved between the hills, and they could no longer be seen from the ranch house. But Marley still felt exposed. Small groves of trees were scattered over the hills, and farther on was a patch of real cover. Reaching this, they slowed the horses to a trot, and then a walk.

Such a beautiful day to ride, Marley thought. *Too bad I'm too terrified to enjoy it.* The exertion of the hard gallop had relieved some of the heart-pounding stress, but her mind whirled with worries. What was going on back there? Would the adults be okay? She tried to put the worries out of her mind and concentrate on finding their way.

◆ ◆ ◆

In the game room, strapped into a swiveling chair, Vanessa was fuming. Half an hour ago, she'd gotten a message:

> *Kara63*: Raiding ranch today. Delay evacuation as long as possible.
> *Van79*: Need one or two more days. Need to get to campsite. Will call from there.
> *Kara63*: No. Moving in right now. Delay evacuation of adults.

What idiot is fucking this up? Vanessa thought angrily. *Gonzalez could get away. And if they blow my cover now, someone is getting spectacularly fired.*

But there was nothing to do now but follow the order she was given. She hurried to the game room, strapped herself in, and started playing a loud game with one headphone set beside her ear so she could hear the house. Soon she heard Addams yelling over the intercom. She paused the game and listened as his voice became more and more urgent. The urgency was hard to resist. She slipped the headset over her ear and unpaused the game, hoping to be genuinely startled when someone finally found her.

◆ ◆ ◆

The instructions Marley had memorized took them through several streams to put dogs off their trail, and wooded areas to throw off satellite tracking. All four saddles were equipped with compasses and pedometers, and all four riders paid careful attention to them as they moved from one landmark to the next. Marley and Halen consulted each other at every point of the directions, to make sure they were remembering them right.

They'd gone almost a mile, and were about to emerge from a wooded area into a meadow when Marley heard the beating of helicopter blades above them. They reined in the horses and hung back under the trees.

"This is bad," Marley said to Halen. "We've got .8 miles of open space from here to the next patch of woods. We don't know if there is more than one helicopter, or how far they can see. How long do we need to make that distance?"

"Pretty long," said Halen. "We can't gallop across a meadow."

"Let's just wait here until we're sure they're gone, then," Marley said.

It was a long wait. The helicopters flew over again and again. Eventually the kids dismounted.

"Might be dark before they give up," said Stuart.

"Then I guess we wait till dark," said Marley. "I wonder where Kyle is—he was coming today to take us there." There was nothing to do but wait and worry, and Marley closed her eyes and tried to meditate a little and calm her useless, churning anxiety. The helicopter circled again.

"They're gonna keep looking till dark," said Michael. "Let's loosen the saddles and just hang out."

They did this, but then the horses seemed to think that they should be out in the meadow eating the grass. They could not let go of the horses' reins, and had to keep pulling them back to keep them under the trees. Everyone was hungry and thirsty. There were long spaces of time where they thought the helicopters might have given up, but they always came back.

"Well, this is fucking fun," said Stuart. "Shoulda brought a pack of cards." Stuart and Michael threw rocks at tree trunks to pass the time. Marley braided Charlie's mane. And then his tail.

The helicopters passed again as the sun set, and still they waited.

"It's been 35 minutes," said Halen. "Longest interval so far. But they could be coming back with lights."

"Fifty minutes," said Halen, later.

"I think they're gone," said Michael.

"Yeah, let's move," said Marley.

So four hungry, grumpy humans cinched up four hungry, frustrated horses, and rode out into the meadow. They still had a long way to go, and now they had to find their landmarks by moonlight.

◆ ◆ ◆

"Take the creek roughly northwest for .9 miles." said Marley, as they splashed into a creek.

"Find big boulder with overhanging tree," said Halen.

"Pass boulder, leave stream where bank is rocky," said Marley, pointing. "Go straight north 1.7 miles. About 40 minutes. Look for another creek."

"Creek downstream, west, about 30 minutes. 1.5 miles."

"Sharp turn left with lots of debris on the right bank. Exit the creek to the right and go around the debris," said Marley wearily.

"You guys are amazing," said Michael.

"Stop," said Halen suddenly. "People. Under the trees. On horses." He pointed at two shadowy shapes. They all reined in, hearts pounding.

"Halen?" said one shadowy shape, moving closer.

"Oh, it's Kyle," said Stuart. "Kyle and George."

Relief and joy flooded through Marley, and a small sob escaped her as they all crowded together. Michael quickly spilled out most of their story.

"We were stuck in the woods all fracking day," said Stuart, when Michael paused. "Waiting for those copters to give up so we could get across a meadow. We got moving again about an hour and a half ago, and these two," he waved at Marley and Halen, "have been reciting the directions out of their heads the whole way."

"Damn good thing you learned them," Kyle said. "I was on my way to the ranch to get you guys. I saw the helicopters, and didn't dare go out in the open. Rode back and asked George what to do. We've been watching those birds all day, too."

"Well, you two can relax now," said George. "Just follow us."

Marley was grateful for that, but the directions kept going in her head as they went along. The moon was big and bright in the clear sky, but under the trees the darkness was deep. Riding through rocky streams in the dark made her nervous. Horses slipped and slid a few times on the wet rocks, bringing Marley's heart into her mouth, but no one went down, and no one fell off. Her butt was sore from the saddle. Once, Halen took her reins and she turned around in her saddle and laid her head on Charlie's rump. The high back of the saddle poked into her growling stomach.

They all drank from the streams, horses and humans alike, but Marley felt faint with hunger. The last stream came into view. Charlie splashed into it. The stream flowed out from a narrow ravine, flanked by thick underbrush on both sides. Splash, splash, splash. They made their slow, deliberate way up the stream between looming bushes. As they entered the ravine, the moon was hidden by trees. They hadn't spoken for a long time. They were all too exhausted to complain any more.

The horses plodded dutifully through the water. A small light shone up ahead. The bank opened out, and at long last, they saw the anxious, welcoming faces of their friends.

Some of the boys took charge of the horses while others hustled up a feeble dinner of beef stew and hot chocolate on the propane stove. Marley thought it was the best food in the world, and did not speak until she had wolfed down two bowls and two cups.

Then they shared what little information they had with the others. Mike and Stu related how they'd gone riding to the front gate to visit Trayden and Koster. The boys had gone into the gate house to watch the cameras so that Tray could help Koster work on a broken-down ATV outside. They'd seen tanks approaching on the road, and ran out in a panic to tell the men. After a few seconds of utter disbelief, Koster was on the phone with Addams, and the boys were galloping back. That was all they knew.

"We won't be lighting a fire or making any noise tonight," said George. "We'll just lie low and wait. Maybe the others will show up tonight or tomorrow. If they don't, I'll get far away from the camp and make a phone call and see what I can find out."

Marley noticed that George had a holster on each shoulder, and was carrying a lethal pistol as well as a stunner.

A large, long, rectangular tent of heavy, waterproof canvas had been set up, more or less permanently, on a flat piece of ground near the rocky wall of the ravine. Inside were bunk beds that doubled as storage bins for the bedding.

They waited anxiously, sleepy in the darkness, but no one else showed up. "Hopefully they're just hiding somewhere," said George, "And they don't want to make any calls that could be intercepted." But they all had darker thoughts that were not being expressed.

Marley didn't think she would sleep at all. She pushed her cot up against Halen's so she could feel his body next to hers. She was sure she would lie awake all night, wondering and worrying. *Tanks*, for godssakes. They had brought tanks. And helicopters. And cars and trucks. Lots of people, lots of guns. The faces of all the people she had come to love kept going through her mind. *Oh, please. Let them be alive, at least.*

That last harshly barked order kept going through her head. 'Don't look back. Don't come back. Go.' At last, Marley's exhaustion overcame her and she slept.

CHAPTER 44

◆ ◆ ◆

Subversion must be put down firmly, with
whatever force is necessary.

Those who advocate men's rights have no historical
perspective. Men have all the rights they need.

—CARA TOMASINA, *PRESIDENTIAL ADDRESS*, 2196

JULY 3, 2218, ADDAMS' RANCH, SOUTH DAKOTA:

JADEN BURST INTO THE GAME room, and Vanessa heard him yell, "Found Darlene." A second later, he was unbuckling her from the chair, and whipping the headset off her head. "We're being raided," he yelled at her, and she did her best to look startled and terrified. He grabbed her hand and they ran from the room together, nearly colliding with Addams in the hallway.

"This way," said Addams, and they followed him down the hallway and the basement stairs.

"You are surrounded. Put down your weapons and come out with your hands up," said a voice over a loudspeaker outside.

They did not come out, but hurried through the basement to the underground tunnel.

It won't do any good, Vanessa thought smugly. *They'll be right outside waiting.* It would be satisfying to see Addams taken into custody.

But as Jaden pulled her down the corridor, she heard scraping and sliding, and in the dim light she saw that two of the men were opening a cupboard-like door about five feet above the floor and pulling down a ladder. People were disappearing into the opening, and now Jaden was behind her, lifting and pushing her up ahead of himself. A short crawl on the level, and then a slope. She could see the light from an underground shelter.

How fucking clever, Vanessa thought, sliding down into the dimly lit room full of fearful faces. Behind her, she heard the doors being closed. Addams grabbed a pair of headphones and put them on, and the others looked on anxiously as he listened to the noises and voices above them.

JULY 4, 2218, CAMPSITE, SOUTH DAKOTA:

Marley, George, and the boys waited anxiously for the adults to show up at the campsite. No one wanted to express what was foremost in their minds, and they spoke only of food, cooking, horses, trash, and toilet runs. There was plenty of food for now. They cooked breakfast, then lunch, then dinner on propane stoves. They buried trash in a hole a good distance from the camp. They made toilet runs, but never alone. George went on a long walk with Peter and made a phone call to the Underground, but got no new information.

The day passed. Then another day passed. Marley saw the hope fade from her friends' eyes. George was silent and grim.

JULY 7, 2218, CAMPSITE, SOUTH DAKOTA:

Marley hated the dirt. She hadn't taken a shower since the morning she left the ranch, four days ago. Everyone smelled bad, but no one else seemed to notice or care. She washed her hands and face in cold water, and washed the dishes in a tub of cold water from the creek. Without hot water, nothing felt really clean, but she didn't want to use propane to heat water. She missed her shower room at home, and the public baths with their blue and white tiles, the hot bath and the cold bath and the sauna. She missed her soft bed in the little undersea room, with the stuffed animals hanging in the net in the corner, and for the first time since she left, she felt sickening waves of longing for Mama Sue and home.

Day after day they waited: cooking, eating, washing dishes, feeding horses, talking about inconsequential things, playing card games, and feeling anxious. They didn't dare build a fire. They had dehydrated food to last for months, as long as they had water and heat. But with eleven hungry teens and one big adult, the appetizing food was disappearing fast. The fresh meat, milk, and eggs were gone. The nuts, dried fruit, and jerky were dwindling. They had a large supply of vacuum-packed, ground cereal grains, which cooked fast in water, using little of their propane. They were all doing their best to fill up on this before eating anything else. Marley's pampered palate was already bored. She began to think of gathering some wild foods, but it was too early for nuts and berries, and she seriously doubted that eating weeds would make her feel better.

JULY 3, 2218, ADDAMS' RANCH, SOUTH DAKOTA:

Vanessa and the others crowded around Addams in the dimness of the shelter as he listened to microphones through his headset. Lights flickered on a board in front of him, each light labeled with a location. Most of the rooms in the house were on there, and the barn, and several trees outside the house.

He must be hearing a confused cacophony with all those lights going at once, Vanessa thought.

Addams reported, softly and tersely. "Vehicles all around the house ... sounds like a tank ... bullhorns ... come out, you're surrounded ... gas canisters inside ... bullhorns ... no one in there ... destroy and burn ... loud crashing ... timbers breaking."

They waited.

"The house is burning," Addams said grimly. "Tank engines ... roaring fire ... timbers falling."

Lights on the board went out as microphones were crushed or burned up. Finally, only two lights flickered on the board from microphones placed well away from the house.

"They've destroyed our home," Addams said. Vanessa heard Dahlia, Samika, Carlos, and Maya weeping quietly.

"I just hope everyone else got away safely," said Addams.

July 8, 2218, campsite, South Dakota:

Marley walked over to join Halen, Kevin, and George, who were in a huddle.

"We're going to the ranch to see if we can figure out what happened," Halen told her.

"Addams told us not to come back."

"We won't go all the way back. At least, we'll check it out from a safe distance first," said Halen.

"We should not go all the way back, no matter what we see," George said. "We don't want the satellites to spot us coming out from under the trees, or going back in. But we can take binocs, and maybe climb a tree to get a better look. Just to see if it's empty, or crawling with feds, or what. And while we're away, we can make another phone call. Maybe some Undergrounders know what happened."

George and Halen rode away together, and returned hours later with somber faces.

"They totally razed the place and burned it," Halen said. "And the feds are still hanging out there. The tanks are gone. They've got a trailer. They're just hanging out waiting, like they think someone will show up."

"We called the Railroad," George said. "They haven't heard from Addams or anyone else who was there. They're making a plan to move us out of here. In two days, we'll ride away from the camp again and make another call. By then maybe they'll have a plan, and they'll tell us what to do next."

"Come get some dinner, then," Marley said. "We'll take care of the horses." She grabbed Halen's reins, and turned her face away so he couldn't see her crying. There was very little talk that evening. Marley could see the same thoughts, fears, and questions in everyone's eyes.

◆ ◆ ◆

The next day, Kyle, Tyrone, Halen, Jackson, George, and Marley made an expedition away from the camp to call the Railroad. They each rode a horse and led another horse. They would ride about half a mile to a meadow and let all the horses graze for a while. They had a store of hay and oats in a tent at the camp, but they wanted the horses to have some fresh grass.

Marley rode Charlie, with a young, feisty black mare called Tar Pit following behind on a rope. She had wound Tar Pit's rope around her saddle horn, which made her feel like a real cowgirl.

They rode out into the meadow, and Charlie's head went right down to get a mouthful of grass. Marley pulled her feet from the stirrups, swung her leg over his head, and dropped onto the thick sward. She replaced Charlie's bridle with a halter and rope, loosened the girth, and pulled off the saddle. She tied both ropes to the saddle and watched the horses graze.

It was yet another hot, dry day under a vast, deep blue sky without a cloud in sight. She breathed deeply, turning her face to the sun with closed eyes. She thought of her friends—seeing them dead, or in custody, or some dead and some in prisons, grieving. They had taken on all these risks for her, and others like her. It weighed on her like boulders, crushing the breath out of her. Her mind reached out for Addams and Dahlia, and Jordan and Jaden, and floundered in the empty space of not knowing. Would she ever know who was still alive, and where they were?

I cannot bear this. It's too much for me. I cannot live with this. She tried to let the anxiety and grief flow through her mind without resistance, and concentrate on the warmth of the sun on her face, the in and out of her breath, the munching of the horses. Searching for peace in the moment.

Jackson came around with the food he had brought in his saddlebag. They didn't have a lot of good stuff left. The big cooler at the camp had run out of battery power and dry ice, but the food it was keeping cold was already gone. Dinners were soup or stew made with rehydrated food, heated on the propane stove, or vacuum-packed meals in some kind of packaging that made them last forever. There was milk powder and juice powder and mashed potato powder and scrambled egg powder. They were all longing for something fresh now. Marley had been gathering greens, but there was no dressing for them, so she put the bitter and tasteless ones into the soup with all the dehydrated things.

Jackson and Halen joined her, and they sat in the grass, eating the last of the crackers with the last packages of cheese dip and peanut butter.

"The food sucks, but the company's good," Halen said cheerfully. But Marley could see the sadness behind his smile. She sat close to him and rested her head on his shoulder.

"The company is sad and worried," she said. He put his arm around her, and they ate crackers in silence.

George came over and sat down with them. "I talked to some people," he said. "We're not safe on any kind of road in any kind of vehicle for about 30 miles around the ranch," he said. "They've got checkpoints on every road, and they're searching every single vehicle, even coming off the mag roads."

"Our friends have arranged a way to get us out of the area on horseback, to a ranch about 40 miles away. We'll have to ride through desert badlands where there's no water. But they think it won't occur to the authorities that we would do that, so that's what we're going to do."

"How can we ride through a desert without water?" Marley asked.

"Well, we can't," said George. "Which is why they're not likely to be scrutinizing that area. But our friends are going to bring us water in pickup trucks. They're looking for places where our trail can get close enough to a road that they can bring water for the horses and for us. Our first meeting place will be about five miles out. They'll bring us more portable containers, too. We'll use the GPS, and we'll have to communicate to make sure we don't miss them."

George left them and went to talk with the other boys. They gave the horses another hour to graze, and then saddled up again and rode back to their camp.

CHAPTER 45

◆ ◆ ◆

Those who argue for the old ways in the face of our achievements are
manifesting mental illness. They need treatment, not discussion.

–Shohima Katha Iolanda, *Enlightenment*
for a New Century, 2200

July 8, 2218, Addams' ranch, South Dakota:

Vanessa wondered why the agents were still on the ranch. The headphones lay on the table now, so anyone could hear whatever sounds came
through them. Voices came through at intervals every day, but rarely close
enough that they could make out words. It must be the feds, then, right?
Who else would be hanging out around destroyed buildings? Perhaps an underground hideout had occurred to them. Barilla knew about the basement
tunnel, and if they inspected carefully, they could find the secret door to the
shelter. The entrance to the basement inside the house was probably buried
under smoldering wreckage, but they could come in through the exit in the
cottonwood grove. Unless the locals had failed to get that information.

"Maybe they're hanging out until the fire goes out. They don't want it to
start a prairie fire, and they don't have enough water to put it out," someone
said.

"Maybe they're searching the ruins for our entrance. Maybe they suspect
that we went underground."

"They weren't close enough to know that anyone was in the house when they got here. They're probably assuming we all got away. Maybe they're waiting for someone to come back to check things out."

"Or they suspect we're holed up, and they're trying to starve us out."

Some small talk came through from a surviving microphone in a tree. Just enough to discern that the speakers were feds.

They must be wondering why they haven't heard from me, Vanessa thought. They must have gotten whoever was at the gate house, and maybe the men who were out in the pastures. Trayden, Koster, Greg, and Ian. They would be working on whoever they caught to get information. And four kids had taken off on horses for the campsite without a guide. Melissa had been bragging about how she could recite all the instructions, but she'd never actually been there. Surely the agents would have caught them before they got far, gotten the instructions out of them, and snagged everyone at the campsite.

She was still angry about the miscommunication. She would find out who flubbed up the timing. But right now, her current situation was overwhelming her mind. Packed in like sardines with these people all day, every day, she had to keep her act on every minute, while wondering if they suspected her.

People curled up in corners, trying to get some personal space in the crowded room, playing games and reading books. They ate snacks all day and all night out of sheer boredom, with only the clock to tell night from day. A shower curtain hung around a waterless toilet in the corner, with disinfectant in a pump bottle for their hands. Cases of bottled water were stacked high against a wall, but the water was only for drinking. The smell of dirty humans was becoming overpowering, and the feeling of being dirty was torture.

Did they suspect her? Everyone was trying to figure out what had happened, and how it happened. They had nothing else to do but sit here thinking about it, and throw out speculations. There were whispered conversations that she was not a part of, and she wondered intensely what people were saying.

"What would make them suspect us now? After all these years? Our precautions are so tight."

"They've been on high alert since the Tennessee thing. Maybe the kids going to the campsite tipped them off? If they were watching closely, they'd have noticed four going and two coming back for several days."

"But what would make them scrutinize this ranch that closely? We know they don't have the personnel to watch everywhere all the time."

"You think we have an infiltrator?"

"No. Definitely not. Everyone here is solid Underground or too young."

Maybe they suspected, and didn't want her to know they suspected. She was definitely the least solid person here, but nobody was saying so. Samika, Maya, and Carlos were in a huddle. The initial storm of grief had passed, but now they clung together as they worried and waited. Dahlia was on Addams' lap, her head on his shoulder, his big arms encircling her. The Jays sat next to each other against a wall, trying to kill each other in some virtual reality game. If they suspected anyone, it would be Vanessa.

But what of those who were not here? Koster, Tray, Ian, or Greg? Or even George? How well did these people know George? She felt the urge to deflect suspicion onto others. But that could cause offense and backfire on her. Her nerves were frayed. How long could she keep up the act under this pressure? She had never felt so intensely alone.

July 10, 2218, western South Dakota:

Marley shivered as she saddled Tar Pit in the predawn twilight. Everyone was awake—saddling horses, tightening girths, feeding handfuls of oats, slinging on canteens. Marley checked to make sure they all had extra T-shirts to protect their heads and necks from the sun.

George led them out with the GPS, riding Charlie. They passed through familiar meadows and woods, and then the trees stopped altogether, and there was only grass. Sometimes a well-trodden trail went in the right direction, and in the cool of the morning, they trotted at intervals. Often there was no trail and they had to cross open prairie. They kept to a walk and watched for prairie dog holes that could break a horse's leg. The prairie bloomed with yellow and purple coneflowers and the soft pink of milkweed.

The water truck met them five miles out. Buckets were put on the ground for the horses, and filled with a hose from a water tank in the truck. Everyone drank and refilled their canteens. They were given more canteens to sling on their saddles, and bags of apples, oranges, and nuts to eat as they rode. They gave the horses some oats.

The sun rose higher, and now Marley saw fantastic hills and pinnacles of horizontally striped rock, some in warm shades of orange, beige, and brown, and some in cool shades of gray and white. The grass became thinner and sparser, more interspersed with tough, scrubby plants, prickly pear cactus, and bunches of spiky green yucca with tall spires of cream-colored blooms. There were swaths of verbena and purple thistles. In some areas the grass dwindled and disappeared.

As the temperature rose, they laid T-shirts on horses' rumps and necks, and poured water over them. Wet shirts were wrapped around human heads.

Another water stop was arranged. Horses drank, people drank, and canteens were filled. Horses were checked for overheating, and rubbed down. There would be no trotting in the heat of the day.

They rode through a shady little canyon with rocky walls, and out the other end, where a huge vista opened up and they could again see for miles. Marley munched on apples and oranges for energy and water. Her mouth dropped open as a herd of pronghorns bounced gracefully across their path, and far in the distance, she saw a small group of grazing bison.

Tar Pit plodded along quietly. The heat seemed to have sucked the feistiness out of the young mare. Marley laid a wet T-shirt on top of her mane, and squeezed it to make water run down her neck. The sun was high and blazing hot now, and there was not a speck of shade. Their Underground friends had provided lightweight cloaks to keep the sun off their arms.

Hour after hour they rode as the sun crawled across the clear blue sky. Marley slid off Tar Pit and walked beside her for a while. In the afternoon, ominous clouds appeared on the horizon, and swept over them with stunning speed, dousing everyone with cold rain, and frightening them with lightning strikes on all sides. The storm moved on as quickly as it came, and the blazing sun reappeared—wet horses and wet humans steamed, and Marley shivered violently at the sudden change. She was dry again in minutes.

◆ ◆ ◆

Around midday, they made a more extended water stop at a place that looked like a covered outdoor market, long abandoned. They brought the horses into the shade, unsaddled them and rubbed them down, checking for chafing. Marley and her friends had been riding every day for weeks, but their bodies were still not prepared for this. They stretched and massaged each other, and were reluctant to get back into their saddles. George, Marley, and several boys left the place on foot, leading their mounts. Marley walked until she was exhausted, and had to reluctantly get up on Tar Pit again.

Hours and hours later, the sun began sinking toward the western horizon, and the heat was less direct and brutal, though the ground all around them had been soaking it up all day, and Marley felt as if she were riding through a huge oven.

They met the water truck for the last time, and pushed on to cover the last five miles to the ranch. The horses plodded along dutifully, following their leader. George and some of the boys traded off taking the lead and paying attention to the GPS. Those following sat wearily in their saddles, not so much riding as being carried along.

Marley tried different positions to take the weight off her aching butt, but Tar Pit did not like her shifting, and tossed her head angrily. "I'm sorry, girl," said Marley, patting her neck. "I'll try to keep still."

They reached the ranch as the sunlight was fading away. They had traversed a little over 41 miles. Marley slid off Tar Pit and leaned against her, fumbling for the girth buckles.

"Never mind that," said a kind voice. "Leave the horse to me. You go inside."

"Thank you," said Marley, almost inaudibly.

The kids were warmly welcomed, and offered baths, showers, food, and beds. They gratefully accepted all of this, and Marley fell quickly to sleep in Halen's arms.

JULY 11, 2218, SOUTH DAKOTA:

Marley woke up to the luxury of a comfortable bed, and Halen sleeping beside her. She kissed him until he woke up. They showered, dressed, and went downstairs. Their hosts were two men and three women, who introduced themselves to Marley again.

"We're just letting everyone sleep as long as they need," said an older woman with deep red hair in a ponytail. "Help yourself to what's on the table, as much as you like," the woman said. "We're just making more as people come down."

"What are we doing today?" Marley asked.

"You're just recovering," said the woman. "This big group needs to split up now. A car will be coming for three of the boys, late afternoon today."

"Oh," said Marley, sadly. These boys were like her family now, and she had expected to go all the way to the Island with them. She put pancakes on her plate, took a slab of butter, and doused them with maple syrup. "Who's going?" she asked.

"I believe it's Robert, James, and Peter," said the woman. "And four more boys tomorrow, and the rest of you the next day. Smaller groups are the safest way right now. You'll all see each other again when you get to the Island."

Eventually all the kids came downstairs, restored by a good night's sleep except for some residual soreness. *We're a tough bunch after all these weeks of riding,* Marley thought. *A few months ago, I could not have done that at all.*

◆ ◆ ◆

"I need something to do," Marley said. James, Robert, and Peter all had several inches of hair now, and they were up for traveling openly as girls instead of hiding like luggage in the car. The men and women helped Marley transform her friends into passable girls—styling, coloring, and adding hair extensions, drawing on tattoos, and putting them into padded bras and loose-fitting women's clothing.

In the afternoon, a car and driver came for James, Robert, and Peter. There were many hugs and tears. And the next day, two more small cars came for Tyrone, Kyle, Michael, and Stuart.

"I'll miss you guys so much," Marley said, squeezing each of them in turn. "Don't forget that liner goes on before shadow."

"Oh, fuck yourself with a carrot," said Stuart, with a perfect city-girl accent. It was his favorite phrase now.

◆ ◆ ◆

The house felt empty that evening. The next day, two cars came for the six of them who were left. The salon supplies at the house had been depleted by the other boys. So Marley sat up front with the driver, and Halen and George hid in the back out of sight. Kevin, Jackson, and Benjamin were stowed snugly and covered up in the other car. They got onto mag roads for about an hour, and met up again at an isolated country home, surrounded by fields and small copses of trees. Their hosts, however, worried about satellite surveillance in the area, and thought they should stay indoors.

The hosts were a normal male couple—Tomas and Shane—who had been active in the Railroad network for six years. Their large, finished basement was full of amusements for cooped-up guests: a huge screen for movies, all the latest games, and bookcases that covered an entire wall but still didn't quite hold all the books. They had art supplies and crafting materials too.

"I guess we can stand hiding indoors for a bit, after what we've been through lately," said Marley. "Your crafting stuff is glossy. I'm just gonna sit down here making things." Tomas showed Marley all the supplies, and soon he was busy making jewelry while Marley painted.

Benjamin pulled Kevin over to the crafting area, too, and Marley saw a spark of interest in Benjamin's eyes as he looked at the paints and brushes. She invited the boys to sit, and put pads of paper in front of them. Benjamin reached eagerly for the tools and became immediately absorbed in painting. Kevin stood by, bored, until Tomas pulled him away, assuring him that Benjamin would be okay and he could go play games.

For a while, Benjamin seemed to be just playing with colors. Then scenes emerged as his deft brown fingers worked over the paper. He painted scenes of blood, an angry woman seething with hatred, dead boys, and pistols. He painted them over and over again, wordlessly. Tomas got up quietly and brought Shane down to see this. Shane watched the boy paint, and then gently encouraged him to paint different aspects of his experience. Paint Axel. Paint Kevin. Paint yourself.

Benjamin painted Kevin huge and powerful, fighting with a huge, powerful woman—a clash of the Titans—while three tiny boys looked on, powerless and afraid. He painted his beloved brother Axel, and Gerald—the big, strong, beautiful boy he had worshipped from the moment they met. Then he obliterated them with the blackness of grief.

Kevin and Jackson spent most of their time on the games, shooting and killing bad people and monsters.

CHAPTER 46

◆ ◆ ◆

The mixed-sex family was dysfunctional at its very core.
Women were enslaved in the drudgery of housework.
Sexual abuse of children was common, and physical abuse
of children was widely accepted and promoted.

—Iolanda Voorhees, 2073

July 14, 2218, Addams' ranch, South Dakota:

Vanessa was sitting by herself in a corner of the shelter, as far away as she could get from other people, playing on a game device. She glanced up when Addams spoke.

"I've heard absolutely nothing for twelve hours," he said. "Maybe one of us should go out and look around." But he continued listening on the headphones for a while longer. Vanessa went back to her game.

Suddenly Addams shouted in the stillness. "Fuck, that's Ian! Ian!"

Of course Ian couldn't hear him. Addams whipped off the headphones and turned to the group. "He's telling us to come out," he said.

Everyone dropped what they were doing and scrambled to open the doors. A ladder along the edge of the sloping tunnel allowed them to climb back up, one at a time. The sliding door into the basement tunnel was open. Ian and Greg were in the tunnel, handing people down to the floor. The young men's faces were grim and sad. They did not speak until everyone was out.

"Trayden and Koster were shot down at the gate," said Ian shortly. "The kids got to the campsite, and they've all moved on now. Feds left yesterday. Greg and I have been hiding out here, trying to account for all the horses without getting caught."

Vanessa heard sobs break out around her as her companions were hit with grief and relief together. She felt obliged to hug Samika, who was standing next to her. Addams simply said, "Greg," and reached for the young man and held him wordlessly.

"They took their bodies away," Greg said, barely able to control his voice. "I didn't even get to say goodbye to them."

Keeping his arm around Greg, Addams faced the group. "Listen up, everyone," he said. "We must save this grief for later, and get somewhere safe as fast as we can. Feds will be watching this place, ready to swoop in as soon as they see someone, and they may have seen Ian and Greg already. We're going to grab a vehicle and get to a safe place. And I need to hold all the phones."

Vanessa suppressed her alarm. The others were bringing out phones and handing them over, so she thought she'd better go along, too.

"Of course I trust everyone here," Addams said, stuffing devices into his pockets. "But we've been compromised somehow, and I need to take you all somewhere that no one here knows about. It's not my call to reveal this location to anyone else, and I have to be able to guarantee secrecy. We need to stay out of sight for a while. And we need to get legal people here to take care of the horses."

"We hiked over to Williams' ranch with the bottle baby, and left it there," said Ian. "That's the only time we left the ranch. But they told us the roads all around here are crawling with cops. There are checkpoints on every road, and they're searching every vehicle."

"Well, that stinks," said Addams. "Especially because it's *us* they're looking for. So we need to stay off the roads as much as possible—take ranch roads and off-road. We'll get the transport from the garage. It'll be a tight fit, though."

What garage? thought Vanessa.

"We brought two ATVs," Ian said. "I think we can cram five on each." They were moving down the corridor as he said this, toward the trap door in the cottonwood grove. Ian, in the lead, stopped everyone just before the exit. "It's bad out there," he said.

"We know," said Dahlia softly. "We heard it happening."

July 20-21, 2218, Montana:

Marley and her group spent a week with Tomas and Shane, while the men contacted friends and arranged to drive them farther. They were respectable yunies and were not likely to be hassled driving a car, especially on a mag road. Tomas and Shane drove George, Marley, and the boys to two different homes for the night in two separate cars. The next day, those friends drove them in separate cars to a campground near the small town of Libby in the mountainous northwest corner of Montana.

◆ ◆ ◆

The country around Camp Biding Time was what Underground people called a "cool spot." Authorities were relaxed, and cared little about anyone's personal life. The small police departments of the sparsely populated towns of Libby and Eureka were careful not to hire anyone too enthusiastic about the law. On paper, everything was lawful, but in practice, people did pretty much whatever they wanted in the countryside around these towns.

The campground was owned and managed by two couples who were legally married to each other's spouses, with homes legally owned by the married couples. But the façade mostly ended there. They had seven naturally born children, four girls and three boys, raised in this remote little corner of the country virtually untouched by mainstream North American society.

Arriving just before dinner, Marley found herself beset by questions from all these children, the most open and friendly bunch of kids she had ever met.

"Calm down, all of you," said Ariella, the eldest at fifteen. "Let the girl catch her breath." Frederick wanted to show Marley some of his artwork, and Elanora wanted to show her a frog she'd just caught at the edge of the pond.

"We've had Railroaders coming through here as long as I can remember," said Ariella. "And we all just love new friends. We're a little envious, too, because everyone we meet is going to the Island, and we've never been there yet."

"We'll be going there, soon, though," said Brian, not even giving Marley a chance to ask a question. "Me, Bel, and Ari—we all want to go there to study and get awesome jobs."

"And we have zillions of friends there," said Belinda. "Because we make friends with everyone who comes through here, and we usually keep in touch with them after they get there."

Kevin, Jackson, and Benjamin arrived shortly after, and most of the kids ran over to introduce themselves, leaving Marley with Brian and Ariella. Marley watched anxiously, expecting Benjamin to shrink away from the friendly kids and cling to Kevin.

But he didn't. She was ready to hear Kevin say, "Ben doesn't talk," when the younger boy said, "Hi, I'm Benjamin."

"Would you like to hold my frog?" asked Elanora.

"Yes," Benjamin said, and they transferred the frog, taking great care not to squeeze it or let it jump away.

◆ ◆ ◆

At dinner, the newcomers tried to sort out who everyone was. Rosalie and Darwin were the parents of the four girls: Ariella, Belinda, Clarissa, and Elanora. Savannah and Aristo were the parents of the three boys: Brian, Derek, and Frederick.

The next morning, the camp kids took Marley and the boys out berry picking. Camp Biding Time nestled in prime huckleberry country, and they had arrived at the peak of the season. The camp children had been busy every day, bringing the bounty back to their moms, and taking some of it to Libby to sell to people who were eager to make jams, jellies, and wine.

Marley learned to recognize the ground-hugging, tangled bushes with reddish-green, oval leaves. She learned to look under the leaves for the drooping berries, and to sit down and take her time picking. At first she stuffed almost all of the plump, purple, sweet-tart berries into her mouth. She had never tasted huckleberries before. The kids came home smiling, with blue tongues and fingers, and plenty of berries in the buckets.

JULY 14, 2218, ADDAMS RANCH, SOUTH DAKOTA:

Though Vanessa had passionately hated the ranch house, even she was shocked at the thorough and deliberate annihilation of a place she had lived and slept. And despite having had ten days to accept the loss of their home, the ranch residents were freshly grieved by the utter devastation that now met their eyes. Rooms that had sheltered countless freedom-seekers now lay open to the sky—the dormitories, the gym, the game room—beams, furniture, and walls reduced to desolate heaps of grotesque, unrecognizable, blackened shapes, covered with gray ash as if dirty snow had fallen. The barn where generations of horses had been conceived, born, nursed, and groomed lay in wasted ruin like the remains of a giant's abandoned campfire under the merciless sun. Dahlia's face was wet with silent tears.

Five people crowded into each four-seat ATV and jolted over the rough prairie to a place Vanessa had not seen before. The garage had been built between hillocks and covered by the prairie, obscuring all traces from above. The door was painted in prairie colors, and Vanessa did not recognize it as a door until they were very close. The men jumped off the ATVs and opened up the broad door. Inside were dirt bikes, snowmobiles, and a larger transport vehicle. Addams started this up and drove it out, and the ATVs were put away.

"Jaden up front," Addams said. "Everyone else cram into the back."

As people began climbing into the vehicle, Vanessa saw Addams and Jaden consulting over a map book. She climbed into the back. Ian closed the tailgate and climbed over it. Vanessa waited in silence with the others for long minutes. What were they doing? Weren't they in a big hurry to get away?

Jaden appeared at the open back window with a bucket of paint and a brush.

"I'm closing this and blacking out the windows," he said. "Sorry, guys. This location is strictly need-to-know, you guys don't need to know, and Addams has to vouch for that. I'm only riding up there to navigate for him. It's gonna be a rough ride too—mostly off-road."

He shut the window over the tailgate, and Vanessa saw the brush sweeping black paint over the window. Vanessa wondered if she were in danger. No one was acting suspicious, but how would they act if they were? *Maybe they're as good at acting as I am,* she thought. She felt naked and vulnerable without her phone, or any idea where they were going.

Was Addams really taking these precautions only to preserve the secrecy of the hideout they were going to? He had said the group was compromised. If he suspected her, would he accuse her? He was acting calm, but she could see that his anger ran deep, and surely he was determined to figure out who was responsible for the deaths of his friends and the destruction of his home.

CHAPTER 47

◆ ◆ ◆

We all know that men have no control in the presence of naked girls and women. So in a society with men, modesty is protective as well as oppressive. But now, girls don't need that protection. Women and girls can control themselves.

–Democracy Online, Public bathing discussion, 2138

July 24, 2218, Camp Biding Time, Montana:

"A new boy has just arrived," Savannah shouted over the din in the dining room. Everyone present stopped talking and turned to her.

"He's from Ontario," she continued in a normal voice. "He's from a Natural community, like Halen. I want you all to be sensitive and nice."

Halen's and Marley's eyes lit up immediately.

A boy like Maddy, Marley thought.

As Savannah opened the door and motioned the boy in, Halen and Marley saw the look of culture shock on his face that they had both experienced themselves. This was his first look at a roomful of boys and girls together, the boys just blatantly being boys, like the boys in the camps—the boys in the porn movies.

Halen got up and went over to him immediately. He took his hand, and then impulsively gave him a hug. Marley could see the connection as Halen warmly welcomed the disconcerted young man. "I'm a pretty city boy, too," said Halen. "But if you want to fit in with these ugly fuckers, I can help you out. I'm Halen."

A huge smile broke out on the boy's face, and his deep brown eyes sparkled with a new light. "I was Jasmine. But I'm Jason now," he said.

Their hosts had prepared a big dinner of rice and beans, flavored with a few chicken legs, roasted potatoes, carrots, and cabbage—the only way they could afford to feed their growing crowd of growing young people. As Jason sat down for dinner, he was immediately plied with questions.

"Let him eat first, forsakes," Halen told the others.

Later, with a fire going in the stone fire pit in the middle of the room, Jason was pressed to tell his story. He was born into a Natural circle community near Toronto, Ontario. He knew a hidden boy a few years older, and one a few years younger, but none his own age. He loved all his circle sisters, sharing many interests with them, and he was usually the bestest of three or four girls at any given time.

But around the age of twelve, when he began to venture outside his own circle, the restrictions of his life began to chafe him. He longed to play sports, and take off his excessive clothing, but he knew very well that he couldn't.

"So I grew up with all these girls, and we all had besties, and it was all fine, until they started liking each other—and me—in a different way. Girls were crushing on me because they thought I was a girl, and that was awkward. I didn't even like the girls that way. I wanted a boy to love, and I watched boy porn and boy movies, and I was really lonely. My moms didn't want me to leave. They wanted me to just keep going as a girl, and a woman, study architecture like I wanted, and find a normal yunie to love. They thought I could pull it off with hormones and hair removal, and they just kept talking about that like it was a great idea. But I was going nuts being a girl and wanting to be around boys.

"I love babies and little kids, too. I was always babysitting the little girls in the circle. I thought they were the cutest damn things. And I found those movies of baby boys, too, and wished we had little boys in the circle. And I was reading all this subversive stuff, and thinking why the hell can't men have their own babies, too?"

"Our dads had their own babies," said Derek.

"Yeah," said Jason. "I was totally amazed when your mom told me that. I didn't think people could get away with that anywhere on the continent."

"This place is pretty special," said Belinda. "But it's also in the middle of nowhere."

"Anyway," Jason continued, "right about when I turned 16, I felt like I was going fucking crazy, for real. I just had to get to some place where I could be myself or I was gonna lose my mind."

"I know how that feels," said Halen.

"It just really sucks that I had to leave my moms and everything I was doing in school." Jason's voice had an edge of anger in it now. "Why don't men have the same rights as women? Yeah, I know all the crap they tell us—I've only heard it a million times at least—but it never made any sense to me." Then his voice took on the tone of a teacher. "Our roles are determined by nature. Women can't be men and men can't be women. Society will crash and die if we don't stay in our proper places. Blah, blah, blah. You guys know it all, right?"

Five heads around the fire nodded. For Marley, the term "men's rights" had always conjured up images of violence and abuse. It had never occurred to her that men could love babies as much as women did.

"Well," said Jason, poking around in the fire with a stick, "the subversives say that's all a load of matriarchal propaganda, and they just invented all of it to give women power over us. I don't want to *be* a woman, for godsakes. I just want the same rights as them. People just have to stop believing that crap. They kept telling me that boys are violent and aggressive, and dirty. And they couldn't even tell they were talking to one. But I'm not the least bit violent. At school, the mean girls used to bully me for being a Natural, but I never hurt them. I never wanted to hurt anyone. Everything they say about boys and men is total bunk."

Marley noticed that Kevin, flanked on both sides by his little brothers, was listening intently to Jason, and when Jason uttered these statements, he seemed to recede into himself and she thought she saw smoldering anger in his eyes.

"How did your moms take it when you decided to leave?" Marley asked.

"Pretty hard," said Jason. "They love me so much, but it's like they really couldn't understand what it felt like for me. Finally I convinced them that I was really suffering and going nuts, and I had to get away. So they got me on the Railroad. They cried for days. I did, too."

Marley felt the heart-hurt in those words. She had been at a parting like that, and the memory brought tears to her eyes.

"Did you come here all by yourself?"

"Yup. Stole my mom's car and ran away. I guess I shouldn't describe all the stops. Took about two weeks to get here."

Derek had gotten up and now stood behind Jason. He began pulling Jason's long, dark hair back from his face.

"Can we make you a boy, now?" he asked.

Jason laughed. "Damn, I'm not a real boy yet? I'm still a puppet? Well, go ahead. I want to be a real boy. I want to look like all of you."

Some of the camp children ran away and brought back scissors and boy clothes.

"Don't cut his hair," Marley admonished. When Jason looked crestfallen, she added, "They can cut it to your shoulders, and you can braid it up. That's what Halen's been doing. You can tuck it under a cap to look like the other boys, but you may still need to pass as a girl."

Then Marley hung back and watched the transformation. Thick brown locks fell to the ground, and Ariella's deft fingers cornrowed the remaining hair close to his head. Then several boys gently and respectfully helped Jason out of his long, modest dress into a shirt and shorts, like valets dressing a young lord. And then a few of them placed their hands on his bare arms in a reverent way as if to say without words: *You and your body are good.*

Jason was speechless and trembling. Only his moms had ever seen him in so little clothing. Marley looked up at Halen, and saw tears.

JULY 14, 2218, SOUTH DAKOTA:

Vanessa tried to keep her balance as the transport bumped and jolted over rough prairie and ranch roads, which were little better. She kept being jostled and thrown against the passengers on either side of her. There was nothing to hold on to, and the corrugated metal floor was supremely uncomfortable to sit on. Dahlia and Samika got queasy after an hour, and Samika would not stop crying. As the sun went down, the darkness in the back of the transport became total.

◆ ◆ ◆

When Vanessa felt the blessed smoothness of a real road under the wheels, she thanked the gods that Addams and Jaden had decided to take a real road in the dark. She was sure she had bruises all over her body. The ride seemed interminable, and having no way to measure time was making her crazy. At least it was smoother now. Occasionally she could see the glow of headlights through the painted windows.

She was startled by the sudden scream of sirens. A vehicle was speeding up close behind them, headlights sending in enough light that she could make out faces again. The faces were frightened. She felt the transport slow down, pull onto the shoulder, and stop.

Thank the gods. Thank the gods. My people are here. I have to keep my cover, though. Be scared. Don't show relief.

Doors slammed. Officers shouted, and flashlight beams shone through the black paint. Then tires squealed under her and the passengers tumbled back in a pile against the tailgate as the transport pulled away, accelerating faster than she thought it could. The vehicle rumbled and creaked at a speed it was not designed for. Then it slowed again, very quickly, and the five passengers slid back to the front. They were bumping over the rough again, very fast, and then came to a sudden stop. Vanessa heard the pursuing sirens come closer, pass, and fade into the distance down the road.

Fuck, fuck, fuck, Vanessa thought. *Don't panic. Don't burst into tears. Look relieved like the rest of them. Good thing it's dark in here.*

Thankfully Addams found another road instead of off-roading in the dark. Then came a turn, and a rougher road. And then they stopped again, slowly this time. Vanessa heard the two men get out. Jaden opened the back window and let the tailgate down.

"Gods, I'm so sorry," he said. "That must have been horrible."

Vanessa climbed out. An isolated farmhouse was visible in the moonlight. She could just make out dilapidated outbuildings, forlorn in the midst of abandoned cornfields long ago retaken by the prairie.

"We've got food and everything we need here," Addams said curtly. "I have to report to our contacts that we're all compromised for now. We're all dead in the water until we figure out what happened. I'm sure it's not any of us. But we all need to stay inside the house, and keep our eyes on each other at all times so that we can all vouch for each other. No going off alone. I know you all understand."

'I'm sure it's not any of us,' he'd said. But did he mean that? He had Vanessa's phone, and he would surely check through all the phones. She had no contacts listed, and she erased her history every time she made a call. That would not be suspicious; it was just normal Underground procedure.

JULY 26, 2218, CAMP BIDING TIME, MONTANA:

On a screaming hot summer day, the cool pond beckoned. The suggestion of a swim had barely left Belinda's lips before the kids were running toward the water, stripping off clothes and leaving them in the grass. Again, Marley had that feeling of being in an uncharted social wilderness. She had grown up with social nudity. So, apparently, had the boys from the boys' camps, and so had the free-spirited, unschooled camp children. But for Marley, there had never been boys around. And hadn't she been taught that the sight of a naked woman made hetero boys and men crazy and violent with lust? But the campground girls didn't seem at all hesitant or fearful.

They must have done this numerous times before, Marley thought. *That's all propaganda, right? Right?*

She shook off her fears and left her clothes in a small heap in the grass. She removed her locket so the photos inside wouldn't get wet, and ran for the water. The campground boys seemed unphased, but Kevin, Jackson, and Benjamin were staring frankly at Marley and the other girls. When she splashed into the water, Jackson asked very politely if he could touch her breast. She said "just once," and he did so, very gently.

"It's so *soft*," he said, eyes wide with wonder. Then he submerged himself, grinning.

Laughing, Marley turned to look for Halen. He and Jason were standing well back from the edge of the water with their clothes on, watching. She forgot about swimming for a minute while she tried to wrap her brain around how those boys must feel. Natural boys did not show their bodies, even at home—even in bed, apparently. All their lives, the fact that these boys were boys had been a deep, dangerous secret. Their lives had depended on keeping those *boy parts* under wraps.

To them, it must seem like we're all ripping out internal organs here, Marley thought. *Looks like fun, but we're all about to die.*

She splashed out of the pond and walked up to them. "Well, this is pretty weird, isn't it?" she said. They both just nodded, looking uncomfortable.

"It would be really dumb to say I know how you feel," she said. "I haven't had to hide my body all my life. So I really can't imagine. But we all know that you're boys here. You don't have to hide anymore." And suddenly, a practical solution occurred to her.

"Why don't you go in with your shorts on?" she said. "We can just dry them, for fuck's sake. You don't have to get naked to have fun. And maybe when you're in the water, it'll be easier to take them off."

So the two apostate Naturals went into the water, and took their shorts off below the surface, placing the wet shorts on a rock. Jackson and Derek, lacking Marley's empathy and tact, stole the shorts at the first opportunity, and ran shrieking out of the pond and about twenty feet up the sloping bank, challenging the boys to come out and retrieve them. Eventually Jason and Halen worked up the courage to do so. And so it all ended in laughter and play, and that social hurdle receded behind them.

CHAPTER 48

◆ ◆ ◆

Evolution demands that a male spread his genes as far and
wide as possible. The more obstacles a man can overcome,
the more likely he is to pass on his genes. A woman's
resistance is just another obstacle to overcome. Every
fertile male has rape built into his genetic makeup.

—*The Writings of Iolanda Voorhees*, 2064

July 27, 2218, farmhouse in South Dakota:

"Dinner's ready," Jaden called.

Vanessa was going nuts. She'd been cooped up with these people for two
weeks now, sharing 20th century bathroom facilities and canned food. It was
better than the underground shelter, at least, where they were all in one room.
In this big old three-story farmhouse, the ten of them could disperse to different rooms and have some space between them, though they always remained
in pairs.

The place seemed designed especially to get on her nerves: the peeling
paint, faded wallpaper, cracked and broken linoleum in the kitchen, the
cracked and missing tiles in the bathroom. The electrical wiring had been
replaced—a few years ago, perhaps—but the holes in the walls had not been
repaired, or the fixtures replaced. And the underlying charm of the antique
house only increased the torture. She searched the house for supplies and

tools, but found only a small stash of unopened paint and unused brushes. She busied herself doing what she could with that, but it wasn't much. This was like a special hell for decorators.

"Beef stew again," she said, with mock enthusiasm, sliding into a chair at the kitchen table.

"And canned corn and canned beans," Jordan chimed in.

"And don't forget the canned peaches for dessert," said Jaden. "Always a big surprise."

Vanessa flashed her best smile at the young men. Jaden and Jordan were always friendly, but despite her subtle efforts to charm him, she could not get Jaden to give up the location of the phones or the key.

"Addams has a signal detector, anyway," Jaden said. "And you really don't want to cross him now, after what happened. I'll talk to him about letting people make calls to families some time—we could all do it together."

Most of them politely avoided her, and she could not tell what they were thinking. Now, Jaden sat down next to her.

"How long are we going to stay here?" Vanessa whispered. "Has he figured anything out?"

Jaden shook his head, looking worried. "He's going crazy trying," he said.

Addams strode in, and the others went quiet. He'd been moody and angry continually, for at least the last week, muttering to himself and growling at everyone else. Even the Jays were walking on eggshells around him. He spooned food onto a plastic plate and left the room with it. Most of the others did that, too.

◆ ◆ ◆

Later that night, after everyone was in bed, Ian and Greg crept quietly into Vanessa's room. Ian woke her and shushed her, sitting on the side of her bed.

"I stole the key from Jaden, and got our phones," Ian said quietly. "Jaden won't go against Addams no matter what. But we're going to make some calls. We need to get closer to town where there're other signals so Addams can't tell. We're gonna sneak away in the transport, use the GPS to find the closest town, and call our families. And get someone else from the Underground to come talk to Addams. He's losing it. We're all afraid of him. You want to come along?"

"Yes," Vanessa whispered fervently.

"It's our watch, and we just checked, and everyone else is asleep," said Greg. "Just meet us downstairs—we don't know which phone is yours. And for godssakes be quiet."

"I'll be right down," said Vanessa, sitting up.

At last, she thought. She slipped into her clothes and left the room, pulling the door quietly closed behind her. She crept downstairs, testing each stair for creakiness before she stepped on it. She found her phone among the collection in the cupboard and slipped it into her pocket. It felt very good to have it there again. Stealthily, the three of them left the house, taking care with the squeaky floors and the sticky front door.

JULY 28, 2218, CAMP BIDING TIME, MONTANA:

As the heat of the Montana summer melted one day into the next, the kids had to go higher up the mountain to find huckleberries. They took ponies barebacked into the pond, and Marley learned that ponies could swim.

She practiced meditation daily to keep herself living in the present moment, where everything was fine. She tried let go of the grief and worry, the dangers ahead, the haunting faces of her dear friends who were imprisoned or dead, and she might never know which. Her days were busy and happy. But at night sometimes, as she lay curled up with Halen, they dampened their pillows with tears. Marley had not seen the tanks coming. She had not seen the place they'd called home razed, burned, still smoldering under the broad blue sky. It all seemed unreal to her sometimes.

"Would it hurt less if we knew what happened?" Marley whispered. "Would it hurt less to know they're all dead than to wonder like this?"

◆ ◆ ◆

Benjamin was spending more time away from Kevin with the younger boys. Derek, Benjamin, and Jackson spent their days mostly outdoors, exploring the forest-covered mountain, fishing, swimming, and building a new tree fort. On rainy days, they played electronic games and chess and cards. Derek was partial to science experiments that made things burn and explode.

Marley was happy to see Benjamin bouncing back. Perhaps a scar was growing around his bad memories, encapsulating them, protecting the rest of his mind. She saw a bright, happy personality emerging, and she thought, *I'm meeting the real Benjamin at last.*

But Kevin was often alone now. He did not participate in things of his own accord. Marley took care to invite him to go swimming, berry picking, exploring, or even just to watch a movie. When not invited, he would wander off by himself and practice target shooting with a .22 that belonged to Savannah.

JULY 30, 2218, CAMP BIDING TIME, MONTANA:

Jason and Marley got along famously. On long walks, they compared their experiences of Toronto and Fair City—the schools, the girls, the Naturals. And he asked her about Kevin, and what had happened to him. She told the terrible story, as far as she knew it. And then they spoke of other things. Coming back, laughing and chattering, from one of these walks, she noticed Halen looking grumpy.

"Come for a walk with me," he said. So she did. They wandered down the trail together, into the shady forest.

"You don't *like* him, do you?" Halen asked.

"Of course not, silly," said Marley, laughing. "Wouldn't do me much good anyway, would it? He's like a girlfriend, like a bestie. You know he's had nothing but girlfriends all his life. He's attracted to boys, but not used to them at all. That's pretty weird for him."

"You just seem so connected," Halen said. "It makes me jealous. Makes me want to pull you away from him and kiss you, a lot."

"Oh, you're silly," Marley said. Then she threw her head back, looking up at him, her dark eyes sparkly, teasing. "Catch me," she said, and took off running down the forest trail. He chased her, caught her easily, and pulled her to the ground, panting with desire. His hands went under her shirt, finding her breasts, caressing—her nipples were hard. She was wet. She felt a sudden urgency she had not felt before. She grabbed at his hair, pulling his head toward her, roughly, wanting to explore his mouth with her tongue. *Animalistic. Shameful. Man-lover.* Shame swept through her as she felt the strength of his body, his arms, his strong hands moving urgently down her body, finding her wetness. He was pushing his hard male organ hard against her, like he wanted to drive it right into her. And suddenly he was everything she had learned to fear—the strong, violent man, controlling, forcing, raping. She recoiled, suddenly struggling, pushing him away, frightened.

"Marley! Marley, I'm sorry. It's okay. It's okay. Don't be scared." He was looking into her panicked eyes, backing off, but stroking her hair. "Don't be scared of me. It's just me. Just Maddy."

"Oh, Maddy," she said. She was weeping with the confusion of her feelings. "My Maddy. My Halen. It's just, suddenly, you were a *man*. It felt like you wanted to rape me."

"Not a man," he said. "Not a man. Just your bestest friend."

July 27, 2218, farmhouse in South Dakota:

It felt wonderful to be out of that house. Vanessa cradled her precious phone in her hands as Greg drove the transport several miles down the dark dirt road. The nearest town was quite far away, but now houses began to appear along the road.

"We should be out of range of the signal detector," Greg said. "But these houses will cover our tracks if we're not." He pulled over and stopped, and they all made text calls.

Vanessa had just hit send when Ian, sitting next to her, deftly whipped the phone out of her hand.

"Sorry, Darlene," he said. "We've been working undercover here, and we're bringing in this whole cell."

"What?" said Vanessa, in complete shock.

"We're feds. We've been in deep cover on that ranch for two years, with Tray and Koster."

"Prove it," said Vanessa. Her mind flashed back, searching for clues in her memories of Tray, Koster, Ian, and Greg. Why would Barilla not tell her there were other feds at the ranch? Did Barilla not know? Was that why the timing of the raid had gone awry?

Greg laughed. "Well, we're not carrying ID's," he said. "That would just get us killed. So what does her message say, Ian?"

Ian read the message: "I'm okay. Love you and miss you. I miss the dog, too. Give him a biscuit for me."

"Cute," Greg said.

Ian was looking at where it was sent. "Hey, that number looks like … I thought your family was in New York. This looks like one of our numbers. Fuck, Greg, that's a fed number. I think she's a fed, too."

They were both staring right at her, and Vanessa's mind was whirling.

"Why did you bring me out here with you?" she demanded.

"We thought you'd come, because you kept harping on how much you wanted to call your moms. We wanted a hostage for security. Are you working out of New York?"

Vanessa said nothing. Barilla would be getting her coded message and her location. Local feds and cops would be there soon, and then she would know for sure if these men were telling the truth.

Who did they call? she wondered. *If they're not feds, and they think I just called the cops on them, they wouldn't be just sitting here, waiting for them to show up. Trayden, Koster, Greg, and Ian—all undercover on the ranch, way ahead of me and Barilla.* But her mind was still whirling, trying to make sense of it or find a hole in their story. She wasn't about to start chatting freely with them.

"Okay, don't talk," said Greg. "But we've called it in, and they should be here in half an hour to meet us. Then we'll all go bring in the rest of them, including you, if you're really one of them."

"So Trayden and Koster were working with you?" Vanessa asked.

"They let the feds in, and we let these people think they were dead," said Greg. "We arranged the raid after you brought in Gonzalez."

"So you got the people at the campsite?" Vanessa asked. "Why didn't you all just arrest everyone right out of the shelter?"

"Wanted to see what Addams' next move would be. What else he might lead us to. And he brought us here. Always good to locate their hideouts."

They sat and waited. Headlights appeared from the direction of the town. Several cars were approaching, the off-road-capable type frequently used in this part of the country—six of them. They swerved off the road, making a circle around their vehicle, illuminating it with the headlights and blinding the occupants.

"Everyone out of the car, hands where we can see them," said a voice over a bullhorn.

The three of them got out of the vehicle, showing their hands, and Vanessa strained her eyes to see something beyond the glaring headlights. She heard doors opening, and saw some flashlight beams added to the light from the cars. Then she heard the popping of stunners, and closed her eyes, bracing for a stunner shot.

Too many shots for her to count fired within seconds, but none hit her, and she heard grunts, and bodies falling to the ground all around her. Her eyes flew open. Ian and Greg had grabbed her hands, and were handcuffing them behind her back. Flashlights were on the ground, beams illuminating the grass in various directions.

Black-cloaked figures stepped into the light, holstering stunners. Someone was killing the headlights, and now Vanessa could see bodies on the ground beside the cars.

One of the black-cloaked people threw back his hood. "Well done, guys," Addams said, nodding at Ian and Greg.

"Those two are undercover agents," said Vanessa desperately. "They called us in."

"No, they didn't. *You* did," said Addams. All signs of craziness were gone now. "Give it up, Darlene. We all thought it was you. We just had to find a way to make you blow your cover."

"How did you even get here?" Vanessa couldn't help asking in her confusion.

"We had cars out in the barn. You might have noticed if you weren't so busy bitching about the linoleum."

Dahlia checked under Vanessa's clothes for a key pouch, and found nothing. Everyone from the farmhouse was there, and Vanessa looked from face to face, seeing naked hatred now in every pair of eyes. Raw fear buzzed through her body.

"Can't we just kill the bitch now, Addams?" she heard Greg say as Adams pushed her into the back of a car. The door slammed, and she did not hear the answer.

CHAPTER 49

◆ ◆ ◆

Espie is five years old. How pretty and full of life she is. I long
for the world to come back together for her—for the sexes to
come back together. Will she ever know and love a teenage boy?
My precious little Bonito will be ten next year, and I will have
to part with him, as the other mothers have parted with their
boys. He is one of the very last of the natural-born boys.

—MARLENA MADISON, UNPUBLISHED JOURNALS, 2072

JULY 31, 2218, CAMP BIDING TIME, MONTANA:

WHEN EVERYONE GATHERED FOR LUNCH, Rosalie relayed the short message
she had received by Underground messaging. "Trayden and Koster were killed
in the raid," she said. "The others are alive and in hiding."

Well, now we know, Marley thought. She served herself a bowl, and went
outside to eat and process this information. Kevin was outside, too, sitting
under a tree by himself. She walked over to sit and eat with him.

"Beans and rice again," she said. "Who'd a thought?"

"We should complain to the management of this railroad," Kevin said,
with his familiar brief half smile. "We're not getting the service we paid for."

Marley smiled back. His sense of humor was still there, just not very
lively. More like an old habit.

I'm just meeting the real Benjamin, she thought. *Will I ever meet the real Kevin?*

"I wish I could say something to make you happy again," said Marley.

"Nothing to say," Kevin said. "I lost everything that was important to me. I don't really have any reason to live now. But here I am, living."

"Benjamin's doing better. Not clinging to you all the time now. You were there when he needed you. You saved their lives—Jackson and Benjamin and George."

"I'm glad that I'm of use to people. I guess that's all I have now."

"It's something, right? Something to live for every day, to be of use to someone. To make dinner for people, feed the ponies, weed the garden. And maybe a blue sky and sunshine, and a swim in the pond. Can you live for those things, maybe? Just one day at a time?"

"I guess that's what I'm doing. Or … not. It's not a conscious choice, to go on living. My heart just keeps beating."

Jason came over. "Is this private? Or may I join you?"

"Have a seat," said Marley.

He sat cross-legged on the ground, facing Kevin and Marley. Two tan, beautiful, dark-eyed boys, Marley thought. But what different lives they had led. "You've heard my story," Jason said. "Why don't you tell me yours?"

"It's not a good story," said Kevin shortly. "I've told it once."

"Some parts are good, aren't they?"

"How the *fuck* would you know?"

"I've heard your story. I just want to hear you tell it."

"Why? So you can watch me re-live all the fucking hell?"

"Maybe. You hate it, but maybe that helps you heal. And remembering the good stuff might help you heal, too."

"I'm not going to *heal*. Stop talking like a fucking shrink, you pampered asshole."

Marley had never heard this kind of anger or rudeness from Kevin before. What did he have against Jason?

"Okay, I get it. I had a soft life, lots of luxuries. So did Melissa here, and Halen. And we still had good reasons to get away from it. You got to grow up with other boys. You got to go camping with them, and fishing, and swimming. You had men in your life. You had a beautiful lover."

"*Had*," Kevin spat at him. "Is that supposed to make me feel better, that I had all that? All that good stuff I can't go back to? I'll never see my friends again, and my fathers, and I'll never see Gerry again ... and I let him die. I didn't save him, and I didn't save Axel. That little boy died in agony. And all for what? What they say about men is *true*. You think it's not because you haven't seen it. You haven't felt the rage. Killed people. But it's true. Men are brutal, violent, bloodthirsty *animals*."

Kevin looked up from the grass and right into Jason's eyes for the first time, and his eyes burned with baleful anger. "I know because I *am* one."

"Kevin—" Marley began, but Jason stopped her with a look.

He pushed Kevin roughly, rocking him back, and said, "Show me, you little pisshead." And Kevin sprang up of the ground and attacked him, bowling him over onto the grass, and landing punches on Jason's face and body.

Marley jumped up with a shriek, and the other people outside turned to look. Marley had seen girls in a serious fight, but never boys. It scared her. Lips and noses were bleeding, and they didn't seem to notice. They were really *damaging* each other.

They scrambled up, threw punches, knocked each other down, and grappled on the ground. Halen and two older men ran over, grabbed the boys' arms, and pulled them away from each other. Both boys were breathing hard and wearing a lot of each other's blood. Kevin struggled and fought the restraining arms for a minute, and then gave up.

"I think," Jason gasped. "I think we should go for a run. You want to run with me?"

Kevin nodded, panting.

"Okay, let go of us, you guys," said Jason to the men holding them. Darwin, George, and Halen released them. "Last one to the hollow pine's a dirty het," said Jason, and they both took off sprinting toward the track that looped through the forest.

Halen went to Marley, whose eyes were stinging with tears. "Are *you* okay?" he asked.

"I'm okay," she said. "I just don't really understand what happened." Her lip was trembling. "But Jason just made that happen. He pissed him off on purpose. And it may have been a good thing. Poor Jason just took a beating, though—I don't think he knows how to fight."

"Is that why you're crying?" Halen asked.

"I don't know. But he totally asked for it. He was baiting Kevin until he snapped. I can't stand that Kev is in so much pain."

"I know," said Halen.

About an hour later, Kevin and Jason were back at the house, exhausted from several laps around the track. They'd taken a dip in the pond to wash the blood off, bruises were beginning to darken on their faces, and one of Jason's eyes was swelling shut. Darwin did some first aid on them, matter-of-factly, and no one asked any questions.

Jason and Kevin went for long runs through the woods every day after that. They also gathered wood and started chopping, stacking it up high against the cold winter. Marley watched them swinging axes—shirts discarded in the sun, sweating, and growing stronger and tanner every day as the wood pile grew.

The cuts healed and the bruises faded, and occasionally, in fleeting, unguarded moments, Kevin laughed.

July 28, 2218, South Dakota:

"Fed jackets, ID's, pistols, stunners, anything else useful into the trunk of this car," said Addams, indicating the cop car in which Vanessa was imprisoned. Everyone worked quickly gathering those items.

"Cops' phones go into their own cars so they'll be traced together," said Addams. "We'll drive these six cars about five miles in six different directions. Undergrounders are on standby to pick us up. Take a wheel off the cop car and take it along. Toss it out at least a mile away. They won't be getting any calls from these people until they wake up and walk somewhere.

"Maya, Samika, and Carlos, you're driving the transport, farm car, and a cop car back to the farm. Hide them in the barn. Drive out in the cop car and ditch it. Everyone send me the code when you're safe. We're heading for BB."

By sunrise, Dahlia and Addams had received all the coded messages. The Jays, Samika, Maya, Carlos, Ian, and Greg were all safe under various Underground roofs. Addams and Dahlia had ditched the cop car, but they did not take time to remove a wheel. Addams wished he could just slash it, but on the continent, air-filled tires were unheard of. He transferred Vanessa into the Undergrounder's car, gagged her, and the three of them hid in the back. The Undergrounder was driving them all to Belligerent Beef Ranch in central Montana.

August 1, 2218, Camp Biding Time, Montana:

Marley had tagged along on a shopping trip into Libby with Savannah, Rosalie, and Ariella. She told the women about her mission to teach camp boys to pass as girls.

"I haven't had a chance to go shopping since I thought of it," she said. "We mostly worked on speech and manners because we didn't have a lot of stuff at the ranch."

"But speech and manners are the most important, I would think," said Rosalie. "They need time to sink in. And there's not usually a girl available to teach them."

The women perused the shelves, happily picking out temporary tattoos and nail colors. Rosalie piped up again, suddenly. "We should record lessons that Undergrounders can access online. They wouldn't need a city girl then. They could use the time when they're holed up in a house recuperating, or when they're traveling with nothing to do."

"That's brilliant," said Marley.

◆ ◆ ◆

That night, Marley and Halen snuggled into their bed in a tiny private cabin barely bigger than the bed itself. Halen had overcome his shyness, and Marley loved to look at him, all of him, in the light of a hurricane candle in a sconce on the wall. She blew out the candle and got into bed with him.

"Mad Halen?"

"What, Little Fat Boy?"

"You know, um—what happened in the woods? I talked to Rosalie about it."

"Did you? I talked to Darwin."

She laughed softly, nervously. "Oh, did you?" she said. "What did Darwin say?"

Halen didn't answer. He was too busy kissing her neck, and cupping her breast, softly teasing her nipple. Marley felt the heat rising inside her.

"I want to try the mating thing," she whispered. "Rosalie says it's a nice thing. And I think I actually want it, too."

"Really? Do you?" said Halen. "It's okay if you don't. But Darwin said if I went in very slow and gentle, it wouldn't hurt you. And it would help if you orgasmed first."

Marley moaned as his mouth moved down her body, and he brought her to a wild, whimpering climax. "I want to try it now," she gasped. "I want to feel you inside me."

She felt his hard organ pressing against her, and she reached down to guide him in. Slowly. Gently. It hurt a little, but she wanted it, and she opened herself to him.

"Oh, *gods*, Marley," he gasped into her hair, and his arms tightened around her. "This is the best feeling *ever*."

"It's good, it's good, it's good," she said. And then Marley laughed, happily, with relief at the banishment of her fear and the discovery of something wonderful. Halen's gold-flecked eyes were dazed with pleasure as he captured her laughing mouth and stopped her talking. And she knew now, in her body and soul, that this love was a very good thing.

CHAPTER 50

◆ ◆ ◆

Some day heterosexuality will be completely eradicated, and all this
subversion will drift away like smoke from an extinguished fire.

–Aspera Vas Cortine, *Inaugural Address*, 2103

July 29, 2218, Belligerent Beef Ranch, Montana:
Addams passed under the square archway of Belligerent Beef Ranch. At
the center of the arch, the huge face of a horned bull glowered down at the car
with heavy eyebrows pulled down low over angry eyes. But at the ranch house,
they were warmly welcomed by old friends. Persephone and Garudi had been
hard at work turning an unused freezer room into a cell for Vanessa. They had
drilled through a wall to install ventilation, and driven to town to purchase
a large piece of carpeting that almost covered the concrete floor. They'd furnished the cell with a comfortable bed, an armchair, a portable commode, and
a bookshelf full of books.

"We tried to make this comfortable," Persephone said to Vanessa. "I do
hope you won't try to use anything in here as a weapon or a tool of escape,
because it would be a shame to take any of this away. I'll bring you some dinner in a few minutes."

Vanessa just nodded. She was locked in and left alone.

Then Dahlia and Addams sat down for dinner with their host and hostess.

"Thank you so much for doing this, dear friends," said Dahlia. "I hope nothing bad comes to you because of it."

"We don't get much heat here," her friend Persephone assured her. "And you know we want to be here for you in times of trouble. Whatever comes, comes."

"I feel like I can relax for the first time since the raid," said Dahlia, and tears stood in her eyes. "It was so, so hard, spending all that time closed up with that woman, knowing what she was, but acting like I didn't know. I feel like I've been performing on stage all this time. Bottling up my grief because I couldn't bear to show it in front of her."

"You can grieve now," said Persephone's husband, Garudi. "We don't need you to be good company. We just want to give you whatever you need."

◆ ◆ ◆

Over the next week, the other members of the group found transportation and they all reconvened at Belligerent Beef Ranch. Gathering at the big dining room table, they drank a toast to the escape of George and the young ones, shared memories of Trayden and Koster and the ranch they had loved, and shed many tears, together and alone.

Greg had gone quiet. He had suppressed his feelings and played his part during the past weeks, and now he slid into a quiet, deep depression over the loss of his twin and his lover, and the life and home they had all shared. Ian, who had grown up with Trayden, also felt this loss deeply, and could hardly bear to speak of his camp brother. Garudi offered to put them to work, and they agreed, thankful for a distraction. Most hands on the ranch were busy with haying. Garudi put Ian and Greg to work on horseback, moving cows and calves into different pastures, and checking and mending fences.

Addams did the work of communicating with the Underground, making sure that anyone who could have been compromised by Darlene was aware of it and took precautions. Infiltrators like her were their biggest danger.

"We have to just kill her," said Jaden hotly, releasing anger that had brewed for weeks. "She got two of our friends killed. And who knows how many others are imprisoned or even dead because of her. And she would do it again and again. We should kill her and publicize it as a warning to others. People should be terrified to attempt infiltration. It's the only way to stop it."

Not to mention that she charmed you and played you, Addams thought. Jaden's crush on the girl had not escaped his notice.

"We only kill in self-defense," he growled. "I understand what you're saying, Jay. But we don't want to put any truth into that terrorist bullshit they say about us."

"It *is* self-defense," said Jaden. "And defense of others. Just because she's not killing anyone *right now*—"

"And she has others do it *for* her," Jordan added.

"We can keep her for a while so they wonder where she is," Addams said. "We can publicize everything about her so she'll never be able to work under cover again. We can demand the names of other informants for her release."

"But what about everything else she knows, though?" argued Jaden. "We traced her back to where she started. But she was part of the Railroad for what, two years? She could still compromise lots of good people and places, especially now her cover is blown and she has nothing to lose. We can't afford to release her and have her talking."

"You're right," Addams said. "You're absolutely right. But I don't want anyone in the Underground killing anyone in cold blood. So what do we do with her then? Keep her prisoner forever?"

"You think she doesn't deserve that?" Jaden growled. "I'm sure lots of people are stuck in work camps for the rest of their lives because of her, and two good friends are dead because of her. Dead is forever, isn't it?"

AUGUST 5, 2218, CAMP BIDING TIME, MONTANA:

One evening, when all the family and guests were gathered for dinner, Savannah announced some good news. All the other boys were now safely on the Island. The survivors of the raid were in a safe place as well.

"The one called Darlene was an infiltrator," said Savannah. "She has been uncovered and deactivated."

Darlene, Marley thought. *All that time.* Anger welled up in her as she remembered Darlene being so friendly and sweet, and sharing confidences with her. *Two-faced, lying, evil bitch.*

"What does 'deactivated' mean?" she asked.

"I don't know," Savannah said, frowning. "The message didn't say. Infiltrators have been killed before now, but I don't think Addams would do that. We have lists of dangerous people, with fingerprints, pictures, DNA and all that. Undergrounders can use those to check people out, and it helps. But Darlene could do a lot of damage with what she already knows. I'm thinking he's keeping her somewhere secure."

JULY 29, 2218, BELLIGERENT BEEF RANCH, MONTANA:

Vanessa looked up from the book she was reading as Addams entered her spacious concrete cell.

"Are you going to do the right thing and let me go?" she demanded.

"No," Addams said brusquely. "You should know that a lot of people want you dead. They want to make you an example and a warning to others like you. And when I think about Tray and Koster, I want to kill you, too. But killing in cold blood goes against my ethics, and I won't do it. But we can't let you go, either. The only alternative seems to be keeping you here forever. You're a grave danger to a lot of innocent people."

"It's my job," said Vanessa, calmly, with a hint of condescension. "And I'm not a danger to the innocent—only the guilty."

"Two very good young men were killed in that raid," said Addams with tightly controlled anger. "And many more were put in grave danger of death or life in a work camp. And my family is grieving."

"Because you're all *criminals*," said Vanessa. She found Addams' attitude alarming and confusing. "You all *chose* to break the law, and you all knew what you were doing and what the consequences could be. Even the kids. They all knew what they were doing was wrong: running away from their camps, indulging in hetero sex—arrogant teenagers spitting in the face of the greatest society that has ever existed. And now you're going to kidnap a person for enforcing the law? Are you really that crazy? You're all working to destroy our society, and I'm just doing my job to protect it."

"Spare me the philosophy," said Addams. "I've heard the rationale before. I'm just really sorry that you believe in that crap so strongly that it makes you dangerous to innocent people. I've devoted my life to helping people find freedom and happiness. And your beliefs make you a danger to those people."

Addams paused for a few moments as yet another wave of grief and rage rolled through him. He focused on breathing. This delicate little woman sitting in front of him was deadly as a viper on the loose. But here, now, he could snap her little neck with his hands. He breathed. Vanessa watched as he mastered his feelings, her fascination spiked with raw fear. In that moment, her life hung on that mastery.

"You really believe you're preserving something good," said Addams. "And maybe it's not your fault you believe that, but you're operating on false ideas. Bad ideas hurt people."

Vanessa's eyes were still fixed on his face. She wished to all the gods that he were just a ranting, raving, terrorist lunatic. His control was somehow enraging. And the way he saw himself and her, as if she were pitifully misguided and he—this *man*—were a defender of the innocent. Fear grew inside her that he really meant all this, and would never let her out of here because he simply could not see her as she saw herself: the defender of goodness and order in an almost-perfect society.

"You're just a *man*," she said hotly, her fear and frustration bringing on a surge of anger. "How dare you talk as if you're superior to me? You just want the old days back so you can dominate women and rape them and murder them as you please. You just want all the violence and poverty and starvation of the past. You want to see women suffer in childbirth."

"No," said Addams. "No, I don't. But I think there's a better way than this—a way that doesn't sacrifice the freedom and happiness of so many. And if I turned you loose, I'd be responsible for all the death and grief you would cause. We'll talk again."

And with that, he left her.

AUGUST 8, 2218, CAMP BIDING TIME, MONTANA:

Rosalie took Marley into her office and set her up to send an untraceable message to Mama Sue.

Marley pulled out her locket from under her shirt and opened it. Mama Sue and Mama Jo smiled at her from the locket. She wished she could tell Mama Sue all about her adventures and her new friends.

Mama Sue always listened to me, she thought. *I never thought she was really interested, but she listened. I do miss her. I wonder if she misses me?*

Mama Sue -
    How are you doing? I miss you. Maddy and I are in a very
safe and lovely place. I have not got to Mama Jo yet.
    Love, Marley

Then Rosalie went to a deeper level and set her up to audiochat with her friends on the Island. The Underground had various levels of encryption and access for different levels of trust.

"Okay, let's see who's here now," said Rosalie. "I told them four o'clock, their time."

"Hey, guys. It's Melissa," said Marley, wishing she could see their faces.

"Melissa! This is James. Peter's rounding up Kyle and Stuart. We're loving it here. There isn't just one island—there's lots and lots of them. Some of them are attached together with walkways. Some of them are big tall ships with a million rooms in them, and there's huge flat barges, with palm trees on them, or cows. Okay, the guys are here now. Say hi to Melissa, guys."

The other boys greeted her, and James continued, "We've only been on a few of them. We're living in rooms on one of the big ships. People drive around in little open cars and they ride bicycles a lot. There's awesome fruit and the coolest flowers."

"There are girls everywhere," Peter broke in. "They're all so pretty and so nice. Not disgusted or scared of us at all. I'm in love with four of them— maybe five now. My favorite one is whichever one I'm talking to."

Marley laughed.

"Ty is off with some boy he likes," said James. "It's so amazing here. People just tell you if they're normal or hetero or *both*. Did you know people can be both? And we've seen women with babies inside them, and men with beards. And best of all, I found my friends—the ones I thought died last summer, and the summer before. They're *here*."

"Wow," said Marley. "That's the awesomest, happiest thing ever. We're doing well here, too. This place is gorgeous, with the glossiest people. We're doing fun things and just working on getting over all the horrible stuff that happened."

"Us, too," said James soberly. "We were all sick about it when we got that news. Fucking Darlene. So little and pretty. It's really creepy to think that someone who seems so nice could be completely different inside."

"I know," said Marley. The conversation paused as they pondered this.

"We have a new boy with us, called Jason," Marley continued. "He's been really good for Kevin. I can't quite tell if they're just good buddies or crushies. Ben's talking again, and hanging with the boys that live here. And Jack's just fine. And Halen and me are fine, too. But we really miss all you guys."

"I'm sure you'll be here soon, Mel," said Kyle.

"Yes," said Marley. "Yes, I'm sure I will."

◆ ◆ ◆

Marley and Halen walked out into the warm, peaceful twilight of Camp Biding Time.

"I'm so glad I dared to come with you, Halen," said Marley.

"I'm so glad you dared to have lunch with a weirdo Natural," said Halen. "I wanted to kiss you right then, you know."

"Did you?" said Marley, laughing. "Well, you can kiss me right now."

And he kissed her in the slanting evening light.

END OF BOOK ONE

INSIDE FENCES
ESCAPE FROM ENLIGHTENMENT BOOK TWO

◆ ◆ ◆

2205, PACIFIC OCEAN OFF LANGARA:

A LARGE COMMERCIAL FISHING VESSEL cut through the waters of the northern Pacific, far out from its port in Langara, the northernmost of the Queen Charlotte Islands. The ocean reflected a deep blue sky, in which a tiny speck had appeared, and was growing larger.

A dark, slender man and a beautiful woman leaned on a deck railing, eyes fixed on the approaching speck.

"It's our helicopter, Jo," the man whispered. "That's the last vehicle we have to travel in. We're almost there."

"Imagine us, walking around, being a couple right out in the open," she said. The wind whipped her straight, light-brown hair around her face, which glowed with happy excitement.

The sound of helicopter blades cutting through the air now reached their ears, but they heard movement behind them as well.

Jo turned, and her heart sank sickeningly at the sight of two large, tall women, one blonde and one dark-haired, wearing fishing crew uniforms, but with holstered stunners on their hips. Infiltrators. Undercover agents.

"Are you waiting for that helicopter?" the blonde one asked in a sneering tone.

"No, just watching it," said Jo, with all the calm she could muster.

"Hand over your IDs," the other, dark-haired agent demanded.

The couple took out the fake IDs they had acquired in South Dakota ten days ago, newly minted to match the new hair colors they had obtained at the same time. The blonde agent scrutinized the IDs, comparing them to the device in her hand, scrolling a little.

"You're not part of this crew," she said. "And you're both under arrest." She brought out handcuffs, while the dark-haired agent pulled her stunner and held it trained on the couple.

"We're guests," said Jo. "The captain invited us to go along."

"You look like a dirty *het* couple to me," said the agent with the stunner. "Waiting for that helicopter to take you to your imaginary hetero utopia. Turn around, now. Hands on the rails. If your story checks out, you have nothing to worry about, right?"

Oh, not now, not now, Jo thought. *We've come so far, and we're almost there.* But she turned and put her hands on the rails. If she didn't, the one with the stunner would just render her unconscious.

The helicopter came closer.

"Jorga, if that bird gets in range, give it lethal fire," said the blonde agent, clipping a cuff around the man's left wrist. She yanked his arm down behind his back and cuffed the other wrist. Then she reached for the woman.

Jo trembled as the agent grabbed her wrist and clicked on the cuff. She wanted to bolt, but there was nowhere to go. She heard two rapid stunner pops behind her, and felt a painful yank as her captor fell unconscious with a firm grip on the cuff attached to the one on her wrist. She whipped around again to see a crew member she knew as "Gin" holstering a stunner inside her shirt.

"Damn infiltrators," Gin spat. "I thought these two were a little off from the start."

The pilot had hovered out of pistol range, but now brought the helicopter in close. A rope ladder dropped, unrolling as it descended almost to the water.

"He can't climb the ladder," said Jo desperately, indicating her partner's cuffed wrists.

"Hold on," said Gin. She disappeared into a doorway. Jo waited tensely beside her man. The helicopter hovered, beating air down on their heads. The ladder hit the railing, and Jo grabbed it and pulled it over.

"Get on the ladder—I'll hold you on," Jo said frantically to her partner.

"But I can't climb up into it," he said. "We can't ride all the way hanging on the ladder."

"I'll keep my arms around you. Climb with your feet. Those two will wake up," she urged, fearfully eyeing the unconscious agents.

Gin reappeared with bolt cutters. "Get up there, now. I got this," she barked at Jo. As Jo obeyed, Gin pressed hard with the cutters, severing the chain that connected the cuffs. "We'll get the bracelets off later," said Gin, as the man swung his arms free.

"Thank you, thank you, thank you," he said, grabbing the rope ladder.

"Just get up there," said Gin. "Now I have to come, too."

◆ ◆ ◆

Vasalisa
Escape From Enlightenment Book Three

48391940R00162

Made in the USA
Lexington, KY
29 December 2015

29025704R10097